SUMMER IN PARADISE VALLEY

A brand new heart-warming, uplifting romance

ANGELA BRITNELL

Choc Lit

A JOFFE BOOKS COMPANY

Choc Lit
A Joffe Books company
www.choc-lit.com

This edition first published in Great Britain in 2023

Cover art by Berni Stevens Cover Design

ISBN: 978-1-78189-586-3

CHAPTER ONE

Lyndsey's mother had cleverly maneuvered her into a corner.

'Have you asked Becca what she thinks of the idea?' Lyndsey asked, on a resigned sigh.

'There's no need. She'll be thrilled.' Maureen Carne's declaration sounded as convincing as a fox swearing blind to a suspicious chicken that it had no ulterior motive in hanging around the hen house.

That's a 'no,' then, Mother. Lyndsey's relationship with her younger sister, Becca, had always been tricky, to say the least. There were long-standing resentments on both sides, so it suited them both when Becca's marriage to an American country music star put four thousand miles of Atlantic Ocean between them.

'She had a baby six weeks ago, she's got a moody twelve-year-old stepson to cope with and her husband's going off on a concert tour for three months. Do you honestly think she's going to make a fuss over who offers to help her out?' Maureen shrugged, remaining at a safe distance on the other side of the kitchen table.

'Three months!' Lyndsey's voice turned shrill. 'Are you mad, Mum? I can't possibly leave Cornwall and disappear off to Tennessee for all that time. In case you've forgotten, I've a business to run.'

'I know that, but Nicola's very capable and you can work online from Becca's house, can't you?' Her mother was now begging.

During the pandemic, Lyndsey was forced to adapt her home organizational business, The Right Place, or go under. At the time, she'd recently taken a lease on a small shop in Truro, so immediately switched to opening by appointment only, and developed strategies to avoid having to enter her clients' living spaces. It'd been tough, but she'd survived, and business doubled as soon as things opened up again. When, a couple of months ago, it became impossible for her to cope with all the work herself, she hired Nicola May, a similarly minded young woman, who was a huge asset.

'I *could* manage, although the six-hour time difference will be challenging . . . but not for three months . . . no way.' Lyndsey was emphatic. 'For a start, Becca and I would kill each other long before then, and you know it.' She allowed herself a small smile when her mother didn't disagree.

'You know I'd be there myself in a heartbeat if it wasn't for your father.' Maureen dabbed at her suspiciously dry eyes with a snowy-white lace hanky. 'I'd love nothing better than to get my hands on that sweet baby.'

Lyndsey gritted her teeth. 'I know you would.' Her stoic father had dealt with being on dialysis three times a week for over two years while he waited for a new kidney, and a month ago they miraculously found a match. The surgery was successful, but it would be months before he fully recovered his strength, and that was without any setbacks, so there was no way her mother could leave him.

From the start of this conversation there'd been only one possible outcome. 'Okay, if Becca agrees, I'll go — but only for a couple of weeks to start with, and we'll see how that pans out.'

That concession brought a wide, self-satisfied smile to her mother's weary face. 'I knew you wouldn't let me down.'

How could I? The guilt buried deep inside her never went away. Simply by her unexpected arrival, Lyndsey wrecked all of her mother's youthful plans. Instead of leaving Cornwall and becoming a smart, high-earning solicitor, life's curveball meant she still lived in her cramped childhood home and had only ever been able to work a raft of low-paying jobs. Looking back, Lyndsey wondered how her parents managed to raise two girls on limited resources, without ever making their children feel deprived. These days, she helped them as much as she could, knowing her dad's disability pension didn't go far, but it was like pulling teeth to persuade them to accept anything from her. Almost worse was the fact neither of her parents ever complained.

Once, as a teenager, she foolishly brought up the subject with her mother and lived to regret it. Maureen's normally placid, easy-going temperament disappeared when Lyndsey naively asked if she ever wondered how different her life could've been had she not been saddled with raising a baby on her own at nineteen. Her mum turned on her with a fierceness she'd never forgotten, insisting that she never regretted falling in love with Luis Reyes, and that far from considering herself 'saddled' with Lyndsey, considered her unplanned baby to be an absolute blessing.

It hadn't convinced Lyndsey, though she'd kept silent about her determination not to repeat what she saw as her mother's mistakes. Teenage boyfriends who sarcastically labeled her an ice queen were swiftly dismissed, because she knew the brief heartbreak that ensued was far better than the alternative. She'd become single-mindedly focused on carving out a secure, financial future on her own terms — if it was to the exclusion of everything else, then so be it.

She watched her mum whip out her mobile to ring Becca. Although Lyndsey only fully heard one side of the ensuing conversation, it convinced her that her sister was no more thrilled than she was. Once the call ended, Maureen turned back around with a bright, forced smile.

'She's over the moon.' The no-nonsense declaration dared her oldest daughter to disagree. 'Becca says don't forget the Minstrels.'

Their love for the delicious creamy chocolate was one of the few things they had in common.

'You'll have to lower your standards while you're there, remember, or there'll be uproar.' The warning came with a wry smile. 'I expect having to share a bedroom with Little Miss Messy when you were girls is why you're so . . . particular.'

Particular was a tactful way to phrase Lyndsey's obsession with neatness and order. These days she found it somewhat ironic that the trait that irritated and amused so many people in her life over the years now made her a very comfortable living. After university, she initially trained as an accountant and worked at a firm in Falmouth for almost ten years, but the moment she read the Japanese woman Marie Kondo's bestselling book about the art of decluttering and organization, a light bulb went off in her head. Becca almost died laughing when Lyndsey announced her plan to start The Right Place.

'It would be a different thing up in London, but you can't seriously expect to find enough gullible Cornish people to pay you to tidy up their cupboards, surely to God, Li-Li. And we both know you don't have the guts to leave and give this business idea a try somewhere bigger. I suppose you think this is your "right place."' The last two words came with sarcastic air quotes.

Her sister's negative attitude, along with the childish nickname that started when two-year-old Rebecca couldn't pronounce Lyndsey, had grated on her. She hadn't tried to defend herself, possibly because there were more than a few grains of truth buried underneath the standard sibling rivalry. Apart from her three years at Plymouth University, which was barely over the Cornish border so might not count, she'd never lived or worked further than about a twenty-mile radius from St Lanow. She'd never dug too deep about why that was.

'Becca's a slob,' she protested, and noticed her mother didn't argue with that true statement. She dreaded to imagine the state her sister's large, sprawling house would be in with a baby to juggle on top of everything else. It was probably best *not* to imagine it until she landed in Nashville, or she might change her mind halfway across the Atlantic and demand the pilot turn the plane around and fly her back to London.

'You two always were chalk and cheese.' Maureen shook her head. 'Becca should've been Luis's daughter, not you. Your dad was the most laid-back person I've ever met.' Her soft blue eyes turned misty.

Lyndsey was swept with a wave of sadness. She had no memories of Luis Reyes, a handsome smiling man from Dominica, who she only knew from a few treasured photographs. When she was younger, it confused her when Maureen explained that Paul Carne wasn't her biological father, although Lyndsey considered the kind, patient man who raised her absolutely her father in every other way. Luis had left the sunny Caribbean behind for a summer job at one of the big hotels in Newquay where he hadn't been able to resist the charms of a certain bright bubbly chambermaid. Maureen Nancarrow was making some much-needed money over the long summer vacation following her first year at university. Two months into their whirlwind romance, Luis's tragic death in a motorcycle accident shattered the naïve young couple's plans for a future together. The Reyes family wanted nothing to do with his pregnant girlfriend, and left the Nancarrow family to pick up the pieces.

'Luis would be so proud of you.' Maureen sounded wistful. 'And Paul is, too, so you're extra lucky.' Her bright smile inched back.

'I'll check on flights and get something booked.' Lyndsey tried her best to sound positive, rather than resigned.

'You're a gem,' her mother declared and threw her arms around Lyndsey. 'I knew I could rely on you.'

She would grit her teeth and do the best possible job of keeping her sister's home and family afloat. Packing a life vest would be crucial.

* * *

Griff kicked back in the rocking chair, popped the top on a cold beer and took a satisfying, deep swallow. Contentment washed over him as he watched the glowing ball of sun disappear behind the rolling hills, the backdrop to Paradise Valley. When he left his suit-and-tie life, it hadn't totally been by choice, but now he'd no regrets. He certainly didn't miss the six-figure salary, his luxury apartment overlooking the bright lights of Nashville or his string of equally career-driven girlfriends. Now, the noisiest thing he heard most evenings was an owl hooting in the trees.

'Hey, Griff. You got a minute?'

'Oh, hi, Deke.' He must've been miles away in his head, because he hadn't heard his next-door neighbor approaching. 'Come and sit down.' His friend joined him on the porch and dropped into the other chair with a groan. 'How're things at the madhouse? How's Nora? I'm guessin' you aren't getting much sleep?' Dark, puffy rings circled the other man's eyes.

'Sleep? What's that?' Deke scrubbed a hand over his gray, drawn face. 'She's the light of my life, though, and got me wrapped round her tiny fingers already.' His tired brown eyes brightened.

A stab of envy pierced Griff. If anyone had asked when he graduated college how he pictured his life at forty, it would've included a loving wife and a couple of kids, but if the right woman had crossed his path yet, he must've been looking the other way.

'Beer?'

'Hell, yeah.'

He pulled a can out of the small fridge he kept on the porch and tossed it in Deke's direction.

'Cheers.'

They drank in silent companionship for a few minutes as a moth fluttered around the porch light. They watched a shy, wide-eyed deer venture in from the woods to check out Griff's budding vegetable patch.

Before moving here three years ago, he'd never done any gardening. For a start, Nashville apartment life wasn't conducive to it, plus he never had the time or the interest. But thanks to Harold Morton, one of his neighbors across the road, he'd discovered the immense satisfaction of growing his own produce. Harold considered Griff his star pupil and freely shared seeds, young plants and advice. All of the tiny transplants — cucumbers, summer squash, tomatoes, jalapenos and bell peppers now starting to sprout were courtesy of Harold's magnificent greenhouse, a purchase on Griff's wish list for the future.

Apart from getting him outside more, the garden encouraged Griff to cook properly for himself, too, instead of relying on the typical bachelor fare of frozen pizzas and Cup Noodles.

'You off on tour again soon?'

'Yep, next week, and it's a long one to Europe and Japan. Three months. I sure hate leavin' Becca and the kids.' Deke grimaced. 'Becca's struggling to cope, and I'm worried sick about her. She's so damn stubborn, though, and won't admit she's having a hard time. Yesterday I suggested talkin' to the doctor and I'm not gonna repeat what she said back at me.'

'Tricky.' Griff didn't know much about new mothers, but suspected that anyone who hinted they weren't managing would get an earful. 'And Theo?'

'He's another story.' Deke buried his face in his hands. 'God, I was naïve to think he'd settle in and accept Becca and then Nora, too, after what he'd been through. Ashley was cruel to drag him here from California and dump him on me the way she did. Not that I didn't want him. Don't you go thinkin' that.'

They'd never discussed his friend's first, brief marriage but, with every depressing detail splashed over the tabloids, he and everyone else in the world knew Deke's ex was a piece of work. Ashley had been a wannabe model and actress in Los Angeles, working as a cocktail waitress, when Deke's band turned up at her club one night, celebrating their first performance on one of the celebrity talk shows. She calculatedly hitched her star to his, and by the time Deke realized her shallow depths, they were married with Theo on the way.

Six months ago, Ashley had arrived in Paradise Valley out of the blue with twelve-year-old Theo and the boy's paltry belongings in tow. She blithely announced to Deke and his new, pregnant bride that she was emigrating to Australia with her new husband and didn't intend taking her son with her.

'I know. He's a good kid. He'll adjust. Give him time.'

'Becca might kill him before that happens.' The grim pronouncement was mitigated with a faint smile. 'Twelve's a crappy age at the best of times. Don't get me wrong, Griff, I'm sympathetic for the kid, and guilty as hell for not being the father he needed early on. I'd cancel the tour if I could, but I can't let the band down, or our fans.' He looked shame-faced. 'What does it say about the type of guy I am that I don't put my family first?'

'When you get back, you can work on sorting it out properly.' Griff skirted around Deke's question. He understood more than most about priorities, but he'd never shared the full story of how he ended up here, so it was probably wise not to say too much.

'Becca's sister's comin' at the weekend to help out for a couple of weeks.'

'That's good, right?'

'Maybe. Maybe not.' Deke shrugged. 'They've never been close. Lyndsey's a neat freak, and although I love every inch of my incredible wife, I'm not tellin' you something you don't know when I say housekeeping's not her thing.'

Griff suppressed the urge to smile. Every time he'd been inside Grey House, named after a family who moved here from Kentucky to settle in this part of Williamson County, it was what his mother would call 'up to neck.'

'To be fair, it's not mine either, so we're two of a kind. I'm not *as* messy as Becca, but I got into lazy habits living on my own all those years. I've learned to ignore the chaos,' Deke said, 'but it'll drive Lyndsey crazy. I'm pretty sure their mom must've guilt-tripped her into coming in the first place.' He drained the last of his beer and crumpled the can. 'That's enough of my griping. I'd better not hang around, as I'm on bath duty tonight.' He stood up. 'I can't believe I almost forgot. I came over to ask you a favor.'

'What d'you need? I'll do pretty much anything except babysitting.' Griff held up his workmanlike hands. 'I'm terrified of droppin' her.'

'We wouldn't do that to you. If it's any consolation, Nora terrified me too, at the beginning.' Deke chuckled. 'Lyndsey flies into Nashville early Saturday evening, but we won't be here to meet her. We've already committed to go down to Memphis for my twentieth high school reunion. I'm getting some sort of award and performing after the dinner. Becca really wants to take the kids and be there to support me.'

Griff didn't make any comment, but that struck him as more than a little strange. No matter how well the sisters did or didn't get along, the woman *was* traveling four thousand miles to help out, voluntarily or not.

'If you wouldn't mind hanging around next door for when the taxi brings Lyndsey from the airport, that'd be great,' Deke went on. 'We don't want her arriving tired and jetlagged to an empty house.'

'Sure, I'd be happy to.' An idea hit him. 'Why don't I simply pick her up at the airport?'

'I couldn't possibly ask—'

'You didn't. I offered. Give me her flight number, and show me a picture, so I don't get arrested picking up some random woman.'

Deke pulled out his mobile and scrolled through his emails before stopping. 'Here we go. I'm forwarding the email with her travel details. I don't have a photo, but might be able to find one.' He tapped some more then passed over the phone. 'Here you go. That's her website and her picture's at the top.'

'The Right Place?'

'Yeah, she organizes people's homes and whatever,' he said, with a derisive laugh. 'She better not start on ours, or there'll be fireworks, and they won't be up in the air.'

Griff peered at the screen. The statuesque woman with her cap of close-cropped jet-black curls, dark honeyed skin and sharp green eyes was night-and-day different from Becca. Deke's petite wife with her pale freckled skin, wide blue eyes and flyaway blonde hair looked as if she'd blow away in a stiff breeze.

'Wow, she's stunning.' He hurried to backtrack, in case his words were taken the wrong way. 'I don't mean Becca's not—'

'I know that, you idiot. We've all got different taste. Good thing, too,' Deke said. 'It's a bit of a sad tale. Becca's mom had Lyndsey when she was young, a few months after the father was killed in a traffic accident. When Lyndsey was a toddler, her mom married Paul Carne and they had Becca about six years later.'

'Oh, right. Don't worry, I'll be at the airport in good time on Saturday ready to introduce Ms Lyndsey to the delights of Paradise Valley.' They exchanged smiles. There were only five homes, including their own two houses, in their tiny community. The tour wouldn't take long.

'Thanks, I really appreciate it. We both do.'

'Hey, that's what friends are for.'

After Deke left, Griff abandoned his spot on the porch and retreated back into the house. A prickle of anticipation ran through him, although he couldn't put a finger on why.

CHAPTER TWO

Lyndsey scanned the arrivals area for the mystery man she was supposed to meet. She would've preferred to take a taxi to Becca's house and get herself settled in peace, but was overruled by her brother-in-law. Now she had to be polite and quasi-friendly to their neighbor, Griffin Oakes. Without any sort of description from Deke, she'd formed a picture in her head of a grizzled old man with a thick, unintelligible Southern drawl. She'd no doubt be forced to graciously tolerate his astonishment at her Britishness.

'Ms Carne? Griffin Oakes.'

She felt curiously light-headed as she glanced up. *Not old or grizzled then*, she thought. As she took the tall, lanky stranger's outstretched hand, his strong grip sent a bolt of awareness zinging through her blood. Broad shoulders filled out a soft green collared shirt, and a wide embossed leather belt circled the dark jeans hanging on his narrow hips. The thick tawny hair fastened back in a neat ponytail emphasized his razor-sharp cheekbones, and she couldn't pinpoint why his wide-set eyes struck her as unusual until she studied them closer. They were different colors — one a startling cerulean blue and the other a rich dark brown. Fixed on her now, their intensity made the skin on the back of her neck prickle with heat.

'What's your secret?' he asked.

'Secret?'

A slow smile inched up his lean face, deepening the laughter lines fanning out from his eyes. 'Well, ma'am, you look fresh as the proverbial daisy and all these other poor souls look as though they've endured Dante's nine circles of hell.'

'I took a natural sleep supplement at Heathrow, hydrated well and ate my own nutritious snacks on the plane.' She sounded prim, but couldn't bring herself to lower her guard. Not when the man's deep, syrupy drawl was doing things to parts of Lyndsey that had been asleep so long they might as well belong to Sleeping Beauty. 'Would you mind very much if we got a move on, please?'

'Don't you have a bag to collect?'

'Oh no, I never check in any luggage. It's unnecessary if you know how to pack.'

'If you say so.' The casual response was laced with wry amusement. 'It's rush hour, so the traffic will be crazy until we get off the interstate. You want me to take that?' He pointed to her roller bag and small backpack.

'No thank you, Mr Oakes.'

'Call me Griff. Everyone else does, and yeah, my mom had a thing for Greek mythology — especially griffins. I promise under this regular ole shirt and jeans, I'm not hiding the body of a lion, and last time I checked I didn't have an eagle's head.'

Lyndsey managed a tight smile and avoided commenting one way or another on his appearance. 'Perhaps you can lead the way to your car?'

'Yeah, I expect I can manage that.' He sauntered off, leaving her to follow along behind. Despite his easy unhurried stride, people moved out of the way. Under the affable surface, something about his energy hinted he wasn't a man to be messed with.

Outside the terminal building, the cool early evening air bathed her face, and she must've sighed, because her appointed chauffeur for the evening stopped walking.

'You okay?' He tilted her a worried look.

'Absolutely. It feels so amazingly good after hours of breathing recirculated air.'

'You picked the right time to come. May's a pretty month, although it's a toss-up between that and October, when the color can't be beat.' His lazy smile returned. 'We'd better get cracking. My truck's over there. It's not fancy, so don't expect too much.'

Lyndsey kept to herself that her expectations about this whole trip weren't high in the first place. 'As long as it's road-worthy, it'll be fine.' She took a wild guess that the beat-up pick-up truck he stopped next to might've been black in the dim, distant past, but now boasted a variegated color scheme of gray interspersed with rust.

'It's sturdier than it looks.' One corner of his mouth twitched. 'A bit like me.'

She didn't comment on either statement.

'Give me those, unless you can't be parted from them.' He gestured to her bags. 'I'll wedge them behind our seats.'

He left her no choice. Lyndsey winced as he squeezed in her roller bag, no doubt leaving marks on the bag's pristine dark blue leather.

'Off we go.' After a few loud protests, the engine fired into life and the truck lurched out of the car park.

She never usually took naps because they messed with her sleep schedule, but her eyes soon drooped.

* * *

'We're here. This is Paradise Valley.'

Lyndsey jerked awake, momentarily confused. She peered out of the window as the truck slowed down. 'Really?' The narrow dead-end road with its scattering of disparate houses wasn't what she'd expected. She'd seen pictures of Becca's house, but not in context, and assumed it was in a wealthy enclave of similar properties. The name 'Paradise Valley' was the only thing with pretensions here.

'Yeah.' Griff sounded amused. He steered the truck up a long tarmacked drive and stopped. 'Welcome to Grey House, your home sweet home for however long you're stayin'. Hop out and see it close up.'

It was easier to follow his suggestion than answer his veiled question. She'd love to know how long she was staying, too.

* * *

Griff pretended to admire the well-proportioned red brick house in front of them rather than Lyndsey. He caught a drift of her subtle perfume, nothing in-your-face or lingering, but distinctive enough to throw him off-kilter.

'Becca told us this property was in the same family for generations until Deke bought it a few years ago,' she explained.

'Well, the land it stands on was, but the original building was a simple log cabin. From what I've dug up of the history, Thomas Scott Grey, his wife Kathleen and several other family members made their way here from Kentucky back in the mid-1800s, after deciding this area was perfect to settle in and farm tobacco. They bought around fifty acres of land, named it Paradise Valley and built half a dozen cabins for them all to live in. This particular house was built by a descendant of the Greys around the turn of the twentieth century. Are you an architecture nut at all?'

'Not really, although I know what I like when I see it, and this certainly is a lovely house.'

'The white columns, wide porch, low-pitch gabled roof and evenly spaced multi-paned windows are all signatures of Greek Revival style,' he explained, and pointed them out to her. 'We like our classics here. You'll even find a full-size replica of the Parthenon in downtown Nashville.'

'Grey House has been here a while . . . from an American point of view.' Griff cracked a smile. 'I guess it still counts as a new house to y'all?'

'Sort of.' A hint of mischief lit up Lyndsey's rather serious face. 'It's okay, I won't brag that parts of my family's cottage in Cornwall date from about 1550, the village church from the mid-1200s and the local pub has been in business about two hundred years.'

'Bragging's un-British, isn't it? You're only stating facts.' For a fleeting second their eyes met and he expected a smart quip in response, but she only shrugged her stiff, slender shoulders. Griff cleared his throat and tried his best to stay on track. 'Ruth Mae and her brother, Scotty, were the last of the Grey family to live in this house. Neither of them ever married or had any family of their own. He passed away a few years ago, and by then there was no money left and the building was very run-down. Miss Grey was forced to sell it to Deke, and he's done a whole lot of work on it since then. He's even turned the abandoned tobacco barn behind the house into a music studio. If you have the chance to get out and about here, you'll see plenty of similar barns still standing. Ones built specifically for tobacco usually have gabled roofs and some form of ventilation used to dry the crop, like hinges attached to some of the cladding boards, so they can be opened.' He became aware of her bemused look. 'Sorry. I'm droning on. It's a bit of a hobby of mine to track down old barns. I take pictures of them and try to dig up their histories.'

'Don't apologize. It sounds interesting.'

'History fascinates me. It's where we're from, isn't it?'

'Yes, it is.' He picked up on a hint of sadness in her brisk tones. Griff could've kicked himself for forgetting Deke's explanation about his sister-in-law's mixed heritage. Changing the subject seemed wise.

Griff turned away and pointed to a dilapidated wood cabin at the end of the road, its neglected garden choked with weeds and waist-high grass. 'That's where Ruth Mae Grey lives now. Deke told me once that should've been included in the sale, but he let the old lady hang onto it because he felt sorry for her. Did Becca mention Ruth Mae to you?'

'No. Should she have? I mean, she didn't mention you either.' A heated flush bloomed in her sculpted cheeks. 'Becca and I . . .'

'It's all right. You don't have to explain.' Difficult family relationships he totally got; he hadn't spoken to his own brother in years. 'Miss Grey is bitter and resentful, which is understandable, I guess, but it's a shame. There are only five houses in total here, so you'd think we could all get along and help each other out.'

'What a pretty little place.' She pointed to the neat, single-story house opposite with its fresh white paint, glossy sky-blue front door framed by lush, colorful hanging baskets and surrounded by an immaculate garden.

'Yeah, Harold Morton and his partner William Puckett live there. They're both retired teachers and enthusiastic gardeners.' He chuckled. 'If they get chatting with you, don't be surprised if they bend your ear about British history and the royal family. They're huge Anglophiles. I'm afraid Becca's been a bit of a dead loss for them . . .'

He hesitated. Deke was concerned about his wife's lack of interest in their neighbors, but it wasn't Griff's place to gossip about Becca to her sister. 'She's been too busy for socializing.' He left it there. 'The gray brick house to the right of William and Harold's place belongs to Tiffany Hunt. She's in her early thirties and a physical therapist over in Franklin. Tiffany moved here from Minnesota last year. If you ask her why, she'll say it's mainly because she was tired of digging her car out of the snow every winter. We sure don't get much of the white stuff here.'

'It's rare in Cornwall, too. We're surrounded by the sea on three sides, so it tends to be mild and damp. Great for the gardens.'

'Yeah, it would be.' It was on the tip of his tongue to say he'd love to see them one day, but she might take that the wrong way. 'Poor ole Miss Grey disapproves of us all for different reasons.' A wry smile sneaked out. 'Deke's a degenerate musician with a foreign wife. I'm a long-haired layabout.

Harold and William — well, you can probably imagine what *she* thinks of *them*. They're about equal to Tiffany in Ruth Mae's mind — the old dear considers her a damn Yankee — that's the derogatory name for a northerner who comes to the South and stays.' He stopped talking when Lyndsey stifled a yawn. 'I'm sorry, I've been rattling on again—'

'Please don't apologize, but I'm certain you've got better things to do with your Saturday evening than babysit me, so shall we get on inside?'

After traveling, all he ever wanted was a hot shower and bed. Making small talk with a stranger would be his worst nightmare too, and he'd bored her long enough. 'Yeah, sure. Deke asked me to show you where a few things are, so I'll do that, then get out of your hair.'

Griff walked back to the truck and retrieved her bags. He headed up the three broad steps onto a spacious wraparound porch.

'I love this. We don't generally have anything like this back home. It's not worth the expense of building it, because the English weather is so unpredictable.' Lyndsey's amusement brought added light to her face and stirred an unexpected frisson of desire in Griff's gut.

She ran a hand over one of the four glossy red-painted rocking chairs lined up facing the road. 'Do people really sip mint juleps on porches like this, or have I been reading too much Southern Gothic literature?'

'Some do, I guess, but I'm more a cold beer or Jack Daniels man myself.'

'Where is your house, anyway?'

'If you bend down and peer through those trees you'll see the roof line.' Griff gestured over to their right. 'It's not fancy like this place.' He cracked a smile. 'Like my truck, the cabin's made for practicality, not good looks.'

'I see the house now.'

An invitation to come see it anytime danced on the end of his tongue, but he swallowed it back down. He dangled a brass key on a guitar-shaped keyring in front of her. 'You want to do the honors or me?'

'Go ahead, please.'

'I even know how to make a real British cup of tea, if you want one? Becca's given me lessons.'

'No, thank you. I'm sure my sister still drinks the PG Tips we grew up on, and that's not my preference these days. Sorry.' A hint of apology crept into her voice. 'It's kind of you to offer, though.'

Griff got the impression that for her to unbend that much was a rare occurrence. He unlocked the cherry-red front door and pushed it open, standing aside to let her enter first.

'Oh.'

No wonder she looked dumbfounded. If he didn't know better he'd be convinced a tornado had recently blown through, wreaking a trail of destruction. The hall's traditional black-and-white chequered tile floor was buried somewhere under a sea of abandoned shoes, coats and baby paraphernalia.

'How about I show you the kitchen?' Griff offered. Anything to get her out of there as fast as possible. 'Deke assured me there's plenty of food in the fridge and the freezer is well stocked, so you shouldn't starve.'

'Thank you.' Lyndsey's voice was faint with dismay.

He steered her down an equally cluttered hallway and into the spacious kitchen diner, part of the addition Deke had built at the back of the house.

'Wow, this is an amazing space.' Her bright green eyes darted around.

Griff agreed with the unspoken criticism. It *would* be a whole lot better if the sleek pale wood countertops and long farmhouse table were visible. This time, the culprits were piles of dirty dishes wedged between wobbling stacks of magazines, newspapers and junk mail. The deep butler's sink under the window was crammed with more dirty dishes, and he dared not contemplate what his feet were sticking to on the wood floor. He ran through the basics of where things were as fast as he could, relieved when she didn't ask any questions.

'I'll show you your bedroom.' Deke had been explicit about which guest room he'd picked out for Lyndsey. *I tidied it as much as I could and cleaned the en suite bathroom.* It both amused and saddened him to picture the famous front man for a chart-topping band scrubbing the toilet for his fussy sister-in-law.

'There you go.' He flung open the door to reveal a generous sized room, simply decorated in blue and white, and clutter-free apart from a stack of brown cardboard boxes in one corner. It was a huge improvement on everywhere else, and he caught Lyndsey's small sigh of relief. 'Is there anythin' else you'd like me to show you?'

'No, thank you, I'll be fine.'

'At least let me give you my phone number.'

'That won't be—'

'You might have an emergency before your family gets back tomorrow afternoon . . . even if it's only how to work the remote control for the TV.' She didn't respond to his feeble joke. Griff dragged out his mobile. 'Okay?'

'Of course. I'm sorry. Again.' Lyndsey's shoulders drooped.

'It's okay. You're tired, and it's all a bit overwhelming, I'm sure.' An understatement, but she wouldn't appreciate him probing any further. She retrieved her phone from her backpack so they could swap numbers. 'Don't bother to come down, I'll see myself out.'

'Thanks again for the lift.'

'You're welcome. I'm sure I'll see you around while you're here.'

'I'd say that's quite possible. Goodbye, Mr . . . Griff.'

The unexpected spark of humor flashing in her emerald eyes brought his fascination with her flooding back with a vengeance.

CHAPTER THREE

Lyndsey finished scrubbing a tea-stained blue pottery mug and gave it a good rinse off in boiling water before pulling off a couple of sheets of kitchen roll to dry it thoroughly. She preferred to be more environmentally conscious and use a tea towel, but the dirty germ-ridden object hanging by the sink made her shudder. After one long stare at the green-and-white PG Tips box, she pushed it out of sight and opened her reusable linen bag, stuffed with a selection of herbal tea bags. Her normal morning choice was ginseng matcha, because its energizing herbs and whole leaf green tea gave the perfect kick-start to the day. At least, that was normally the case, but this morning it would face an uphill battle. Despite the soothing camomile tea she drank before falling into bed last night, she'd been wide awake by three. Now it was only eight o'clock, and she was struggling to keep her eyes open. With a resigned sigh she made her drink.

If she stayed here in Becca's untidy kitchen a moment longer, she might do something unforgiveable, like clean it, so she'd better find somewhere else to drink her tea.

She strolled back through the house and stepped out onto the porch, hoping that a dose of fresh air might lift her lethargy. Lyndsey padded down the cool wooden steps onto the dewy grass, and stopped to sip her tea. The almost musty bitterness was definitely an acquired taste. Idly, she watched two gray squirrels squabbling over something at the base of a large oak tree.

Gardening wasn't really her thing, but even she could admire the huge azaleas in full flower along the front of the house, their frothy white blossoms resembling a delicate lace veil. The rest of the garden, with its lush dark green grass framed by mature trees, suited her immensely, because she'd never been a fan of fussy, overly manicured gardens. That probably came from her being a fervent disciple of William Morris. She'd adopted, as her own mantra, his famous quote about having nothing in your house (or outside of them, in this case) that you do not know to be beautiful or believe to be useful. A tiny smile played around her lips. Morris was the original selective minimalist, before anyone heard of Marie Kondo.

A buzzing sound interrupted her musings and she jerked her head around, searching for a bee before realizing it was coming from her phone. She yanked her mobile out of her dressing gown pocket and spotted a new text from her sister. Becca didn't do short and sweet, so the voluble message began with rambling expressions of guilt for not being there to meet Lyndsey the night before. Right at the end came the pertinent part. Everyone had woken up early, so they'd already left Memphis and were now well on the way home.

Lyndsey's stomach tightened. In an hour or so, her challenge would really begin. She tossed her barely touched tea on the grass. It was time to get her armor on.

* * *

Griff selected a rectangular piece of glass and held it up to the light, shook his head, and set it back down again. The solid white, milky opalescent glass was completely wrong for his latest project, but his mind kept straying from work today.

Earlier, when he was out on the porch drinking his first cup of coffee, his eye caught a flash of white through the trees. He stood up to take a look, thinking it might be a mockingbird in flight, because the white patches on their wings became more visible in the air, along with the outer tail feathers. Olivia, his most recent ex-girlfriend, called his interest in bird-watching another of what she scathingly labeled his 'old-man hobbies.' But this morning's sighting wasn't a bird of the feathered variety, but the tall, erect shape of his new neighbor in a sensible, white dressing gown. Griff had almost called out to her, but drew back at the last second, reluctant to make her uneasy about being observed.

He'd thought nothing of it when she suddenly disappeared back in the house, until he received a text from Deke a few minutes later. No doubt Lyndsey got a similar message to say her family were on the way home. Within the next half hour, he heard a vehicle and peered out in time to see Deke's shiny black Mercedes minivan swish by. A few months ago, his friend laughingly bemoaned becoming a suburban, middle-aged man when he bought the large vehicle to accommodate his growing family.

Griff forced his concentration back to his latest commission. The three leaded stained-glass panels were for a new high-end Nashville restaurant, his most lucrative and prestigious job yet. The two rectangular pieces, each about a meter high, would be set either side of a pair of reclaimed oak doors. The third — a half-moon shape — was set to be fixed over the door. They weren't due until mid-July, but each would take at the very least a dedicated fifty to seventy hours of work. This morning's task was to finalize the pattern, which so far only existed in his head. It was a meticulous process, which, if it wasn't done correctly, would result in an expensive mess later. Before he got into this particular art form, he'd always been mathematically minded, so the precision needed at this stage came easily to him.

He opened his laptop and soon lost himself in the design, only straightening up when his hunched shoulders started to ache. Two hours had flown by. The loud growls from his stomach reminded Griff that he'd skipped breakfast, so the question now was whether or not to take a break to grab a bite of lunch before he printed off the patterns. Several sharp taps at the door pushed the decision aside for a moment.

'It's me,' Deke's deep gravelly voice boomed out. 'Safe to come in?'

He'd been forced to train his friends not to simply wander into his workshop. Although he was scrupulous about cleaning the space both during and after he was working, he didn't need them potentially breathing in lead dust or cutting themselves.

'Yeah, no problem.' Griff rubbed a tight spot on the back of his neck.

'Sorry.' Deke winced, seeing him at his workbench. 'I didn't mean to interrupt your work.'

'It's fine. I'd got to a good stopping point and was thinkin' about getting lunch. Did you have a good time in Memphis?'

'I guess, although it's kinda strange to see everyone twenty years on from graduation. Several of the kids I palled around with back then treated me different.' He lifted his shoulders in a shrug. 'I doubt I'll go back for the next one.'

Griff could see that classmates who'd settled into more regular lives might be either in awe, or resentful of their former classmate's success. 'That's a shame.'

'That's life, I guess . . . anyway, I didn't come over here to complain. Thanks again for picking up Lyndsey. How did it go? Bit scary, isn't she?' Deke chuckled.

'We did okay. She was tired and a bit grumpy, but jet lag does that to us all.' He couldn't have his friend picking up on his mad, inexplicable attraction to the enigmatic Englishwoman.

'Becca wanted me to invite you over for dinner before I leave . . . does Tuesday work for you? I'm on the Wednesday evening flight out of here.'

Griff pulled out his phone and pretended to study his calendar. 'I might be able to fit y'all in. I'm guessing your kids have livelier social lives than me. I'm not complaining, though. I've had my fill of all that.' In the past, an evening spent at home meant he was either working overtime or sick.

'Yeah, I can understand that. I've been touring off and on for almost twenty years and it gets old.' His eyes darkened. 'I shouldn't complain, because thousands of singers and songwriters would give their eye teeth to be in my position. But the band's been working round the clock rehearsing. I've barely seen Nora since she's been born and I'm surprised Becca and Theo remembered who I was when we went to Memphis.' Deke shook his head, as if tossing out unpalatable thoughts. 'I'm ramblin'. Ignore me. I'll throw some steaks on the grill about six o'clock on Tuesday, if that suits you? It'll fit in with feeding time at the baby zoo.'

'That'll work. Anything I can bring? Beer?'

'Yeah, that'd be great.' Deke rolled his eyes. 'When we were talkin' about it at the house, Lyndsey threatened to whip up a kale salad as her contribution. I had to break it to her gently that no red-blooded American would eat that with a juicy steak.' He headed for the door. 'Thanks again for the taxi service. See ya.'

Griff's appetite had disappeared. He'd plow on with his work, in an effort to stop thinking what might happen when he crossed paths with Lyndsey again.

* * *

'If I want you to wash the bloody dishes, I'll ask you — okay?' Becca snapped. She snatched the dishcloth from Lyndsey's hand and tossed it on the counter.

Their mother's optimism had clearly been misplaced.

Lyndsey still couldn't wrap her head around the drastic change in her sister's appearance since last year's wedding, when Becca made a stunningly beautiful bride, elegant and glowing with happiness in a froth of designer white satin and lace. She'd expected the post-baby weight, tiredness and perhaps the lack of make-up, but not the aura of defeat dragging down Becca's frail shoulders.

She dug deep, took a couple of steadying breaths, and prepared to apologize.

'Lyndsey's come to help us, honey.' Deke stepped in. 'We don't want her rushing off on the next plane back to London and—'

'You mean, *you* don't.' Becca turned her wrath on her hapless husband. 'It suits *you* to have her here, so you can swan off to Europe with less of a guilty conscience.'

The color rose in his face, but he said nothing. Presumably he was used to her sister's changeable moods. Even as a child, she was all sweetness and light one minute, like butter wouldn't melt in her mouth, but when anyone crossed her, she blew up in a heartbeat.

A thin, reedy cry startled her, and for a moment Lyndsey couldn't think where it was coming from. Deke turned away and reached into the car seat, balanced on the kitchen table, and fiddled with the complicated straps. They hadn't wanted to disturb Nora's nap when they first arrived, but obviously her niece was ready to make her presence known.

'Nora, sweetheart, it's time to meet your Aunt Lyndsey.' He wriggled the fractious baby out and into his arms.

'Li-Li doesn't do babies, do you?' Becca's dismissal stung, and to make matters worse her sister had reverted to using that stupid childish nickname.

She flinched under Deke's sympathetic gaze. 'It's true, I haven't had much to do with them before now, but I certainly want to get to know my niece.' Doing her best to convey an impression of confidence, she smiled broadly as Deke placed the feather-light baby in her arms. The little girl's eyes flew open and Lyndsey braced herself for another piercing wail. Instead, Nora stared up at her, unblinking. She'd never fallen in love at first sight before, but it hit her now like a freight train with faulty brakes. 'Oh, Deke, she's got your brown eyes,' she murmured. 'Her adorable mouth is all you, Becca.' Her finger stroked Nora's plump cheek. 'Her skin's so soft,' she whispered. 'She's perfect.'

For the first time since they laid eyes on each other again, she and Becca exchanged smiles instead of unkind words.

A sudden blast of loud music reverberated through the ceiling, and Nora's face screwed up and turned bright red. She let loose an ear-piercing scream.

'For God's sake, we've hardly been back five minutes and Theo's at it already,' Becca complained to Deke. 'Are you going to tell him to stop or do I have to?'

'I'll go,' he said wearily and hurried away.

'Give her here.' Becca snatched the baby away from Lyndsey and paced around the kitchen in a vain attempt to soothe her. 'Bloody boy,' she hissed. 'His usual trick is to wait until Nora's sleeping, but everyone at Deke's reunion was fussing over how cute she is, so now he's making us pay.'

Lyndsey was sympathetic. She'd been in Theo's position once when blonde, adorable Becca melted peoples' hearts but an awkward eight-year-old half sister with attitude, not so much.

'I caught a glimpse of Theo when you came in, but didn't get a chance—'

'A glimpse is all we get half the time, too,' Becca scoffed. 'The last thing Deke said to him as we got out of the van was to come and say hello to you — fat lot of good that did.'

Lyndsey had only met the twelve-year-old once, at last year's wedding in Cornwall when he glowered all the way through the ceremony. It'd wrenched her heart when she spotted him standing alone with his hands jammed in his trouser pockets watching Becca and Deke enjoying their first dance, misery etched deep into his face.

'Deke usually manages to smooth things over, and I expect he'll cajole him into joining us for dinner, but I don't have a clue how I'll cope when he leaves,' Becca confessed. 'At the moment, we have an uneasy truce. I don't attempt to parent him, and in return, he's not outright rude to me.' She pushed a wisp of blonde hair out of her eyes. 'It'll be even more horrendous in a couple of weeks when the schools start their long summer holidays and Theo's around full-time. Won't that be wonderful?' Sarcasm oozed out of her.

Before Lyndsey could dredge up a suitably reassuring reply, Deke returned, steering a thin, hunched-over boy towards them. Theo's lank dark hair fell in front of his face, but she didn't need to see his face to feel the waves of resentment radiating off him.

Their mother was right about Becca needing help, but she wasn't the only one, and even the Angel Gabriel might balk at this particular challenge.

CHAPTER FOUR

'Why don't I take our little diva out for a walk?' Lyndsey offered. A solid hour of her sister pacing around the kitchen had failed to placate the unhappy, red-faced baby. 'The fresh air might help—'

'So you know everything about babies now, do you?' Becca turned on her, hollow-eyed and angry.

Since she arrived three days ago, she'd learned to keep her expression neutral around Becca and say as little as possible.

If her sister needed someone to vent her frustration on, Lyndsey would have to take it. That was no novelty, because she'd been forced to do the same thing all Becca's life. It'd been drummed into her when her sister was born that it was her job to help take care of her. She would've been happy to do that, but a kernel of resentment took root when it seemed Becca's wants and needs always came first. When Becca cried and fussed and threw tantrums — something she unfortunately did on a regular basis — Lyndsey was aggrieved when their parents insisted that Becca was simply 'sensitive.' If Lyndsey misbehaved herself, that was considered straightforward naughty.

'Fine. Help yourself.' Becca thrust the squirming, tightly swaddled baby at her and Lyndsey settled Nora in the crook of her arm, automatically rocking her from side to side.

'Oh God, I'm a terrible mother.' Her sister collapsed on the nearest chair and covered her face with her hands. 'I'm sure Deke can't wait to leave tomorrow. Why wouldn't he?'

'You know he's torn up about going, and will miss you all dreadfully.'

'If you say so. I bet you've got your return flight booked already, too?'

'I promised I'd stay at least a couple of weeks, and I've no plans to leave anytime soon. I also think you're doing an incredible job.' Becca's wary look said her sister didn't trust the genuine compliment. 'Honestly. It's tough. My work can be challenging, but it's nothing compared to what you're trying to juggle.'

A faint smile lifted her sister's gloomy expression. 'Miracle worker with babies, too, I should've expected it.'

They'd been too engrossed to notice Nora falling quiet; her tiny face was now slack in sleep.

'Would you prefer I stayed here and helped get things ready for tonight?' she whispered. For his last night at home, Deke had invited Griff to join them for a steak dinner. There was an unwelcome flutter of excitement in her stomach at the thought of seeing him again.

'There's oodles of time to worry about that.'

'So, in that case, why don't you go upstairs and have a rest?'

'I think I will. I'll show you where the pram is.'

Becca's meek agreement shocked her, but she allowed it to slide by and followed her sister through to the utility room.

'There you go.' Becca gestured to an impressive navy-blue vehicle wedged in between a mountain bike and a set of golf clubs. 'It's a Bugaboo stroller. That's the same model as all the younger royals. All-terrain wheels and a suspension system to rival a Rolls-Royce.'

She continued rocking Nora while the stroller was wriggled out of its appointed spot. Her niece's eyes briefly flew open when Lyndsey deposited her gently inside, but fluttered closed again when Becca tucked a soft pink blanket in around her.

'We'll be fine. Go lay down.' She shooed her sister away, and pushed open the back door to wheel Nora outside. Down at the end of the drive she turned right; supposedly there was a path running between two of the houses that looped around a couple of nearby fields and made for a decent walk.

'Yoo hoo, Becca's sister, hello there!'

She turned to see a short, plump man with a shock of white hair and red wire-rimmed glasses scuttling towards her.

'Harold Morton, at your service.' He shook hands vigorously and hardly gave Lyndsey a chance to introduce herself before he switched his attention to Nora. His cherubic face lit up as he peered in at her. 'How's our little poppet, today? She's such a sweetheart.'

'You wouldn't have said that a few minutes ago. She's been screaming the house down for the last hour. I'm surprised you didn't hear her.'

'Griff told us you'd come all the way from England to help out, and we've been longing to meet you.' He pointed to the pretty white house behind him. 'My partner, William, and I would love you to come and have tea with us one day.'

'I'd be delighted.'

'We were so sad about the Queen — such a lovely lady.' He sighed sadly.

'I met her once.' Lyndsey's confession made his blue eyes sparkle.

'Oh my, I can't wait to hear about it.'

Snuffling noises drifted up from the stroller and Nora started to stir. 'Oh dear, I'm sorry, but I'd better keep moving.'

'Of course. You're welcome to pop in anytime, although I know William will want to make his famous scones, so you might give us a little notice.'

'I will, and thank you for the invitation.'

'Naturally, Becca is welcome, too, when you do come, but . . .' Two blobs of heat flared in his plump cheeks. 'We did ask her once before — through Deke — but we never heard anything back. I'm sure she was terribly busy and still trying to settle in.'

It struck her as sad that Becca hadn't got to know her neighbors, except for Griff, and even he was more Deke's friend. She pulled herself up short. She'd absolutely no right to condemn her sister. Becca had married a man she'd only known a few months, moved four thousand miles away from everything and everyone she knew, acquired a stepson and had a baby — all in little over a year. No wonder she was struggling to find her feet. Lyndsey had lived in her flat near Truro for over five years and still barely knew the names of her neighbors. She'd certainly never been invited to tea with any of them. *You haven't invited any of them in over the doorstep either*, she thought.

'Off you go, and we'll see you soon.' Harold smiled at Nora in farewell, then trotted off back to his house.

She started off again, taking a good look around as she walked. The narrow road dead-ended at these few homes. It was a pretty enough spot but paradise? That was stretching it.

Why the original settlers described this as a valley was a bit of a mystery, although she supposed the ridgeline of gentle hills in the distance could conceivably give that impression. Perhaps the Grey family's life in Kentucky was hard and this place offered something different. People needed the right place to flourish, too.

She was sounding daft. Her brain must still be jet lagged.

In another few weeks the temperature would heat up even more, but today, she relished the warm sun on her skin. Back home she was one of the few people who soaked up Cornwall's rare, brief heat waves, her only complaint being they never lasted long enough for her liking.

She'd worked hard to become indifferent, showing no interest in anything to do with the Caribbean side of her heritage, but the occasional pang of resentment sneaked in that her biological father's family wanted nothing to do with her. A few years ago, her mother tentatively suggested they made another attempt to reach out to them, but Lyndsey stamped on it immediately. She had no intention of being rejected again.

Stopping Nora's stroller at the curve in the road, she studied Ruth Mae Grey's dilapidated cabin. The roof sagged. Strips of wood were nailed over a broken window. The narrow porch was missing several uprights and on the verge of collapse. Nobody should be living there, let alone a solitary old woman. Her gaze landed on an elaborate stone bird bath rising up from the middle of the unkempt grass. Too ornate for its mundane surroundings, the intricately carved mermaid with long hair reaching the top of its tail held a scalloped seashell in one elegant outstretched hand.

'What're you starin' at, girl?'

She hadn't noticed a stooped figure dressed all in black and holding a battered watering can.

'I'm sorry. I didn't mean to be rude. I was admiring your bird bath. You must be Miss Grey.'

'Who says so? I don't know you from Adam.' The woman hobbled across, leaning heavily on a stout wooden stick. 'I s'ppose you're with that party who turned my family's house upside down?' Her dark hooded eyes scrutinized Lyndsey.

'My sister and her family live in Grey House, if that's what you mean.' She could give as good as she got; old or not, Miss Grey clearly hadn't mellowed.

'They've no right to use that name.'

'I'm sure they only wanted to honor the heritage and history behind the building, not offend you. I'd love to hear more about it one day.'

Her adversary snorted.

'I'm not surprised your family chose to settle here. It's a pretty spot.' She applauded herself for the slight lie when the faintest hint of softening worked around the woman's thin, tight mouth. 'I'm Lyndsey Carne, by the way. I've come from England to help take care of my new niece. Her dad's going on tour tomorrow for three months.' She pointed in the stroller. 'This is Nora. She's about seven weeks old.'

Lyndsey managed to hide her surprise when Miss Grey shuffled closer and peeked in at the sleeping baby, stretching out a finger gnarled with arthritis to stroke the pink blanket.

'We came out for a long walk, but I haven't got very far yet, not that I'm complaining. Harold Morton stopped me first for a pleasant chat, and now I've met you.'

Miss Grey pulled back her hand as if she'd been stung. 'I don't have nothin' to do with him or his *friend*,' she boasted. 'Or that Yankee woman and the long-haired man who looks like he's never done a day's work in his life. They're not the kind of people my kinfolk would want living on their land.'

'Times change,' she murmured. 'They all seem really friendly. I'm sure they'd be good, helpful neighbors if you let them.'

'I don't need anyone's charity,' Miss Grey bristled. 'Don't you go bothering me none again.'

Lyndsey resisted the urge to point out she hadn't started the conversation in the first place. Politely she said goodbye and carried on down the road. Something needed to be done for the frail, lonely old woman, because that's what she was at the end of the day. A smile played around her mouth. As if she didn't have enough on her plate already. She really needed to add getting tangled up with a dangerously interesting man and a bitter old woman.

* * *

Griff strolled out on the patio and sniffed appreciatively at the mouthwatering scent of smoke and steak. 'Boy, nothing smells quite like that!'

'The meat's just gone on.' Deke glanced around from the grill.

'You ready for a beer?'

'Stupid question.'

Griff peeled one off the six-pack he'd brought with him, and tossed it over, smiling as his friend caught it adroitly in one hand.

33

'Leaving tomorrow is gonna suck.' Deke sighed and shoved a hand through his shaggy, blond hair. The occasional gray thread ran through it these days, something his manager had urged him to cover up for the sake of the band's younger fans. Deke's response had been blunt and unprintable.

'We'll all keep an eye on your family, you know that.' Griff tried to reassure him. 'Once you get on stage again, you'll be okay.'

'I suppose. When I was a kid growin' up, I taught myself how to play guitar and spent all my time listening to country music. I loved the way it told stories. Still do. I'd tune in to the Grand Ole Opry on the radio every week and dream of playing there one day. I've been fortunate enough to do that many times now and the band was even inducted into the Opry a couple of years ago, which was a huge honor.' Deke's face settled in a frown. 'I'm startin' to question if the effect it's having on my family and private life is worth it.' He drank deeply of his beer.

Griff wasn't sure how to respond. He was living proof that achieving so-called success wasn't always what it was cracked up to be.

'I'm in a self-pitying mood tonight. Ignore me.' Deke shook his head 'Why don't you go in the kitchen and tell the girls the steaks will be about fifteen minutes?'

'Sure.' He left his friend tending the meat, but when he pushed open the back door and stepped into the kitchen, Griff seriously considered walking straight out again. The two sisters stood in the middle of the floor, facing off like gunslingers at the O.K. Corral.

'I could clear the table so we've got room to sit down and eat,' Lyndsey said.

'I'm sure you could, but Mum promised you'd do whatever I wanted, and I want you to hold Nora,' Becca tossed back at her.

'Fine. Pass her over.'

'We've discovered my clever big sister has yet another talent — baby magician.' Sarcasm oozed out of Deke's wife.

The squirming, tightly swaddled baby was thrust into her aunt's outstretched arms.

'That doesn't surprise *me*. Lyndsey strikes me as a very capable woman, and I'm sure there's a prescribed regimen for putting a cranky baby in its *right place*.' Griff's humorous emphasis on the last two words, echoed the name of her business. A dark flush of heat raced up Lyndsey's smooth, rich dark skin. 'Is there anything I can do to help? Deke said he'd be about fifteen minutes.'

'You could lay the table, if you like.'

'No problem.' He winced as Lyndsey's expression turned to stone. It pissed her off big time that her sister was happy enough to accept *his* help.

Griff grabbed a couple of dirty plates off the table and added them to the dishwasher before methodically clearing away everything else, stacking papers, baby toys and clothes on the counter. He didn't dare ask where their proper homes were, because that would kick off another argument.

'Here you go.' Becca passed over a stack of mismatched plates. 'I'm going to drag Theo out of his bedroom.' She marched off, bristling with determination.

'I wouldn't like to be in the kid's shoes.'

'Me neither,' Lyndsey agreed.

'I never meant to make fun of you earlier. I'm sorry.'

'Don't worry about it.'

His gaze fixed on the little girl snuggled against Lyndsey's body and woefully inappropriate thoughts about doing the same came to mind. It did no damn good whatsoever to tell himself it was nothing more than a case of being celibate too long.

'Right, the steaks are done.' Deke strode in carrying a hefty white china platter, and the mouthwatering aroma shifted Griff's mind off sex to the fact he was ravenous. 'Where's my lovely bride?'

'I'm here.' Becca hurried in to join them, her stepson trudging along behind like a man going to his execution.

'You're starving, aren't you, Theo?' Her smile and voice were both a little too bright.

It didn't take a psychic to sense Deke's annoyance when the boy stayed stonily silent.

'Sit by me, Theo.' Deke's tone made it clear he didn't expect an argument. 'I'll take Nora, Lyndsey, so you can eat.' He set the platter down and reached for the sleeping baby.

Griff totally got that his friend wanted time with his new daughter before he left, but Theo's angry, flashing eyes said his son saw it as another kick in the teeth.

Becca grabbed a pile of cutlery out of the drawer and tossed it on the table for them all to grab.

Before Lyndsey had a chance to sit elsewhere, Griff yanked out two chairs and gestured for her to sit down.

'No kale salad?' He reached for the bowl of jacket potatoes. 'I'm disappointed.'

'I was banned.' One of Lyndsey's smiles broke through. 'We do have roasted broccoli, though. I need something green, even if no one else does.'

'I'm not allergic to green stuff.' Griff scooped a heaping spoon of the broccoli she offered on his plate. 'My vegetable garden's shapin' up to be pretty good this season. I don't give it all away, either. I eat a bunch myself.'

'Glad to hear it.' She hesitated. 'I'd like your opinion about something . . . and maybe your help.'

'You can have both. Willingly.'

'Don't be too hasty. You might regret the offer when you hear what it's about,' she said with a husky laugh, leaning in closer. Her arm pressed against his, and he couldn't avoid breathing in her warm scent. 'I met poor Ruth Mae Grey this afternoon when I took Nora out for a walk and that woman needs our help.'

'She actually spoke to you?'

'Yes. It started by her telling me off for staring at that incredible bird bath. The one that looks like it belongs in the grounds of an English stately home.'

'You're spot-on about where it came from. Deke told me it was imported from some fancy estate, and used to be a fixture at the front of Grey House. It was the one thing Miss Grey insisted wasn't sold with the property.'

'That explains it.' Lyndsey's smile widened. 'I'm afraid she went on to verbally tear all of you apart.'

'I can imagine.' He hated to put a dent in her generous nature, but needed to inject a dose of realism. 'You've got a kind heart, but there's no way Miss Grey will accept help from any of us. We've all tried at different times and been snubbed. She wouldn't give me the time of day the one occasion I said hi to her.'

Lyndsey gave a subtle nod towards her sister. 'Becca thinks I'm crazy, and maybe I am. I don't usually . . .' She looked distinctly embarrassed.

'Get involved? Hey, it's what folk do for neighbors, friends, family. The world would be a better place if we all stuck out our necks a bit.' Recklessly he covered her left hand that rested on the table with his own. Griff's heart raced when instead of pulling it away, she hooked one of her fingers through his.

'So, are you in, or am I on my own here?'

'What do you think? Yeah, we'll have a go.' He didn't think for one minute they'd be successful, but couldn't resist anything that dangled the possibility of spending more time with Lyndsey in front of him. 'We'll try killing her with kindness.'

'I wasn't suggesting we murder Miss Grey.'

'I sure hope not.' He roared with laughter, setting her off too. Far too late he realized they'd become the focus of everyone's attention. Deke and Becca were exchanging smug smiles and Theo had stopped shoveling food in his mouth to throw them a puzzled look. Even Nora's little head bobbed in their direction.

Griff let go of her hand and dived into his juicy steak with a smile on his face.

CHAPTER FIVE

'This kills you, doesn't it?' Becca rummaged through a dresser drawer overflowing with tiny baby clothes.

'Would you mind humoring me by answering one question?' Deke had only been gone for a couple of days, but Lyndsey missed him as a buffer between her and her sister. After almost a week of existing in the mayhem of Becca's house, she'd already come close to ripping out every hair on her head.

Every room in the sprawling five-bedroom house was bursting at the seams, the dark oak floors hadn't been cleaned in forever and the only word to describe the neutral cream-and-white color scheme was grubby. It struck her as a shame, because the bones of the building were stunning. Deke had done an exceptional job with its renovation and the original parts of Grey House blended seamlessly with the modern upgrades and extension. It was the little touches that most appealed to Lyndsey. The arched top to an elaborate doorway. A single dramatic tall window overlooking the gently curved staircase. The exquisitely carved crown mouldings. None of those things could truly be appreciated in the state it was now.

'How would it be to have a little time each day for yourself?' Lyndsey asked.

'That's a stupid thing to ask any frazzled new mother.' She flopped down cross-legged on the floor and started tugging clothes out of another drawer. 'I suppose you'll claim tidying all this lot up would be equivalent to waving a magic wand and having a fairy godmother appear?'

'I wouldn't quite put it that way, but—'

'But nothing.' Becca pulled out a scrap of pink and waved the miniature onesie in the air with a triumphant fist punch. 'Found it.' She angled Lyndsey a hard stare. 'You promised Mum and me you wouldn't nag. If I want your professional help, I'll ask for it.'

If Lyndsey claimed she was raising the subject out of concern for her sister, she'd be laughed out of the room, but she was genuinely worried. Yesterday, Becca grudgingly admitted she bit Deke's head off the night before he left when he suggested finding someone to clean the house and take care of the endless amounts of washing. It sounded a brilliant idea to Lyndsey, but her sister was notoriously stubborn. This was a woman who abandoned her career as an up-and-coming designer with a major London fashion house six weeks after meeting and falling in love with the charismatic Deke at a post-concert party. She followed him to America, and three months later, they returned to Cornwall for their hastily arranged wedding. Before the ink was dry on the marriage license, she fell pregnant.

'Okay, but at least let me help out more, though. It's what I came for, after all. I'm not much of a cook, but I'm perfectly capable of clearing up after meals and I know how to work a washing machine.' She crossed her fingers out of sight while the wheels turned in her sister's head.

'I suppose that would be okay, but don't look too satisfied,' she warned, 'you are absolutely not doing your thing on my whole house.' Becca glanced at her phone and groaned. 'I'll be late picking up Theo if I don't get a move on. You'll be okay with Nora?'

'Of course. Off you go.' Her heart sunk. So far she'd been lucky and Nora had napped every time her sister was doing the school run, but it must be only a matter of time before her niece caught her out.

'If she gives you any trouble, call on the cavalry from next door.' Becca winked. 'I'm sure the yummy Griff would be happy to lend a hand.'

'Griff?'

'Oh, come on, Li-Li, the two of you were thick as thieves at dinner Tuesday night.'

'We were talking about how to help Miss Grey, that's all.' Heat prickled her neck and she avoided her sister's provocative stare.

'If you say so. The miserable old cow won't appreciate it, you know.'

'Have you ever even spoken to her?'

The rhetorical question made Becca's face turn bright red. Her sister's lack of involvement in their small Paradise Valley community was another point of contention between her and Deke. *Contention* wasn't the right word, it was more concern on her brother-in-law's part. He saw huge benefits in his wife having more friends, especially when he was away. But Becca would have none of it, swearing she didn't have the time. Lyndsey could totally see where Deke was coming from. By nature Becca was a social butterfly and the isolation of her present life was draining the joy out of her. Lyndsey used to envy the groups of girlfriends Becca effortlessly gathered around her, but there was no sign of her sister attempting to replicate that here.

'We were talking about Griff before you veered off-topic,' Becca said with a smirk. 'Mum told me about you and Tristan. Whatever got into you? You two were always best mates, but you never fancied him. She says you aren't even talking to each other now.'

Lyndsey said nothing. Last year she'd looked at her life and tried to see it from the viewpoint of someone looking in from the outside. Owner of a successful, but all-consuming business. Helping out her parents. Regular long walks. A healthy diet. She'd seen the same pattern stretching into the foreseeable future with no change in sight. Altering her relationship with Tristan from best friend to boyfriend hadn't seemed a huge stretch.

'You've got to admit, Griff is pretty fit,' her sister persisted. 'Very easy on the eyes. Smart too. If I wasn't happily married, I'd definitely be tempted. He's something of a mystery, and doesn't say much about his past, and that's always intriguing.' Her eyes sparkled. 'I'm not sure how you and I would get on as neighbors, though.'

'Neighbors!'

'Oh, Li-Li, it's so easy to pull your chain,' Becca said with a giggle. 'Must go. Time for another face-off with dear Theo. Take care of my sweet little girl.' She breezed out of the bedroom, leaving Lyndsey standing and staring into space.

* * *

The strident sound of a wailing baby drifted across the lawn. Griff's curiosity won out over common sense and he strolled across the grass to pull aside a few branches of his favorite pink dogwood tree. April's stunning blossoms were gone by now, replaced by vibrant green leaves. May was the lushest of months, to be savored and enjoyed before the searing hot summer kicked in with a vengeance.

'Everythin' all right?'

Frustration suffused Lyndsey's face when she spotted him. 'No, it's not.' She swayed around, jiggling Nora in her arms, but that only made the baby cry even louder.

'Did Becca leave you stranded?'

'School run.'

'Do you want a hand? Or maybe two?' He waggled his hands in the air.

'I'm sure you've got better things to do.'

'Maybe, but I'm happy to try anyway.' Before she could argue, he let the branches fall back in place and sprinted off down the drive. Griff trotted along the short stretch of pavement between their two houses and on up Deke's drive.

'I thought the fresh air might calm her down,' Lyndsey said with a rueful sigh. 'It didn't work.'

'Really?' Griff chuckled. 'Pass her over.'

'You're sure? Good luck.' She thrust Nora in his direction as the tightly swaddled pink bundle emitted another ear-piercing shriek.

He shifted the crying baby so she nestled in the hollow of his shoulder. 'That tuft of dark hair never does stay down,' he said, smiling at Nora's natural mohawk.

'You're an observant man.'

'I sure try to be.' Griff swept his gaze over her and slashes of heat highlighted her sharp cheekbones. He cleared his throat, determined to concentrate on the fussy baby instead of his temptation to flirt. 'I'll try walking her around.'

Over the last couple of years, he'd buried himself in work while he built up his business, apart from a few visits to his family in East Tennessee. Occasionally he got together with Deke and Becca or his other neighbors — excepting Ruth Mae Grey, who pointedly ignored them all. Griff didn't regret settling in this out-of-the-way spot — far from it. The small convenience shop in nearby Adamsville with its homely café, occasional live music and gas station served him well, while the nearest real town, Franklin, was a good ten miles away. Downtown Nashville was the best part of an hour's drive away, but he rarely had any desire to go there these days. Despite staying busy in a good way, as opposed to the hectic hamster-on-a-wheel existence he lived before, he occasionally found himself lonely. Even before he met Lyndsey, he'd begun to wonder if finding someone to share his days, and nights, with might not be a bad thing.

'So, Nora, why're you trying your hardest to outcry the birds?' He chatted as he walked, describing the trees and flowers he recognized, and pointed out a bluebird darting through the air and a couple of blackbirds perched high on the roof. Griff glanced down to see Nora's big brown eyes had fluttered closed, her long dark lashes feathering against rosy cheeks. Cutting out the monolog, he kept moving and finished making a circuit of the house. Rounding the last corner, he spotted Lyndsey with her back to him, but before he could indulge in watching her unobserved he made the mistake of stepping on a twig. The cracking sound made her glance his way, and a smile worked its way across her face.

'You did it,' she mouthed.

Griff nodded towards the porch. They tiptoed across the grass together and he waited until she settled in a rocking chair before lowering himself gingerly into the one next to her. The change of position made Nora stir and he held his breath while she stretched, yawned and burrowed back into Griff with a satisfied sigh. 'Do you hear that?' he whispered.

'What?'

'A peaceful sleeping baby. Unlike that noisy bird.' He smiled at a bright red bird chattering away in the tulip poplar tree next to them. 'That's a Northern Cardinal. They say its call is like two coins hitting each other.'

Lyndsey's eyes twinkled. 'So you're a twitcher . . . like my dad.' Her eyes turned shiny with tears. 'At least he used to be, when he was well enough to get out and about.' Griff saw her straighten her shoulders like a sergeant major, and there was a firmer edge to her voice when she spoke again. 'I'm sure he'll be out on the cliffs with his binoculars again soon. He's recovering incredibly well from the kidney transplant. I check in every day and Mum says he's able to walk further all the time. He made it the half mile or so to our local pub for the first time yesterday.'

'That's awesome. It sounds like it must've been a difficult time for y'all.'

'Yes.' A faraway look spread over her face. 'He'd been sick for so long, but knowing his improved health is down to someone else's misfortune . . .' Her voice trailed away.

'It's hard to be completely happy. I can see that.' Although he shouldn't compare their situations, he'd been similarly torn by the time he resigned from his old job. If he'd received the promotion he fought tooth and nail for, it would've come at the expense of the woman he was then dating. By the time he came to his senses, it was already too late for him and Olivia. Now, with the benefit of hindsight, he saw they wouldn't have lasted the course anyway, but that didn't make his behavior at the time any less dishonorable.

'You're right.' She opened her mouth to say something, but then tilted him a wary smile, as though she wasn't sure he was ready to hear it.

'Go on,' Griff encouraged.

'You looked miles away there for a few moments, that's all. Do you want to tell me why?'

He knew she wasn't referring to physical distance and everything to do with the thoughts racing through his head. If he shared the full story with Lyndsey, would it put a stop to the friendship — or perhaps more — that they kept inching towards? But pretending he had no idea what she was referring to would be a lie, and he was through with those. 'Not yet.'

'I can wait.'

Griff heard a definite hint of promise in her response.

'When I was a little girl, Dad tried to teach me about our Cornish birds, but I'm afraid I wasn't a very good student.'

He could've kissed her for changing the topic of conversation. That would have to wait for another time and place, when he was more certain of them both. 'That's because you weren't interested. If you had been, I'm sure you'd have aced every test he gave. I only really got into bird-watching when I moved here and was curious about the different varieties I spotted every day.' Griff gave a soft chuckle. 'My last girlfriend complained that my interest in decrepit barns was an old-man hobby and saw bird-watching the same way.'

'Rubbish. I'm guessing we're a similar age, so if you're an old man, I must be an old woman and I'm definitely not admitting to that any time soon.'

'If we'd met last year, I could've claimed to be in my late thirties, but the big 4-0 hit back before Christmas.'

She broke into a wide, infectious grin. 'That means I can still gloat about being a spry young thing. I've got another three years before I'm on that particular downward path.'

'Don't fret. It'll look good on you.'

'Flatterer.'

'Yeah. You have a problem with that?' A certain question nagged at his brain, but if her answer wasn't what he hoped for, Griff was afraid he wouldn't be able to do the 'just friends' thing with Lyndsey. *Coward.* 'Or perhaps you've got a husband/partner/boyfriend who *would* mind?'

'No. No one.'

Was it wishful thinking to believe he heard a note of sadness in her voice? Was she like him, and wondering if what they had in their outwardly fulfilled lives was enough? Griff nodded, satisfied with the hint of pink flushing her cheeks.

'So, what do you do for a living anyway?' she asked. 'Becca was cagey when I asked the other day. She said I should ask you myself and promised I'd be surprised. I dreamed up all kinds of bizarre possibilities afterwards.'

'Like what?'

'Oh, maybe you're an undercover FBI agent or an illegal arms dealer.'

He spluttered with laughter and Nora let out a shriek at having her peaceful nap disturbed. Unconsciously he'd stopped rocking the chair, so he set it going again and waited for Nora to settle before daring to continue their whispered conversation. 'If you pop over to my cottage tomorrow, I'll happily show you my secret. I promise it's nothing illegal, and not that mysterious either. Becca's pulling your chain.' Griff held his breath, waiting for her response, then mentally cursed as a jaunty bright red sports car swept up the drive and braked in front of them. Would she have said yes or no, he wondered.

'I see Becca's driving skills haven't improved. I'm amazed she's still got her license. My dear sister used to collect speeding tickets like other people collect stamps.'

'Don't you two look cosy?' Becca leapt out of the car and smirked. 'If anyone didn't know better, they'd think—'

'Shush.' Their simultaneous plea for silence came too late. Nora's eyes flew open and she let out a shrill wail.

Theo clambered out and threw his stepmother a scathing look. 'I'm goin' to my room.' He slouched off, his thin shoulders hunched under the weight of his bulging backpack.

'Damn,' Becca groaned. 'He voluntarily spoke more than two words in the car on the way home today, too. I should've known it couldn't last.'

'Hang in there. It's early days.' Griff's attempt at positivity did nothing to brighten her grim expression. He'd continued to rock Nora and she'd gone quiet again, staring up at him. It crossed his mind she might find his unusual mismatched eyes fascinating, then told himself not to be silly. From the little he knew about babies, he was pretty sure they couldn't even focus well at this age.

'I'll take her, Griff, and let you get back to work.' Becca's weak smile had no effect on the edges of her downturned mouth.

He reluctantly handed Nora over and instantly missed the little girl's heavy warmth in his arms.

'Thanks again for rescuing me,' Lyndsey murmured.

He mouthed the word — *tomorrow* — over her sister's shoulder. A flare of happiness shot through him when she nodded back. Griff kept his expression neutral when Becca slid them both a look brimming with curiosity. If the spark of possibility fizzing between he and Lyndsey had the ghost of a chance, then her matchmaking sister needed to be the last to know about it.

CHAPTER SIX

Nerves fluttered in Griff's stomach. Anyone would think he was fourteen instead of forty. Lyndsey was on her way over to see where he worked — plain and simple — nothing more. But did he want it to be more? He'd tossed and turned all night asking the same question. There'd been a definite connection between them yesterday, but that could've been nothing more than friendly empathy.

Today he crawled out of bed with the dawn chorus, making do with a mug of scalding hot black coffee for breakfast before throwing himself straight into work. Once, Griff had tried to explain the multiple steps involved in making one of his stained-glass pieces to Deke and watched his eyes glaze over. To him, though, it wasn't work, the same as any other job that revolved around someone's passion. His friend had agreed when Griff asked if creating music was really any different. Composing, rehearsing, pulling together a show — none of those conformed to a nine-to-five, five-days-a-week schedule either.

First on his to-do list was turning the design he'd created on the computer into working pattern pieces. By nine o'clock, he finished copying and tracing the three paper copies needed. Then the ninety-five pieces for the first panel all had to be numbered, a slash line added to indicate the grain direction for each piece of glass, and a color designated from the glass choices he made yesterday to match his vision for the completed panels. Now he was done cutting out the pieces with special pattern shears, an exacting process that took all his concentration. After Lyndsey left, he'd attach the labeled pieces to the appropriate sheet of glass with rubber cement — a simple-sounding process that was far from it. For a start, a typical sheet of glass wasn't uniform — the color might be more saturated in one part, or a bubble could've erupted in another section; any glass artist in tune with their craft used that to their advantage. Then there was the practical placement of pattern pieces so the least amount of expensive glass was wasted. Only when all that was complete did he have the luxury of one of his favorite jobs, actually cutting the glass.

'Knock, knock, it's me.' Lyndsey's lilting voice trickled in. 'Is it safe to come into your secret lair?'

'Yeah, come on in.' Before Griff had a chance to open the door, she beat him to it and stepped inside. Her sharp green eyes widened with surprise. Instead of throwing a barrage of questions his way, she silently made her way around his workshop, checking everything out. Stopping at the back wall, she studied the finished pieces hanging there.

'So, I'm taking a wild guess this isn't another "old-man hobby" you use as a cover for your secretive real life? You're a dark horse, Griffin Oakes. These are stunning. Why keep quiet about it?'

'I don't. Not really,' he mumbled and rubbed his hands on his jeans, not knowing quite what to do with them. 'Sit down. Please.' Griff pulled out a high black leather stool. 'It's clean. I haven't been working with the glass or any lead yet today.'

'Is that an issue?'

'Oh, yeah. My first teacher was real strict, and ingrained it in our thick skulls never to cut corners on keeping our work stations clean. We spent a lot of time mopping the floor and wiping down the work surfaces to eliminate glass slivers and lead dust. Dave was a paramedic in his day job and taught us first aid as well, so we'd know what to do when we cut ourselves.' He chuckled. 'Notice I said when . . . not if.'

Lyndsey suddenly reached for his hands and the brush of her warm skin against his sent shivers running through him. 'Now you've satisfied my curiosity about these.' She stroked the mesh of tiny scars that'd become such a part of him, Griff barely noticed them these days. 'I want to know everything. What did you do before this? How did you become such a talented artist?' He spotted an unmistakable flare of heat in her dark Caribbean skin. 'Sorry. Am I being pushy? Becca claims I've got no filter.'

Griff smothered his disappointment when she let his hands drop away.

'When it comes to *my* business, people pay me extremely well to sort out their homes and work spaces. From day one, I make it clear I'm not going to hold their hands and tiptoe around whatever problems they've got. If they can't handle my forthright style, they need to find someone whose personality matches theirs better.'

'Does that mean you lose a lot of clients?'

'Not really, and those I do, it's the best solution for us both. We obviously wouldn't have suited, so it would never have worked . . .' She looked embarrassed. 'I haven't given you a chance to answer any of my questions, have I?'

'No, but that's okay. You ended up revealing more about you. In my book, there's nothin' wrong with being straightforward. I prefer it.' A wave of shyness overwhelmed him. He wasn't fond of talking about himself or his work, preferring both to speak for themselves. 'About five years ago an ex-girlfriend dragged me along to a stained-glass workshop class she'd been given as a birthday present. She hated it. I loved it. I'd never done any sort of art work before, but it felt right, if that makes sense?'

'Absolutely. I was an accountant — a good one — but that was always just a job.'

'Yeah, mine was too, although I hadn't realized it at that point. Watching the teacher turn pieces of colored glass into pictures only he could see in his head blew my mind. I'll show you the first piece I made one day. I've got it hanging in the house.' He grinned. 'It's pretty bad, but if I'm having a down day, it reminds me how far I've come. What about you? What steered you towards home organization?'

It wasn't hard to get caught up in her enthusiasm as she explained about a Japanese woman who started a movement celebrating a minimalist approach to life. 'That was my light-bulb moment. I adapted Marie Kondo's way to be less strict, although when I told Becca that once, she roared with laughter. She thinks I'm directly descended from Attila the Hun when it comes to doing things a particular way.' Lyndsey shrugged. 'Anyway, tell me more about how you got from beginners' classes to this.'

'Every spare minute I wasn't working, I took more classes to grow my skills. I started selling a few pieces at craft fairs and picked up my first commission for one of the fancy McMansions in Brentwood — that's a wealthy area not far from here, with massive showy homes screaming money. The business mushroomed and I didn't have enough hours in the day, or space in my head, for all I wanted to do. So I chucked in my job.'

'Doing what?'

'Senior manager in a health care company, with the fancy downtown apartment, designer suits and tickets to all the top concerts.' He wasn't ready to go into any more details and hoped she wouldn't push. 'I had a decent amount of savings and wasn't responsible for anyone else, so I took the plunge and resigned. Sold my apartment for a decent profit. This place was on the market, and although the cabin wasn't in great shape, the location appealed to me, plus it had a dilapidated shed perfect for converting into a workshop. That's it, really.'

'What's that?' she asked, pointing to a mosaic paperweight fashioned in the shape of a fish.

Griff felt himself blush. 'It's something new I'm experimenting with. All stained-glass artists end up with a lot of glass offcuts we can't use, but I'd never given any thought to how they could be recycled until I went to a craft fair in Nashville and saw an amazingly talented lady selling mosaic pieces similar to that. I gave it a try, and I'm finding myself more and more drawn to it.' He picked up the paperweight and offered it to her. 'It's more affordable, if my bigger pieces are out of a customer's reach. But there aren't enough hours in the day, so if I'm not careful I'll get distracted by this, and not get my commissions done on time.'

Lyndsey studied it closely. 'It's beautiful.'

'Thanks . . . uh, keep it. Please.'

'Oh, I couldn't possibly.'

'Why not?' He gave a sheepish smile. 'I'd like you to have it.'

'Only if you let me pay for it.'

'Okay.' Griff's prompt agreement caught her by surprise. 'How much is it?'

He folded his arms and pretended to think. 'One dinner date should cover it.'

'A dinner date?' Lyndsey's voice rose. 'With me?'

'Yeah. Who did you think? I'm hardly goin' to ask out your married sister, and the only other single woman around here is Tiffany, who lives across the road, and we're good friends, nothing more.' Griff smacked the side of his head. 'I almost forgot Ruth Mae Grey. I could be her toy boy.'

'Idiot.' A peal of full-throated laughter burst out of her.

'Right. Let's stick to my original plan. One date with me, when it fits in with your busy schedule next door.' Griff stuck out his hand. 'Do we have a deal?'

* * *

Lyndsey's heart raced and she panicked. 'I really should go. It's getting late, and Becca will be off to do the school run soon, so I'll be on Nora duty.' She saw disappointment flicker in Griff's eyes and hoped he wouldn't press for an answer. A long time ago, she swore never to be swept away by what

51

people ridiculously called 'love at first sight.' She made sure her sensible head always overruled her heart.

'How're you two getting on? It can't be easy.'

'No, it isn't . . . for either of us, I suppose. If we're too honest with each other, we'll end up arguing, and I'll be on the next plane back home.' She shrugged. 'Do you have any brothers or sisters?'

'One brother, but we're not close. I don't remember the last time we spoke.' Griff's husky drawl faded to an uneasy silence, and she sensed she'd touched a nerve.

'Becca's struggling, and I'm not sure how to help. She and Deke didn't have time to adjust to being married before she got pregnant. Theo coming to live with them right away hasn't helped.' She hurried to make herself clear. 'Don't get me wrong, I'm not blaming Deke for everything, but my sister tends to be impulsive and doesn't think things through.'

'If it helps any, I know Deke's concerned too, and guilty about goin' away. He was pretty torn up when we spoke a day or two before he left.'

'It does. I hope he'll step up and try to sort it when he comes back. It's no good sweeping these things under the carpet.'

A hint of amusement tugged at Griff's mouth. 'That sure wouldn't be the "right place" for it.'

'You can't resist, can you?' Against her will, Lyndsey laughed. 'No one's ever made so many appalling jokes about my business name as you!'

'Glad to hear I'm best at something.'

She suspected that was merely the tip of a very dangerous iceberg of things Griff Oakes was good at. Kissing came to mind, as it always did when they were face to face and she imagined his firm, shapely mouth pressed against . . . Before she got in even deeper water, Lyndsey forced herself to stop.

'I'm forgetting the time. I should leave you to get on with your work.' Around him she tended to forget everything, mooning like a teenage girl overtaken by her first serious crush. This wasn't the sensible, competent woman she'd shaped herself to be. 'Perhaps another day you'll talk me through the process of making one of your pieces. It's fascinating.' Lyndsey could hardly blame him for the frown settling between his thick tawny eyebrows. Blowing hot and cold wasn't her usual style.

'Yeah, I'd be happy to. It might have to wait 'til this project's finished. I'm on a deadline.'

She wouldn't lower herself to beg. As the old saying went, there were plenty more fish in the sea, if she was inclined to use herself as bait. 'I understand.' And she did. Normally she made it perfectly clear where men stood with her, but with Griff, it was like walking on sand where it shifted all the time. 'Cheerio, then.'

Lyndsey strode away, leaving the mosaic paperweight sitting on the workbench, and closed the door quietly behind her.

The short walk back to Becca's house allowed Lyndsey a few moments to calm down. If her sister picked up on anything going on between her and Griff she wouldn't be able to resist the temptation to interfere. Outside the front door she took a few breaths, smoothed out a crease in her pale gray cotton trousers, plastered on a smile and stepped back into the madhouse.

Angry voices drifted out from the kitchen. Becca's shrill tone was easy to distinguish, but she could swear the other belonged to Theo, which made no sense because he should still be at school. She debated whether to creep up to her room and leave them to it, or join them.

'You're not my mother, so I don't have to listen to you.' Theo barreled into the hall with Becca close on his heels. Fury glazed the boy's bright blue eyes. 'If my dad was here, *he'd* understand!' He shook off Becca when she tried to grab his arm and thundered up the stairs like a herd of stampeding elephants.

'I just got Nora off to sleep,' Becca moaned. 'God, he's thoughtless.'

'Whatever is wrong?'

'Oh, Li-Li, I can't do this any longer.' Tears trickled down her sister's pale, drawn face, making a damp patch on the front of her stained, washed-out blue cotton dress. A couple of years ago her glamorous sister wouldn't even have owned something that unfashionable, let alone wear it two days in a row.

Lyndsey instinctively wrapped her arms around her. The simmering differences between them seemed irrelevant now. 'It's going to be okay. I promise.'

'But how?' Becca wailed. 'My life isn't an overflowing wardrobe to be weeded out and organized.'

She wouldn't be stupid enough to say it wasn't really that different, because her sibling's life was also chaotic, over-stuffed and emotionally draining.

'Let's put the kettle on.'

The ghost of a smile lifted the corners of her sister's down-turned mouth. 'You sounded like Mum then, and it made me homesick.' Becca swiped at her red-rimmed eyes. 'I'm not drinking any of your nasty herbal rubbish,' she warned. 'A strong cup of PG Tips was Mum's remedy for everything from skinned knees to teenage broken hearts, so that's what we're having.'

Lyndsey blinked away a wave of emotion. 'You've totally convinced me to join you.'

'You're such a wild thing. We'll have you dancing on the tables of the Wildhorse Saloon yet!'

She hitched her arm through her sister's and steered her towards the kitchen, content to be gently mocked if it brought them closer. Now she could see that many of their clashes were down to nothing more than normal sibling rivalry. Few children who'd been the center of their parents' lives for as long as Lyndsey would've been thrilled to be forced to share them with a new arrival. It wasn't Becca's fault that her openly friendly personality and blonde prettiness made her more popular than her reserved, prickly older sister. But Becca wasn't blameless, because she'd gone out of her way to use that to her advantage. If they could learn to move past all that, then perhaps the help Lyndsey provided with Nora would turn out to be the least important achievement of this trip. Their mother was smart.

'You sit down.' She filled up the kettle and reached down a hefty brown teapot from one of the open-plan shelves. 'Is this Granny's?'

'Yes, Mum gave it to me when I got married,' Becca said. 'She didn't think you'd want it. You don't mind, do you?'

If she were completely honest she'd say yes, she did mind. She'd been far closer to their grandmother, Amy Trerice, and often ran to her nearby house after school to share tea and confidences.

'Of course not,' Lyndsey lied. Once the tea was made, she raided the precious stash of Minstrels she'd hidden in a drawer and handed one bag to her sister, keeping another out for herself.

'God knows I need this.' Becca ripped the packet open and crammed a handful of the crunchy chocolates in her mouth. 'While you were at Griff's, the school rang to say Theo started a fight with another boy during lunch. When the teacher asked him to explain what it was about, he refused to answer, so I had to go pick him up.'

'Why didn't you tell me? I would've come back so you didn't have to haul Nora with you.' She poured two mugs of tea, added milk to them and passed one across to Becca.

'I didn't want to spoil things for you, and I . . . I hate feeling so useless all the time.' Her voice oozed with frustration. 'Before I reached the school, I was determined to be the totally understanding stepmother and stand up for him.' Becca heaved a sigh. 'That part wasn't a problem, so I hoped he'd be able to confide in me when we got home, and I'd make him see we're in this together.' She dropped her head. 'You saw how well that went.' She licked a finger and worked on the stain marring her dress. 'I know I need to be more patient, but it's so hard.'

'I know. I can see how much you have to deal with. I've got a few ideas that might help if—'

'If I'm willing to listen?'

If they don't care for my forthright style, they can find someone else. But *forthright* was one thing. *Dictatorial* quite another. 'Yes, but I'll do the same. Now eat some more chocolate and hear me out.'

CHAPTER SEVEN

Griff stopped the lawnmower and lifted his arm to wipe the sweat from his face with the sleeve of his ragged T-shirt. He pulled out a water bottle from his shorts' pocket and gulped it down, then threw the empty bottle up on the porch to put in the recycling later.

The roar of a car engine disturbed the peace, and he saw Deke's Mercedes swing by with Lyndsey at the wheel. If he was any sort of friend, he'd offer to cut his friend's grass, too. It bewildered him why they didn't pay for a lawn service, but maybe Becca put her foot down over that as well.

You're just dreaming up an excuse to go over there.

He whipped out his phone to fire off a quick text, and in no time at all Becca's response flew right back.

Yes please! You're an angel.

Griff preferred his familiar mower over Deke's fancier model, so wheeled it on down the drive then along the pavement before turning into Deke's. Out of nowhere, Lyndsey materialized in front of him, cool and immaculate in a crisp white shirt and black capris. He didn't think he'd ever seen her wearing any other colors apart from black, white and gray, which struck him as unusual, now that he thought about it.

'You must not be baby wrangling today.'

'What makes you say that?'

'Your clothes are pristine. Not a stain in sight.'

'For all you know, I might've just changed,' Lyndsey protested.

'I was only havin' a bit of fun with you. I've come to mow the yard.'

'I'm sorry, I didn't mean to be—'

'It's okay. You go back to doin' whatever you were in the middle of and I'll get on with it.' He was too hot and sweaty to argue.

'I've just returned from picking up Theo. I actually persuaded Becca to let me do the school run until he gets out next week for the summer.'

'How on earth did you manage that?'

'I could see it added more stress to Becca's day, and I've driven a lot in Europe, so it doesn't bother me being on the other side of the road.' She shrugged it off. 'It helped she was extra fed-up with him when I offered. The day I came over to see you, he got in trouble for fighting at school.'

'Theo? Fighting?'

'Yes, we've never found out why though. He won't say.'

'Can't Deke get it out of him?'

'He doesn't know.'

Griff tried to hide his dismay.

'I know. I think he's got the right to hear about it too, but Becca's stubborn and insists he's got enough on his mind.'

'There's some logic to that, I guess.'

'Anyway, you were sort-of right earlier, before I went to get Theo I was indeed baby wrangling, and I did get messy and I did change. Call me fussy if you like.'

'I'd never do that.' He risked a teasing smile. 'Particular maybe, but there's nothin' wrong with that.' Griff stepped away. 'You don't wanna get downwind of me. I cut my own grass before this and I didn't reckon Becca would mind if I continued as I was.'

'You didn't bargain on me.' A hint of good humor played around her wide mouth, the sunlight picking up hints of deep rosy pink lip gloss. He was swept by a powerful urge to kiss it all off.

'You're right there.' His wry reaction deepened her smile.

'I must go. I'm on baby alert.' Lyndsey showed him her phone with a live feed of Nora curled up in her crib. 'I've just sent Becca up for a shower.'

'I'll bet my last dollar you've been busy around the house every chance you can when your sister's been busy doin' other stuff. Did you start on the kitchen and purge it of unnecessary stuff and scrub it from top to bottom?'

'Even if my sister *was* one of my clients, which she most definitely isn't, that's not the way I work.' The icy glare she aimed his way could combat global warming. 'Organizing someone's house is a collaborative process. *I* throw nothing away. I help my clients choose what deserves to take up a space in their lives and what doesn't.' She angled him a searching look. 'Your workshop is a perfect example of making a space work for you, instead of the other way around. Everything has a specific place and fills a specific purpose, leaving you free to be creative.'

'It's partly a safety issue, but you're right.'

'Is your house the same way? The two don't necessarily follow.' Embarrassment flared in her face, and he guessed she hadn't meant to be so forthright.

An invitation for her to come over and check it out for herself hovered on the tip of his tongue, but he held back. 'This isn't getting the yard done.'

'It certainly isn't. Slacker.' Lyndsey's bright green eyes danced like emeralds in the sunlight. She'd seen right through his cowardly response. 'I'll leave you to it.'

Yeah, you do that. She'd shaken him up like a kaleidoscope, leaving a multi-colored jumble that made as much sense as one of his designs when it was nothing more than sheets of glass waiting for him to work his magic.

* * *

59

Lyndsey fled into the quiet house, cheeks burning. She'd kept out of Griff's way for the last three days since her visit to his workshop, when she deftly avoided saying either yes or no to his unexpected dinner invitation. It hadn't been hard to stay well clear of him, because she barely had a minute to spare in between helping her sister and keeping The Right Place ticking over long distance, in the temporary office area she'd set up in the corner of her bedroom.

'I saw you out there flirting with the help.' Becca, freshly showered, ran down the stairs. 'You'll need to get a move on. At your ages, you can't afford to waste time.'

'Charming. For a start, neither of us has one foot in the grave yet, and for another, we most certainly weren't flirting.' A prickle of heat started at her neck and worked its way up to make her cheeks burn. 'Not really.'

That reluctant confession made her sister burst out laughing. The shimmer of heat she'd seen in Griff's mismatched eyes had nothing to do with today's soaring temperatures. He'd most definitely been on the verge of inviting her to his house before thinking better of it.

'He's very fond of my millionaire's shortbread. I'll whip up a batch soon to thank him for cutting the grass and you can deliver it in person.'

'You bake?'

'Don't sound so surprised.' Becca turned huffy. 'I might be a disorganized mess and a lousy mum but—'

'You are *not* a lousy mum. Nora's thriving and you're trying your absolute hardest with Theo.'

'You didn't argue with the "disorganized mess" bit.'

'If I agree you'll throw a wobbly, and if I don't—'

'You'd be a liar and we both know you're a scrupulously honest person. It's one reason we clash. I've never seen fudging the truth as a hanging offence.'

Almost on cue, the faint drone of the mower stopped.

'Strike while the iron's hot. The poor bloke's bound to be gasping, and I happen to know you've got a jug of home-made lemonade in the fridge. Take out the biggest glass you can find with plenty of ice and he'll be putty in your hands.' Her sister tripped happily on. 'The two of you fancy each other like mad, and by my calculation you've got about two months left to seal the deal, and that's if you're staying until Deke comes home. Are you?'

'I'm not sure,' Lyndsey muttered. 'I'll take Griff a drink, but only because he needs it.'

'Liar, liar, pants on fire.' Nora's thin cry pulsed from Becca's phone. 'No peace for the wicked. I'll knock on Theo's door while I'm up there and mention you've got cold drinks on offer. He'll want cookies, too. There are plenty left in the jar, so you can give our grass cutter some as well.' She gave a wry smile. 'If I forget and call them "biscuits," Theo will deliberately misunderstand and complain when you don't have the scone-like things they eat here for breakfast.'

Before her sister could dole out more unsolicited advice, Lyndsey decamped to the kitchen. She opened the cupboard where the glasses were kept and gave in to a tiny smile. It'd been the truth when she denied throwing anything away, but she *had* surreptitiously cleaned and straightened up in a few places, so far with no negative feedback. The sparkling glasses were now arranged in height order which made it easy to select a suitably hefty mug. Once it was filled with tart lemonade and plenty of ice, she added a sprig of mint from one of the pots of herbs on the windowsill. The fancy addition would make Griff laugh, but she didn't care. She fished a couple of chocolate chip cookies out of the black-and-white ceramic crock shaped like a cow and wrapped them in a paper napkin. Arranging them on a pretty plate would be a step too far.

It was automatic to check her appearance in the mirror and she tucked a rogue curl back behind her ear; of course, it wouldn't stay there long, because her hair was notoriously unruly when it started to grow out of its usual short style. Lyndsey fished out a tube of lip gloss from her pocket and slicked on a fresh layer. Anything more would look as if she was trying too hard. She carried her offerings out onto the porch.

'Well, you sure are a welcome sight.' He'd taken up residence in one of the rocking chairs.

'Me or the lemonade?'

'Fishing for compliments, are we?' Amusement threaded through his deep, smooth drawl. 'I'm happy to dole them out anytime you like.'

'I was joking.' Lyndsey thrust the glass into his out-stretched hand. 'There are a couple of biscuits, too . . . I mean cookies.' She set them down on the small white wrought-iron table by his left hand.

'You're okay. I'm pretty adept in British English these days, thanks to Becca.' He gulped down the lemonade and smacked his lips. 'That sure hit the spot.' Griff leaned forward. 'I'll let you into another little secret about why my British language skills are so exceptional. I'm hooked on *The Repair Shop* program and binge-watch it whenever I have the chance.'

'Oh my God, it's my favorite, too.' She blushed. 'It's the stories behind the items that get to me. Please don't tell my sister, but I've been known to shed the occasional tear. She's convinced I've got a heart of stone and will make fun of me unmercifully.'

'That's not very fair when you've traveled four thousand miles to help out.'

The honesty gene reared its head again. 'I didn't exactly volunteer. My mum talked me into it. She played the one card I couldn't argue with. Becca and I both know she'd be here herself in a heartbeat if it wasn't for my dad's uncertain health.' Lyndsey puffed out a sigh. 'So I'm not a wonderful, generous, loving sister after all.'

'Don't be so hard on yourself.'

'It's one of my worst habits, according to some people.'

'No one's perfect.'

'Really?' Her smile inched back. 'And here I was think-ing I'd finally found the perfect man. How disappointing.'

'Yeah, well, that's life.' Griff chuckled. 'I could hardly be perfect when my eyes don't even match.'

'I noticed that the day we met.' Lyndsey wished she hadn't said that when a hint of satisfaction crept into his smile. 'Is it . . . ? Forget it, that's absolutely none of my busi-ness and incredibly rude of me to ask.'

'You haven't asked anythin' yet.' His dry comment sent a whoosh of heat racing up her neck. 'You could say I'm a member of the one percent club. That's roughly the percentage of people worldwide with heterochromia. I'm sure I don't have much else in common with Dan Ackroyd, Kate Bosworth and Mila Kunis, but weird eyes are one. Thankfully it's a benign mutation, so it doesn't affect most people's sight, and mine's fine. They reckon it's a quirk caused by genes passed down from your parents or by something that happened when our eyes were forming.'

'That's fascinating.' She reddened again. 'I suppose I should go.'

'Did you think any more about my dinner offer?'

'Yes.' No way was she going to admit it'd been on her mind constantly, interrupting work and everything else she was supposed to be focusing on.

'Look, if you're not interested, just say so and you can still have the paperweight.'

Not interested? Lyndsey's heart thudded. If her younger sister could be brave enough, or crazy enough, to throw in the towel on her old life, surely *she* could accept one date with the first man who'd piqued her interest in years? Only it wouldn't be simply one date, or at least she hoped not, and that's the part that frightened her most.

'I'd love to have dinner with you.' Oh, God she was doomed. That was the only thought lodging in her head when a huge, sexy smile lit up Griff, as if he couldn't believe his luck.

'Good.' He nodded. 'You can let me know when it suits Becca for you to be absent from duty.'

'I will.' She appreciated his understanding her family obligations needed to come first. 'I'll take that if you like.' Lyndsey gestured to the empty glass in his hand.

'Thanks.'

'It'll save you sullying the clean kitchen.' She ran off with a swing in her step and his peal of warm laughter followed her.

CHAPTER EIGHT

Griff wriggled his aching shoulders and stretched his arms behind his back hard enough to give his spine a satisfying pop. Even though he'd taken the trouble to design his workshop to suit his height, being hunched over for hours took its toll. In about another hour or so, he should be through with cutting out the ninety-five pieces of glass for the first panel. He glanced anxiously over at his phone, safely encased in a plastic bag, sitting there in reproachful silence, as if telling him it wasn't the phone's fault Lyndsey hadn't called yet. It'd been two long weeks since she agreed to have dinner with him, but he'd known how busy she was, so he needed to rein in his impatience.

'It's me; I've got something for you. May I come in?'

Lyndsey. Did she know he'd been thinking about her — again? He recklessly sprang up from the stool; if he'd been handling a piece of glass, it would be scattered over the floor now in thousands of pieces.

'Uh, yes and no. You can open the door, but please don't step inside.' *Frustrating* didn't cover it, but he mustn't let his desire to be close to her override her safety.

The door inched open and she peeked around, the sight of her smiling face lifting his spirits. 'Sorry, I should've rung first.'

'I couldn't have answered.' Griff lifted up his hands. 'Everywhere is covered in glass dust. You can open the door fully and stand there, that's the best I can offer.'

'Wow, you've been busy.' Lyndsey peered across at the labeled pieces of glass, arranged on a big table over his right shoulder.

'Eighty-five down and another ten to go.' He pointed to the sheet of bright pink glass in front of him. 'That's going to be a dancing lobster.'

Her dark arched brows shot up. 'You've been artistically inspired by seafood?'

'I had to be.' Griff explained about the panels he was making for a new Nashville seafood and steak restaurant. Translating the customer's vision was, in many ways, the most challenging part of the equation; on this occasion the restaurant's owner wanted to inject a note of humor. It'd been a struggle to track down the right shade of shocking pink glass, but he'd finally found some for sale at his favorite online German outlet.

She held up a white plastic box. 'It's a thank you from Becca for your grass-cutting endeavors the other day.'

'Don't tell me — let me guess — it's the millionaire's shortbread she's got me hooked on?'

'Got it in one.'

'Awesome. Would you mind putting it inside the cabin door for me?'

'Oh, okay, but I promise I won't go poking around.'

'Wouldn't bother me.'

'I'll do that then.' Her color flared. 'I meant drop the cake off, not sneak around.'

Seeing her flustered boosted his confidence a few centimeters. Perhaps he wasn't the only one shaken by the attraction between them after all.

'I also wanted to ask if you're free tonight, because a couple of Becca's girlfriends from her yoga class are coming over for a spot of baby worshipping, and bringing pizza and wine with them.'

'Uh, yes I am, but I'm pretty sure Becca wouldn't want me there too.'

'Becca? Oh, she doesn't . . . that's not what I . . . or perhaps you've changed your mind about taking me to dinner? I can see you're busy.' Lyndsey stopped to suck in a breath and covered her face with her hands. 'You must think I'm stupid and—'

'I sure don't. If I wasn't covered in glass dust I'd kiss you. I've been wanting to since the day we met.' The confession spilled out of him and before he could consider apologizing a brilliant smile illuminated Lyndsey's face.

'Thank God.' She heaved a relieved sigh. 'I was afraid it was just me, and I can't make a fool of myself over any man again.' A groan escaped her throat. 'Forget that last part. I can't seem to say anything the right way today.'

'Hey, it's all good.' Griff spoke softly. Honesty was the hardest thing sometimes. 'Yeah, I'd love to take you out tonight.' He'd had enough pretense in his previous relationships, and had worked hard to turn that around. 'I'll finish this cutting work, then get cleaned up. You go over and pop those goodies in my house — I won't be timing you to see how long you're in there. How about I pick you up at seven? Will that work?'

'Oh, yes, please.'

Her lack of dissembling warmed his heart.

'I can't stay out super late though, because I've got a work call with a client at midnight.'

'Midnight?'

'Time difference. Six a.m. in the UK. The lady in question demanded a consultation before she goes into work. She's an emergency room doctor and has the Sunday day shift.'

'Fair enough. I'll make sure to whisk you back home before you turn into a pumpkin.'

'Very funny.' She rolled her eyes. 'See you later.' Lyndsey took off before he could say another word.

If he didn't get his focus back, he'd cut his hands to ribbons and arrive for their date bandaged. After he finished cutting pieces for the lobster, he'd embark on his meticulous end-of-the-workday ritual. The work surfaces needed wiping down with a wet rag before he gave the floor the same treatment with an old-fashioned mop. Olivia had loved to mock him, saying he'd make someone a perfect house-husband one day.

Only then could he shower off the glass dust, shave and choose something to wear. None of that would take long. The tagline for The Right Place website — If You Don't Love it, Lose it — pretty much summed up his life these days, so the majority of his designer suits were long gone. He'd saved a couple of favorites for fancier occasions than he had in mind for tonight's first date with Lyndsey. Taking her to one of Nashville's many upscale restaurants or trawling the honkytonks on Broadway was too mundane. He needed to come up with something that wouldn't mark him out as predictable.

A flash of inspiration hit. Griff smiled, picked up his glass cutter and prepared to cut the lobster's tail.

* * *

Lyndsey hovered in the hall. 'Are you sure—?'

'Yes.' Becca shooed her towards the door. 'Don't keep the poor bloke waiting.'

'Do I look okay?'

'Okay? If you looked any more gorgeous, it would be criminal.' Her sister pushed past, flung open the door and beamed out at Griff. 'There you go, she's all yours.'

Throw me like Daniel into the lion's den, why don't you?

'For you.' He thrust a bottle of wine at her sister. 'I thought one more wouldn't hurt for your girls' night.'

'You didn't have to do that, but thanks.' Becca grinned. 'I assure you it won't go to waste.'

'Thanks for the shortbread, it was awesome.'

'Was? As in, it's all gone?'

'There are a couple of pieces left. I'm not a pig.'

Lyndsey tried not to stare. Griff's thick, wavy hair hung loose around his broad shoulders, and a fresh, close shave highlighted his tanned, angular face. Dark jeans and a blue-and-white striped shirt rolled to the elbow showed off his muscular forearms. He'd got it just right, making an effort without overdoing it. She'd aimed for simple too, with black linen wide-legged trousers and a crisp white shirt. Soft black leather flats. A chunky silver necklace and hoop earrings. After a month without a trim, her hair was on the way to becoming a halo of corkscrew curls, rather different from its usual close-cropped style.

'Are you absolutely sure your friends are on the way?' She frowned at Becca.

'Yes, they'll be here soon. Theo's holed up in his room with a pizza, so I'm sure we won't see him at all. Go now, before I throw you out.'

'Your carriage awaits, Cinderella.' Griff swept into a playful bow.

'You're an extremely daft man at times.'

He grinned, reached to take hold of her hand and led her towards his ancient truck.

Memories of the first time they met flooded back. Her prickliness at the airport should've warned him off, but had no effect on his even-tempered, affable manner. Even then she'd sensed something in Griff that was far more of a threat to her steady, measured life than straightforward physical attraction.

'So where are you taking me?' She hopped into the passenger seat and fastened her seatbelt.

'Not far.'

'That's not very illuminating.'

Griff threw the truck in gear and gunned out of the drive. 'You'll find out soon.'

They took the narrow two-lane road towards Adamsville, the nearest community of any size, but instead of driving straight on through, Griff pulled into an angled parking spot in front of the only shop, a combination garage and grocery.

'So dinner is a Coke and packet of crisps?'

'Sure, if that's what you want.' He pointed at the strings of white fairy lights twinkling along the eaves of an old, single-story wood building with a pitched red roof. 'They put them out to welcome you.'

'Ha, ha, very funny.' Lyndsey jumped out and watched a steady stream of people entering the shop while she waited for him to join her. It struck her as curious that the place was so popular on a Saturday evening, but presumably this Tennessee version of an English corner shop was open and busy at all hours.

Griff took her hand as they strolled across the road. He pointed to a chalkboard outside the door, announcing an open mic night. 'If you're looking for authentic music, it doesn't get more real than this. There's a small stage in the back, and on Saturday nights anyone can come and perform. You never know who you'll hear. It might make your ears bleed, or you could hear the next Dolly Parton or Garth Brooks.' He hooked his arm around her shoulder. 'Are you brave enough to give it a try?'

The question might not have been a hundred percent about tonight's entertainment option, but Lyndsey nodded all the same.

'The music won't start for another hour, but it soon gets filled up, that's why so many folk are here already but we should get a table. Buddy Earl, the old guy who runs this place, is quite a character. The business was struggling when he took it over from his father, but people started moving out here from Nashville, particularly country music folk looking for a getaway, so the local population base for the core of his business increased. Deke is only one of the many celebrities who appreciate the fact they can live a regular life out here without being pestered by fans. Buddy came up with the idea of live music nights, long before another popular venue called Puckett's and other similar places cottoned on to it. You could say the rest is history.'

He glanced at his watch, a heavy, expensive-looking silver one she guessed was a holdover from his old life. 'We've got time to eat first. I don't know about you, but I'm starved. I never got around to botherin' with lunch.'

'Neither did I, unless you count a piece of toast left over from breakfast.' She gave him a rueful look. 'My healthy diet is going to pot here.'

'Doesn't seem to be doin' you any harm from what I can see.' Griff's laconic drawl sent a whoosh of heat rushing through her.

'I tried to give Nora her bottle, but she threw a wobbly and yelled the house down. Then Theo and Becca got into an awful row, because she asked what he planned to do all summer after he gets out of school next week. He absolutely went off the deep end.'

'He's not signed up for any camps?'

Lyndsey heaved a sigh. 'He's refusing to. Deke offered him several that sounded awesome to me. All he sees is them trying to get rid of him.'

'That's too bad. Y'all will go stir crazy if he's at a loose end for all that long time.'

'He's very into video games, but that's about it.'

He opened the shop door and stood back to let her go first.

As they maneuvered their way through a narrow aisle between shelves of groceries, Griff slid one hand down to rest at the base of her spine, increasing her awareness of him a thousand times over. The pressure from his strong, warm fingers seeped through her clothes, making her skin tingle.

'Wow, that is a surprise.' The automatic reaction burst out of her as they entered a spacious room half-full of people.

'Thought it might be.'

The room ran the full width of the building and history was etched into every inch. Underfoot, the time-bleached pine floor had been trodden into uneven dips by countless thousands of feet. Rusty old farming tools decorated the nicotine-stained walls and mellow electric lights converted from oil lanterns hung from the low rafters.

'Let's grab this one.' Griff stopped at the first empty table. 'What's on the menu?'

'It's up there.' He pointed to a list propped up on the bar. 'We love our fried food in the South, and there's everything from hamburgers to catfish and chicken.'

'What're you having?'

'Tonight's special. Fried baloney sandwiches.' His face lit up. 'My mom used to make them when I was a kid. They're a cardiologist's nightmare.'

'Despite how appealing you make it sound, I believe I'll give that a miss and try the chicken.'

'Chicken it is. How about to drink? Beer? Iced Tea? Lemonade? Or a soda?' Griff nodded. 'I'm havin' a beer. Just the one.'

'Beer it is, then.'

As the evening wore on, Lyndsey wished she could capture time in a bottle. First dates could be a nightmare, but she'd be happy for this one to go on forever. The singers varied, but only one young man made her long for ear plugs. The last one up was a young woman whose rich voice silenced the room; when she finished, the rapturous applause almost lifted the roof. In between performances, she and Griff talked nonstop, heads close so they could hear themselves speak over the rising noise level in the room. Her fried chicken was incredible; crisp and well-seasoned, bearing no resemblance to its pale English imitations. Griff persuaded her to try a bite of his thick, greasy fried baloney sandwich which was more than enough to convince her to decline a second. They must have been an acquired taste, because Griff wolfed it down, and she suspected he'd have ordered another if she hadn't been there.

'You ready to go home? I make a pretty decent cup of coffee.'

'I am ready, but I'll have to give your other offer a miss.' His face fell. 'Not because I wouldn't love to, but I need to get set up for my work call. Another time?'

'Definitely.'

Outside in the truck, Griff rolled the windows down. 'In a few more weeks, we'd be offering ourselves as a night-time feast for the bugs, risking this.'

'We'd better make the most of it, then.'

'Yeah, I reckon we had.'

The hint of sadness in his raspy voice made Lyndsey swallow down a wave of emotion. Did she wish for psychic abilities, so she could see further down the line and know if they stood a chance of making this attraction between them work? She swiftly came down on the side of living in ignorance and seizing the moment. Lyndsey leaned over and brushed a kiss on his cheek. The faint hint of soft stubble and the intoxicating aroma of Griff's fresh, clean scent set her senses on fire.

'Let's pretend we're teenagers. Make out like crazy until our lips are sore. Barely make it home in time for curfew.' The husky edge to his drawl made her skin tighten. Lyndsey arched into his searching touch as his right hand slid around to cup the back of her head. Griff's tongue slid along her lips, nipping and teasing until she opened to him. She'd always enjoyed kissing, but considered it slightly overrated. Now the tantalizing, incredibly sexy point of it became abundantly clear. 'If we weren't parked under a streetlight, with all these people coming and going around us . . .'

Half-grateful and half-sorry when he left the sentence unfinished, Lyndsey sighed as he pulled away. Her tingling breasts said they knew exactly where he'd been headed, and were grossly disappointed too.

'Sorry, Cinderella, but the ball is over.' He touched his finger against the throbbing pulse in her neck, stroking her skin and staring as if to imprint her on his mind. 'We'll continue this another day.'

The hint of promise in his words lifted her spirits. 'Oh yes.'

CHAPTER NINE

Griff turned off the hose and eyed his vegetable garden with satisfaction. Almost everything was flourishing. Harold had given him a rough timeline for how long it should take the different varieties he'd planted to grow, and now it was mid-June, so he was starting to harvest his squash, jalapenos and green beans. They'd be followed closely by the bell peppers and tomatoes. But the poor cucumbers were stunted and misshapen — a sad reflection of his stalled attempt to romance Lyndsey.

By now, she must wonder if he'd dropped off the face of the planet. He'd fully intended to ask her out again after their date two weeks ago, but his client brought forward the deadline for the restaurant panels, so he'd directed all his energies into his work. He genuinely couldn't afford to lose or mess up this commission, but if he was being a hundred percent honest, it also let him off the hook. Gave him breathing space to consider his next move.

He'd spotted Lyndsey a couple of times from a distance as she pushed Nora along in the stroller or walked down to the mailbox, but squashed the urge to rush out to say hello. The *hello* wasn't the tricky part; it was what to say next. She must assume he'd had second thoughts, but perhaps she'd had them, too? After all, there'd been nothing stopping her contacting *him*.

Absentmindedly he sipped his coffee and spat out the cold dregs on the grass. If Lyndsey wanted nothing more to do with him, Griff wouldn't blame her, but he'd had enough of being indecisive. The ragged denim shorts and scruffy T-shirt he'd worn to work in the garden had seen better days about a decade ago, but they'd have to do, because the longer he put off going next door, the more likely it was he'd lose his nerve. Stopping to give his hands a thorough wash first, though, wasn't optional. Any visit to the Warners' house came with the risk of holding Nora.

Risk? He'd never admitted it out loud, but he'd become incredibly attached to the little girl. It was endlessly fascinating to see how swiftly she changed, almost from one day to the next, and to watch her character start to form. The last time he held Nora, she'd burst into a heart-stopping smile, her eyes dancing with glee. It felt like she was telling him that, despite any protestations he might make to the contrary, she knew she had him well and truly hooked.

Griff wriggled off his earth-caked boots outside the front door and hurried in to wash his hands at the kitchen sink, making sure to scrub under his dirty fingernails. This room always made him smile and wince in equal measure. It was next on his upgrade list, but for now it was stuck in a 1970s time warp. He found it hard to believe the almost orangey wood cabinets, bright yellow laminate countertops, garishly patterned tile backsplash and avocado appliances were once considered the height of modern design.

He shoved his large bare feet in a pair of sandals and headed back outside. Walking around and up his neighbor's drive, his palms started to sweat and he hastily wiped them on his shorts.

'Oh, so you're still alive. We did wonder.' Lyndsey's clipped tones made him cringe. She stood on the front porch, holding a watering can, immaculate as ever in another crisp white shirt and black shorts.

Where were the bright colors that would look so incredible against her Caribbean skin? He wondered if there was some deep-seated reason why she stuck to white, black and gray.

'Yeah, I'm really sorry. I meant to get in touch, but then I got caught up in work and . . .' The feeble excuse dried in his throat as her stare bored into him.

'I was scared too, you know,' Lyndsey whispered. 'Did that ever occur to you?' She jerked her head back towards the house. 'Our determined matchmaker has been hounding me ever since our date. Becca's convinced I put you off by being my usual bossy self — her words, not mine.' One corner of her mouth twitched. 'I prefer "assertive." Not such a negative connotation.'

'There's nothing wrong with assertive.' Griff shoved his hands in his pockets, nervous as a teenage boy desperate to pluck up the courage to ask the girl he fancies to the senior prom. 'Is there any hope you might give me . . . us . . . another chance?'

'My God, Lyndsey, how long does it take you to water a few . . . ?' Becca appeared in the door, cradling Nora in one arm. 'Oh, that explains it. It's the ghost from next door.' Her frown morphed into a smug smile. 'In case you're interested, Deke's tour is going amazingly and they're playing to sold-out stadiums.'

'That's great,' Griff murmured.

'On the not-so-awesome front, Theo spends his days hiding out in his room to avoid the rest of us.' Becca threw Lyndsey a dismissive glance. 'As you can see, my sister is as pulled together as ever. Even living with me for — what is it now? About six weeks? — hasn't dimmed her natural capacity for being in calm control.'

'It's actually five weeks and six days, if we're being precise,' Lyndsey snapped back.

'Oh, and we're always that, aren't we?'

His heart sank. This is what Deke had been afraid of.

* * *

'We're very busy, Griff, if there's nothing you actually want,' Lyndsey snapped.

'Li-Li!' Becca's voice soared an octave in horror.

Did no one realize she was clinging on to her so-called control by her fingernails? Lyndsey wasn't sure who frustrated her the most — Griff or her sister. Maybe it was herself? It still made her blood heat, thinking about what his kisses did to her. How was she supposed to reply to his plea for them to try again? Her heart said YES, PLEASE, in massive capital letters.

But her head? That usually sensible part of her body, which kept her life on an even keel? It kept giving massive nudges, hard enough to leave significant bruises, making it clear she should stay well away from Griff Oakes for her own sanity. Now he stood in front of her, a frown etched deep in his forehead, wondering how best to wriggle out of playing piggy in the middle with the warring Carne sisters.

As for her business, that was the other thing hanging on by the skin of its teeth. Nicola's frantic message yesterday, sent at a ridiculously early hour because her assistant's panic overrode the time difference, centered around an important client who wasn't happy with the job she'd done. The man insisted on Lyndsey's personal attention. That led to another midnight Zoom call, leaving her fuzzy-headed with tiredness today.

None of this was helped by being forced to portray a cheerfulness she didn't feel every time she spoke to their parents.

'I wondered if y'all would like to go into Franklin and grab an ice cream? Surely you can't resist goin' to Sweet Mary Jane's?'

Lyndsey suspected he'd originally intended to make the offer solely to her but after picking up on the tension was trying to help out. *Cut him some slack*, her heart whispered.

He blows hot and cold. You'll get hurt, her head shouted loud and clear.

'That's kind, but why don't you two go on your own?' Becca said dismissively.

'No. It'll do us all good to get out of here,' Lyndsey said. *Before I kill you.* 'It'll do the kids good, too.'

'The kids? Plural? Theo would rather poke himself in the eye with a sharp needle than be seen out with us,' Becca scoffed.

Lyndsey was tired of tiptoeing around the boy. It was past time he saw himself as part of the family, with all its pluses and minuses. 'If you see to Nora, I'll tackle Theo.'

'Knock yourself out.'

Griff had been watching their to-and-fro conversation warily, but now his smile inched back. 'That's great. I'll need to have a quick shower and change first. I won't take long.' He looked embarrassed. 'I've been working in the garden.' *Couldn't wait another second to see you again.*

The unspoken admission resonated in Lyndsey's head. 'So we noticed.' To her, it didn't matter that he was sweaty and dirt-stained and with his tangled hair tied back with something she suspected was green garden twine. She strode back into the house, took the stairs two at a time and banged on Theo's door. One of the first warnings Becca issued was that her stepson's bedroom was off-limits to everyone but Deke. Predictably, she got no response and knocked again.

'Theo, Griff's invited us all out for ice cream.' She sucked in a deep breath. 'If you don't have the good manners to answer me, I'm coming in.' Lyndsey mentally counted to ten and hoped he wouldn't force her hand. Silence. She turned the knob and pushed the door open.

Instead of the typical boyish mess she'd expected — clothes dropped all over the place and piles of dirty plates and glasses on any available surface — the immaculate room resembled her own flat back home in Cornwall. A twin bed with its plain navy cover tucked in military style at the corners. Alphabetized bookshelves. The gray carpet, free of clutter and recently vacuumed. Theo sat with his back to her, hunched over his desk playing a video game.

Lyndsey considered creeping back out. Before she could decide whether or not to act on her change of heart, he swung his chair around, ripped his headphones off and gave her a fierce glare.

'I'm sorry. I did knock.'

'Get out!' Theo yelled, his voice breaking as it rose in volume.

'I will, but I've got a message from Griff first.' There was a slim chance he'd be more agreeable if the request didn't come on behalf of his stepmother. 'He's offered to take us to Sweet Mary Jane's. Apparently their ice cream is awesome?'

Lyndsey waited. By the boy's conflicted expression and the way he nibbled at his lip, she guessed he longed to say 'yes,' but hated to give in. 'We're leaving in about ten minutes.' She glanced around. 'You and I must be soulmates when it comes to liking our surroundings organized and tidy.'

'I guess.' Theo lifted his thin shoulders in a shrug. 'We're both the cuckoos in our families, too.'

Lyndsey struggled to breathe. It felt as though he'd punched her in the stomach. 'Is that how you feel?'

'Don't you?'

'Could we talk about this later?' That kept the door to the conversation open and gave her the opportunity to think through what might be best to say. 'So, ice cream?'

Theo bent down to shove his feet into an old pair of broken-down trainers. The disinterest in his appearance was a clear difference between Theo and herself, but then it clicked. Revealing his true nature in his obsessively neat room was one thing, but doing the same outside of it quite another. He flicked a lock of straggly brown hair away from his face and glowered at her. There was something forced about the attempt to look annoyed, as though it was expected rather than how he genuinely felt.

'Are we goin' or not?'

A fleeting impulse to hug him and reassure Theo that life wouldn't always be this hard swept through her, but Lyndsey wasn't about to push her luck. 'We certainly are.'

* * *

This wasn't how he'd pictured the afternoon going, but Griff wasn't unhappy. Far from it. Everyone, including him, was more relaxed. They'd been fortunate to nab the last free table outside the ice cream shop, so now Nora was fast asleep in her stroller under the shade of a wide green-and-white striped umbrella. Becca had lost her tight, haunted look and was licking a strawberry waffle cone with a smile on her face. Theo was talking animatedly to Lyndsey about his favorite video games and another one he was in the middle of coding and trying to create.

And himself? He was indulging in three scoops of ice cream to make up for missing lunch — Rocky Road, Death by Chocolate and Mint Chocolate Chip. Lyndsey had teased what a typical man he was, choosing the most chocolatey flavor choices on offer. In return, he laughed at her single scoop of lemon sorbet.

'So, have you finished the project you were working on?' Lyndsey angled around to face him.

'Yeah, I wrapped it up last night.' He cracked a smile. 'About two o'clock this morning, really.'

'You're pleased with it?'

Griff nodded. This was an opening. If he didn't snatch it, the moment could be lost. 'Would you like to see it later?'

A flush of heat bloomed in her rich caramel skin.

'It would mean a lot to me if you came over.' He sensed Becca's ears prick up.

'I'd love to.'

'Good.'

'You know something will happen to put a stop to the plan, don't you?' She gave a wry smile. 'I wish—'

'Me too.' Everything else he wanted to say could wait until they were alone.

They switched to watching the crowds of tourists ambling up and down, checking out the various gift shops and places to eat, and traded guesses about where people came from and what might be in the various bags they were carrying. He gave Lyndsey an abridged version of Franklin's long history, all the way back to when it was founded in the late eighteenth century by an Abram Maury.

'Most similar small towns have disappeared, but thankfully, about fifty years ago, a group of concerned locals started a project to save the older buildings. A heritage group sponsors several popular festivals throughout the year, centered around local crafts and foods. They bring in hundreds of thousands of visitors.'

'I'd love to have a proper look around another day.'

'We can do that.' Griff reached for her hand, and his heart raced when she flashed him a dazzling smile.

'I should warn you, it might involve shopping.' Lyndsey pointed to an elderly white-haired man, hauling a couple of carrier bags in each hand and trailing along behind his wife. 'Do you really want to be one of those poor souls?'

She'd call him crazy if he admitted to being envious of the contentment written all over the man's lined face. Shopping might not be his favorite way to spend the afternoon, but it was clearly no hardship to do this small thing for the woman he loved, possibly since they were in high school. Griff would happily do the same for Lyndsey if she gave him the chance. He realized he hadn't hidden his pensive thoughts as well as he thought when she looked mildly embarrassed.

'I'm bored,' Theo moaned. Next thing, Nora jerked awake and signaled with several pertinent screams that she was, too.

'Time to go, I think.' Becca's resignation was half-hearted.

The glorious smile Lyndsey threw his way resonated with hope and promise. He hoped they might fulfill a few more of their wishes tonight.

* * *

The second the laptop screen went blank, Lyndsey helplessly watched her sister dissolve into heart-wrenching tears.

'I know I should've told Deke the truth, but he doesn't want to hear me moaning all the time.' Becca swiped at her eyes with the back of her hand. 'Did you hear the excitement in his voice? He'd just got off-stage in Tokyo and they wowed the fans there. I should be able to cope here in his absence. It's my job now.'

'Then treat it like one.' The automatic response popped out, and she waited for her head to be bitten off, chewed up and spat out again. Instead, there was silence. 'What would you have done if this sort of situation cropped up in your old life?'

'That was totally different. I handled high-strung models and the artistic temperaments of my fellow fashion designers, standing on my head. Running a massive house, taking care of a tiny baby who seesaws between being sweet as sugar and possessed by demons, plus a stroppy stepson who's determined to hibernate in his bedroom for the next two months until he can escape back to school again — that's another thing completely.'

Lyndsey grasped her sister's hands. 'Take a few deep breaths. We'll work this out together.' A touch of uncertainty sneaked in. 'That is, if you—?'

'Yes. Yes, please.' A wary smile inched across Becca's face. 'You're going to tell me things I don't want to hear, aren't you?'

'Probably.' She found it impossible not to smile. 'The most straightforward thing to solve is the house, so I suggest we tackle that first.'

'Straightforward?'

The obvious disbelief didn't bother Lyndsey because the same sort of response was normal from her regular clients. 'In your last job, did everyone have their assigned work spaces? Did you have cleaners who came in every night? If there was a personnel problem, did your HR person tackle it?'

'Yes, but how does that relate to my problems?'

'Your company budgeted for all those things, because they knew a messy work environment and unfocused staff don't hit deadlines and therefore don't make a profit.' She dredged up a bright smile. 'We'll start with one of my famous lists.'

'But how're you going to have time for all this with everything else you're trying to fit in. And what about Griff? Are you seriously going to sit back and let the best thing that could've happened to you in years, slip away?'

'Let's be realistic. It took him long enough to get in touch again, so I clearly wasn't the only one having second thoughts.'

'You're afraid of rejection.'

'Aren't we all?'

'I suppose.' Becca looked thoughtful. 'But he's such a lovely man and you're super together.'

'Forget Griff for a minute and let's make a start. The linchpin of my philosophy is that your home shouldn't feel like a weight around your neck, but an anchor. A safe, welcoming, comforting place.' She tweaked a smile. 'Have you heard of Marie Kondo, the Japanese woman who set off the modern minimalist revolution?'

'Vaguely.'

'I was a disciple at first, but found her too rigid.'

'She's rigid?' Becca chuckled. 'Wow, she must be way over the top for you to say that. I mean, you iron and fold your knickers, for God's sake.'

Lyndsey ignored the sly dig and carried on as if her sister hadn't spoken. 'As I said, my own philosophy developed from hers, but it's more individually tailored than her one-size-fits-all method. All I want is to free my clients to enjoy their lives more. I'm not aiming for perfection.'

'Good!'

'At least with you I can skip a lot of the steps I normally go through with clients, because I've been living here so I've seen how the house works or doesn't work for your family. I've noticed certain things that are sucking the life out of you, and others that give you joy.'

'You've been spying on me.' Becca bristled.

'Not at all.' Lyndsey exhaled a sigh. 'This is the part where I tell you things you might not want to hear. A few minutes ago, you claimed you were up for that. But if you've changed your mind, say so, and we'll stop right now.'

'I suppose you'd better keep going.'

Not exactly the last word in enthusiasm, but she'd coped with plenty of paying clients who only turned to her out of desperation and certainly weren't a hundred percent invested in the process to start out with. She'd won them all over.

'Right, the first thing we would do is go around the house together, and in each room, you tell me how being in there makes you feel. Does your anxiety rise in that particular space, or do you find yourself smiling? The reasons behind both extremes of emotion are important, because they help me to guide you the right way.' She gestured to her computer tablet. 'I'd make notes as we go, then draw up a plan.'

'That's all well and good, Li-Li, but even if the house is straight, the rest of my worries won't disappear in a puff of smoke.'

'Babies aren't my specialty, so you need to find someone else for that. Are there any support groups for new parents to swap ideas and have a natter?'

'They did mention one when we were at the hospital, but I didn't follow it up because I thought I wouldn't need it.' Her sister looked rueful.

'None of us is an island, Becca.'

'*I* know that, but *you* often seem like one.'

'Me?' Lyndsey couldn't hide her shock. 'Why would you say that?'

Another uneasy silence filled the air. If she didn't push, and brushed it under the carpet now, their relationship would never have a chance to grow the way she'd always longed for. 'Please. I want to know.'

'Do you, really? Honestly?'

She nodded. The tables had turned while she wasn't looking, and it was her turn to hear some home truths.

'Okay. Here goes. You've always made it clear you never wanted a sister, and especially not me. I know there's a big age gap between us, but I used to long for us to do stuff together.' Becca sighed heavily. 'You even keep Mum and Dad somewhat at arm's length. It's like you don't need other people in your life.' She angled Lyndsey a long, hard stare. 'Or maybe it's not that you don't *need* them, but you're frightened of opening yourself to loving anyone because of what happened with Mum and your birth dad?'

Lyndsey opened her mouth to protest, but the urge to defend herself ebbed away. How could the family's adored princess, the much-longed-for baby, ever hope to understand?

'You've made a huge success of your business, and that's awesome, but are you using it as a substitute for having a real life?' Becca persisted.

For a few fleeting seconds, she hesitated. This was her chance.

'Oh, forget it. I should've known this would be a waste of time.' Becca scoffed.

'Will you still let me help you with the house?' Lyndsey asked timidly.

'That's your safe place, isn't it?' She shrugged. 'We'll see.'

She didn't deserve anything more than that tentative half-promise. The failure nagged at her like an aching tooth, spoiling the prospect of the evening ahead.

CHAPTER TEN

Griff wound up the vacuum cord and shoved the machine back out of sight in the hall cupboard. After coming home from the afternoon's ice cream expedition, he'd looked around his home and tried to see it through Lyndsey's eyes. When he was engrossed in work, housekeeping tended to go by the wayside. Although it hadn't been a trash heap on the level of her sister's, it'd definitely been up there on the messy scale. It wouldn't help his romantic prospects tonight if Lyndsey saw him as a candidate for her professional services. But now the house was sparkling — at least by his standards — and it was still only four o'clock. He needed something to keep himself occupied for a few hours, and a putter around in his workshop sounded his best option.

Crossing the sunny garden, he stopped to check out the bird feeder he'd hung from a wrought-iron pole near the porch. A strikingly handsome blue jay pecking at the seeds flew off as Griff approached, giving several of its loud distinctive chirps. Apparently they could do a good imitation of a hawk, although he'd never been lucky enough to hear that himself.

Outside the workshop, he followed his usual habit of kicking off his sandals and replacing them with an ancient pair of brown leather boots. There was less likelihood of losing a toe then, if he was handling a heavy piece of glass and dropped it. He sniffed the faint, distinctive but indescribable scent as he stepped inside his workspace and immediately felt less tense. The ideal job for now, which wouldn't get either himself or the room messed up, would be to sit and draft some patterns on his laptop. Griff hovered over the bin of offcuts and spied a shard of deep amber glass, the color of Lyndsey's skin. The idea for an abstract piece based on her Caribbean background formed in his mind.

He unhooked his protective apron, slipped it on and tied a knot around his waist. First he'd find a suitable piece of MDF to build the mosaic on. The incredible mosaicist who gave him a lesson after he saw her work at a local craft show said that was the best thing to use for a base, as opposed to regular wood that might warp. Some people used glass or slate instead, but he hadn't experimented with those mediums yet.

Griff rifled through his supplies and picked out a simple, small rectangle perfect for what he had in mind. Sometimes he did a preliminary sketch, but today the picture in his head was so clear he'd take a chance and skip that step. He returned to the offcuts bin and picked out a selection of vivid blues for the Caribbean Sea, a shard of sparkling emerald for her eyes and heat-drenched yellows and oranges for the sun. He'd amassed a variety of miniature tiles which were perfect for forming the borders and delved into his collection to find enough complementary colors. Once the piece started to come together, he'd probably add beads or faux jewels, but they could wait. Capturing the essence of Lyndsey would be a challenge, but he was eager to get started.

A quiet tap on the door startled him. Griff straightened, absentmindedly rubbing the back of his neck. He glanced at his phone and was shocked to see it was eight o'clock. Somehow he'd been working for almost four hours without being aware of anything but the design coming to life in front of him.

'It's only me.'

'Hang on a minute.' He grabbed an old towel from his cleaning supplies and draped it over the mosaic. 'Come on in,' Griff shouted, breaking into a smile as she only took a couple of cautious steps inside. 'I wasn't sure you'd manage to get away.'

'Becca's always happy to shove me in your direction. I don't mean . . . She's very fond of you, but right now it's me she's not so sure about.' There was a brittleness to her smile. 'I'm joking.'

No, you're not.

'You'll have to avoid touching anything. I'm sorry. I cleaned up earlier, ready to show you the panels we were talking about, but I was at a loose end late this afternoon and—'

'It's okay. Don't apologize for being passionate about your work.'

He almost blurted out that the only thing he'd intended to be passionate about tonight was her, but that was best left unsaid. Griff gestured towards the three completed panels hanging on the back wall. 'There they are.' The nerves in his stomach jangled as she began to study them.

'Oh my goodness, they're incredible. How on earth do you do this?' Lyndsey peered closely at the lobster. 'Eyelashes?'

'They weren't easy.' He chuckled. 'I wasted an awful lot of glass tryin' to get them right.'

'I can't begin to imagine how long it took. You've got incredible patience.'

Their eyes locked. Griff said nothing, hoping she picked up from his silence that he could be patient about them, too. She broke away and moved along to the next panel: a dancing cow.

'The pink ballet shoes and the tiara are adorable.'

'Yeah, I'm pretty pleased with them.'

'So you should be.'

'Have you eaten yet? I didn't realize how late it'd gotten. I've got a couple of pizzas in the freezer, if that'll tempt you to join me?'

'After the monster dish of ice cream you waded through I'm surprised you could eat again for a month.'

'Hey, I'm a growing guy.' Griff patted his stomach. 'So are you taking me up on my offer? There's a decent chardonnay in the fridge too.'

'I'd like that. Very much.' A trace of wistfulness slipped back into her voice, and for a moment he thought she'd add something else, but her lips pressed shut.

'Why don't you go on in while I get cleaned up here?'

'Couldn't I help? Cleaning is kind of my thing.'

'Thanks, but it's tricky, and it'll go quicker on my own.'

'Fair enough.' A frown creased her brow. 'I can hang around outside if you don't want me poking around your house while you're not there.'

'Feel free to poke around as much as you like. If you want to be useful, you can turn on the oven and stick the pizzas in.'

'Becca would warn you I'm not much of a cook, but I can just about handle that. Do you have the key?'

'No need. It's unlocked. It's pretty safe around here, and I'm in and out a lot during the day. I never leave the workshop open, though. I'd rather lose what's in the house than my work.'

'That doesn't surprise me. I'll see you when you're finished.'

After Lyndsey disappeared back outside, he stood there for a moment. Wondering. Something was up with her, and he longed to discover what it was.

* * *

Lyndsey's first thought was that Griff's description of the house — made for practicality, not good looks — had played down its undoubted charm. Rather like the man himself.

She'd stepped straight into an open-plan living space that must've originally been two separate rooms. The words 'log cabin' equated to dark and dreary in her mind, but here there were three generous windows for the light to flood through, unhampered by curtains or blinds. Lyndsey guessed he'd sanded and varnished the gleaming oak floorboards himself and silently applauded him for not softening them with unnecessary rugs. A red brick fireplace dominated one wall, with an old brown recliner positioned to one side, its leather cracked and faded from years of use. Next to it was a polished brass lamp, angled perfectly for reading, and an end table covered with an uneven stack of books. She couldn't resist wandering over to check out his tastes and was interested to discover everything from how to create a pond to the latest offering by Ian Rankin, one of her own particular favorites. The three-seater sofa covered in plain dark rust-colored linen looked new, but fitted in perfectly. Lyndsey smiled at the large-screen television mounted on the back wall instead of hidden away like so many people preferred these days. She loved the soft buttery shade of cream he'd painted the walls, the perfect choice for showing off a number of paintings. The girlfriend who labeled his bird-watching and historic barn fascination 'old-man hobbies' probably scorned these very traditional, expansive American landscapes, too.

This wasn't getting the pizzas ready, so Lyndsey pulled herself away from the painting she was standing in front of and wandered down a narrow hallway in search of the kitchen. A lover of clean lines and muted décor herself, she winced at the dated color scheme, although she supposed avocado appliances and fruit-patterned tiles might now be considered retro-chic. She pulled two small pizzas out of the freezer and discovered one huge benefit of the old-fashioned kitchen — the cooker controls were straightforward, so didn't need a degree in computer science to work out how they functioned. After sticking the pizzas in to bake, she went on a quest for plates, cutlery and wine glasses, giving her the perfect excuse to check out the impressively tidy and well-stocked cabinets.

'Did you find everything okay?' Griff appeared in the doorway.

'Yes, no problem.'

'Are the pizzas in the oven?'

'Only just.'

'Perfect.' He flashed an endearing smile. 'I need to go shower out the glass and dust. Open up the wine if you like. I won't be long.'

As she finished laying the table, Griff strolled back in, his damp freshly washed hair loose around his shoulders and smelling of something citrusy and tempting.

'I might have to keep you around.' He gazed appreciatively at her and the table. 'Linen napkins? I'd forgotten I owned any, although I'm not sure the cheap store-brand pizza deserves those. Salad and home-made dressing, too? I could get used to this.'

Lyndsey colored. This was exactly the sort of thing Becca picked at her for. Always having to make things just-so. 'I'm sorry, I—'

'No, I'm sorry.' Griff crossed over to her in a couple of strides. 'I should've put my brain in gear before I spoke. I wasn't belittling you. Far from it. I'm amazed you took the care to do this for me . . . for us.' He looked sheepish. 'I usually eat sitting in my recliner, with my food on a tray and a book in hand.'

'Me too. I think it's a common habit of the comfortably single.'

'Are you?'

She swallowed hard, scared to give him an honest answer. 'I think our pizzas should be ready.'

A slow, sexy smile inched over his face, making her blood heat. Naturally he'd read her mind.

'Sounds like a plan.'

To regain some sort of self-control, she hurried across the room to get the pizzas out, then slid them onto two of his attractive brown glazed pottery plates. Lyndsey carried them over to the table.

'I do love your home. It's so you. I can tell you've put a lot of work into it.'

'Yeah, I suppose I have. This is the next project.' He gestured around the kitchen. 'It hurts my eyes every time I come in here.'

'It is a bit . . .' *Garish* and *dated* sounded judgmental. 'In need of modernization?'

'I'm not one of your clients, so you don't have to be tactful with me.' He chuckled. 'It's ugly and you know it.'

'It probably wouldn't win any kitchen beauty contests.'

They chatted easily, touching on their reading tastes, and she asked about the pictures in his living room, making him laugh with her sharp comment on what his previous girlfriend probably thought of them.

'Yeah, you got that right. I've been collecting prints by some of the nineteenth-century artists like Cole, Church and Durand for years now.' He fiddled with his wine glass. 'They never quite fit with my old life, but does it sound crazy to say they've settled in here like old friends?'

'Not at all. Perhaps deep down, you knew the lifestyle you had then was never really you?'

Griff nodded. 'I reckon you're right.' He tilted her a cautious look. 'So you gonna tell me why you were all out of sorts when you came over?'

The perceptive question came out of nowhere and momentarily sucked the breath out of her. Lyndsey hadn't intended to mention her contentious talk with Becca, but now the whole story poured out, from the encouraging beginning to the far-less-uplifting end.

'Are you afraid there's some truth in what she said? Is that what hurts most?' Griff's raspy whisper snaked under her skin.

'Maybe . . . probably.' Lyndsey half-heartedly put her hand over her glass when he offered her the last of the wine.

'People used to say similar things about me.' Griff's confession took her by surprise. 'My career was everything, and I planned to retire as a multi-millionaire before I was forty, with the ridiculous idea I'd then be free to fall in love, get married and have a family.'

'But a lot of people would say you're obsessive about your work now, too. So why is one right and the other wrong?' She genuinely wanted to know, because that was one of the criticisms Becca threw her way.

'It isn't that black and white, honey.' Griff covered her hand with his own. 'Yeah, I love what I do, but I've also got my old-man hobbies and good friends around here.' A shadow crossed his face. 'I'm not the best to ask about sibling relationships, and I'm takin' a guess yours with Becca is equally complicated.'

Lyndsey couldn't help sighing. ' "Complicated" doesn't begin to cover it.'

'Did Becca hit the nail on the head when she brought up your mom and birth father?'

She shrugged.

'The way I see it, his family in Dominica are the ones who've missed out.' Griff caressed her cheek. 'Did your step-dad make you feel unwanted and a nuisance?'

'No! Absolutely not!' Lyndsey's voice turned shrill. 'But . . . I could see how much it meant to him, and my mum, when Becca was born.'

'That's hard on a kid who's insecure. Theo's the same way, yeah?'

She nodded. 'Did you always have to be responsible for your brother? Take the blame for his mistakes? Let him have his own way all the time?'

Griff turned pale, but said nothing.

'Becca's very . . . emotional. Sometimes she would even hold her breath until she fleetingly passed out to get what she wanted. Dad, in particular, never failed to fall for it when she turned on the tears. I always had to be the one to give in.'

'Resentment eats away at you, doesn't it? One day I'll tell you more about my brother, but right now we're tryin' to sort you out.' His forced attempt at a smile failed.

'I don't know how to put things right with Becca. Do you think it's too late?'

'No, it's never that. At least, I hope not.'

92

She suspected he wasn't simply referring to her problems. 'Griff, I hate saying this, but—'

'Your priority right now needs to be Becca and her family. I get that.' He gave a wry smile. 'I'm not a saint, so I'm not gonna pretend it's all good, but I've faith in you . . . and us.' His voice turned to a raspy whisper. 'I've got something for you.' He sprang up from the table, opened a drawer by the sink and pulled out a small unevenly shaped package, wrapped in jade silk and loosely tied with a thin gold bow. 'Your reward for coming tonight.'

Lyndsey took it from him with some trepidation. Cautiously she opened it to reveal the beautiful mosaic paperweight she'd admired the other day. 'I can't take this. It wouldn't be—'

'Right? Yeah, it absolutely would.' Griff clasped his hands around hers. 'Look at it as a promise. When you feel the timing's right for us to pick things up again, you let me know, okay? Hopefully it'll be sooner rather than later, but you have to do whatever it takes.'

She managed a brief nod. Talking would've been impossible. His mouth lowered to hers and she savored the warmth of his firm lips, soaking up every last tempting stroke of his tongue before he pulled away.

'Don't walk me home. Please,' Lyndsey begged, swiveling away from him and striding away before she lost the courage to do the right thing.

CHAPTER ELEVEN

'So, what are we purging today, Attila?' Becca's smile took the edge off her sly dig.

Lyndsey didn't mind. It'd been a long, challenging week, but they were definitely in a better place now. The first thing she'd done when she returned from Griff's that night was apologize to Becca. It shocked her, in a good way, when Becca did the same in return. Her sister's admission that she learned early on how to play their parents to her full advantage somehow balanced the scales.

'How about the dining room?' They were systematically tackling one room at a time. On more than one occasion, her sister's indecisiveness over what to keep and what to get rid of had tried Lyndsey's patience to the utmost, but she'd managed to bite her tongue — so far. She had even talked Becca into agreeing that after each area was weeded out, Lyndsey could give it a thorough clean.

'It's bad,' Becca said with a sigh.

Tell me something I don't know. She'd poked her head in around the door one day and shut it again just as fast.

'Most of the stuff in there belongs to Deke. I daren't throw anything out.'

'Then we'll box it up and take it to his studio. He can sort it when he gets home,' Lyndsey said decisively.

'I suppose that'll be all right.' Becca didn't sound convinced.

'Right, come on then. Grab the rubbish bags from the kitchen and meet me in there.' She touched her sister's arm. 'Think of how much better your bedroom, the kitchen and the nursery look already.'

'Yeah, they really do.' Becca looked shamefaced. 'I didn't realize how bad they were until they weren't, if that makes sense?'

It was the highlight of Lyndsey's week yesterday when Becca gave her an impulsive hug after they'd finished sorting out the nursery. They had boxed up Nora's outgrown clothes for Becca to take to the new parents' group she'd started to attend — and miraculously enjoy — and found suitable places for everything else. It'd stunned her sister how much bigger the space looked afterwards.

'It absolutely does.' She had heard exactly the same from her regular clients multiple times. 'We all get used to how things are — in different areas of our lives. Change is rarely easy, but it can transform us.'

'Like Griff has with you? He's definitely softened you up. I hope you'll give him another go soon. He's worth it, Li-Li.'

Her throat tightened. She hadn't told Becca what exactly happened between herself and Griff last week, not wanting her sister to blame herself. The only excuse now for her not to contact him again was her own cowardice.

'This isn't getting us very far. We've only got an hour, at the most, before Nora wakes up from her nap.'

'Fine. I'll let you get away with it for today, but not much longer.' Becca wagged a finger in Lindsey's face and swanned off.

* * *

Griff leaned against one of the porch uprights and sipped his coffee. He hadn't seen anything of Lyndsey since he nobly — or stupidly — encouraged her to leave. Every time he went into his kitchen he pictured her there, laughing and smiling over their meal. Some days, he swore the scent of her light gardenia perfume still lingered in the air.

Nothing had gone right since she left; he couldn't get her out of his mind. He'd doggedly tried to work on the mosaic panel, but it hadn't come to life as he'd hoped. His creations never did when he wasn't in the right frame of mind. When he couldn't find an off-cut in the right shade of pale pink to represent the Rosa de Bayahibe, Dominica's national flower, he'd decided to cut a piece from a large sheet of glass. Griff had carelessly balanced it on the workbench, then caught the edge with his elbow and sent it crashing to the floor. Like an idiot, he tried to catch it — something his teacher drilled into them never to do — and ended up with a deep cut in the palm of his right hand. Luckily it hadn't needed stitches, so he'd bandaged it himself. Although it was healing well, he wouldn't have the flexibility and strength in his fingers to work again for at least another week.

He trudged down the steps for a wander around the garden, but the sight of the weeds taking over his vegetable patch and the ragged lawn worsened his mood. Harold would be happy to lend a hand, but another idea sprang into Griff's mind — one that might solve two problems at once. He sent off a quick text with little hope of a positive response.

Yes, please. I'll send him over.

Becca's swift agreement surprised him, but he still reckoned there was only a fifty-fifty chance of Theo turning up. The boy would probably dig his heels in and refuse, because the request came from his stepmother. Griff strolled back inside and fetched a cold soda to drink on the porch while he settled down to wait.

Twenty minutes later, when he was on the point of giving up, footsteps crunched on the gravel drive. Theo slouched towards him. Head down. Shoulders slumped.

'Hiya, kid. How's it goin'?'

The only response was a silent glower.

'Your mom says you're at a loose end, so I wondered if you might help me out.' Griff lifted his injured hand. He told him the whole gory tale and watched Theo's eyes widen.

'That sucks. Does it hurt?'

'It's not too bad now.' He shrugged. 'It's a hazard of my job. I thought you might be glad to get out of the house and make some money at the same time.'

'*She* told me I had to come because you're always doing stuff for us. I'm not allowed to take any money.'

He wasn't about to take advantage of the boy that way, but getting involved in the impasse between Becca and her stepson was tricky.

'I'll give Becca a call and see if we can sort something out.'

He picked his words carefully when she answered — not easy with Theo standing next to him listening and glowering. Finally she gave in, the lure of not having to deal with the boy for a few hours proving more tempting than sticking to her guns.

'Okay, we have a deal.' He turned back to Theo. 'I'm allowed to pay you for the hours you put in here, but in return you've got to help out more at home.' He'd heard Lyndsey's voice in the background and suspected the compromise was her suggestion.

'No way,' he scoffed.

'Listen to yourself, Theo.' Griff rested his good hand on the boy's shoulder. 'It's been a hard adjustment for you both since she married your dad, but Becca's trying her best.'

'Yeah, right, sure she is,' he sneered. 'Don't give me any crap about her loving me, either, because that's garbage.' Two angry red circles bloomed on his thin cheeks.

Griff refused to lie. 'She's tryin' to, Theo, but you're not making it easy for her. You love your dad, don't you?'

'Course I do.'

'So do this for him, if nothin' else. Right now, the poor guy's stuck in the middle tryin' to keep you both happy, and that's a pretty lousy position to be in.'

Theo scuffed the toe of one sneaker on the wood floor and didn't meet Griff's eyes.

'Becca's not expecting miracles. You're almost a teenager, after all, and they aren't renowned for being charming and helpful.'

When the kid glanced back up, the faintest hint of a smile lurked in his bright blue eyes.

'I know your aunt is helping out some, but she's got a lot on her plate. You're old enough to work the washer and dryer, unload the dishwasher and stuff like that. Talk to Nora and play with her. She's gonna look up to her big brother, you know.'

'I'm not her—'

'Yes, you are.' His forceful tone startled the boy. 'It doesn't make a shred of difference to a tiny baby. No one's asking you to forget your mom, but—'

'Like she's forgotten me, you mean?' Theo's effort to sound uncaring was contradicted by the tears welling in his eyes. 'She's been gone almost a year, and I've had one email and a couple of texts. All she goes on about are the awesome beaches and what a great guy her new husband is. She never asks if I'm okay.' His voice wobbled.

Griff said nothing.

'Thanks.'

'What for?'

'Not telling me I'm talking garbage. Dad hates me saying that sort of thing.'

'Only because he loves you so much and it kills him to see you hurting.' He decided to take a risk. 'It's none of my business, but do you want to tell me why you got in trouble at school? That's not like you.'

'I'd had enough of Mitch Arnold's digs about me being a loser. He said even my mom knew I was, and that's why she went to live on the other side of the world.' Theo angrily swiped a hand over his eyes. 'He's probably right.'

'That's garbage, Theo.' Griff needed to phrase his reply carefully. 'I've never met your mom, but from what your dad shared with me, she has problems that are nothing to do with you. Ashley struggled with being a mom and reckoned you'd be better off living with Deke. For what it's worth, I reckon she was right.' He didn't add that might've been the only good thing she'd ever done for the poor kid.

Theo jerked away, shoving his hands in his pockets, and stared out at the garden. 'You gonna show me what to do or not?'

'Sure, let's put you to work.' Griff sensed he'd pushed enough for one day.

* * *

Lyndsey gazed proprietorially around the kitchen, more satisfied than she probably should be by the gleaming surfaces and sparkling floor. 'See, Nora, how nice it all looks?' She smiled at her niece, gurgling happily in her bouncy chair. 'Is it time to go out?'

Their new daily habit was taking a walk after lunch. Her original goal was to give them both a dose of fresh air and herself a decent amount of exercise. Neither of which were really happening, thanks to the humid air and the stop-and-start nature of their outings.

'Shall we go see your fan club?' Most days, Harold and William 'happened' to be in their garden when they walked by, and Nora lapped up the attention they lavished on her, bestowing smiles like Queen Elizabeth the First on her favorites. They'd still never seen Tiffany, because she worked during the day. But their most unexpected new friend — although she doubted the woman would appreciate being described that way — was Ruth Mae Grey. After she warned Lyndsey off the other day, it seemed prudent to walk straight by the old woman's house, but she hadn't been able to ignore Miss Grey, stationed by an overgrown bush, close to the street, secateurs in hand. The first time, she stuck to a simple 'Good morning,' to start with, but when Ruth hovered there again the next day, Lyndsey stopped and they exchanged a few words.

Their conversations were never lengthy, but Miss Grey's manner had thawed and Nora was always the beneficiary of a few fleeting smiles. She'd even pried a few stories out of the old lady about her childhood, growing up in Grey House as the adored daughter of one of the prominent families in the area. It'd been a narrow, privileged existence, and gave Lyndsey a glimpse into why Ruth Mae found it so hard to accept the changes she'd been forced to endure later in life. Lyndsey hoped she'd gather up the nerve to offer some help soon, even if it was only cutting the knee-high grass. So far her efforts to persuade either Becca or Theo to join them on their walks were a failure, but she'd discovered with her business clients that gentle persistence often wore people down. That wouldn't happen today though, because her sister had gone off to the nearest supermarket and Theo was helping Griff in his garden.

Lyndsey gnawed at her lip. She missed Griff terribly.

Her phone buzzed from the table and Nicola's name flashed on the screen. She barely had time to answer before her assistant launched into a tale of woe. Their most troublesome client was demanding another personal consultation with Lyndsey tonight. As luck would have it, Madelaine Stanwick wasn't free until eight o'clock, which meant Lyndsey setting an alarm for two a.m. She reluctantly agreed, and was already dreading another night with little or no sleep.

Nora squawked and batted her hands in the air as if to say, *Have you forgotten me?*

'Sorry, sweetheart.' She absentmindedly gave her niece a toy giraffe to hold, her mind still on the business and wondering how much longer she could stretch herself this thin.

'Hiya, I'm goin' to have a shower.' Theo burst in through the back door. His clothes, face and hands were filthy, but he was grinning like mad. 'This guy's a slave-driver.'

Lyndsey glanced over to see Griff lingering on the doorstep, clearly unsure of his welcome.

'I thought Becca would appreciate hearing what a hard worker this kid is.'

The sound of his syrupy drawl again stirred her all over and she nervously brushed away an unruly curl from her face.

'Come in. Please. Coffee?'

'No, thanks, but a glass of cold lemonade would sure hit the spot, wouldn't it, Theo?'

'Yeah, but I'm going to clean up first.' He flashed another smile her way. 'Have we got any of Becca's awesome coconut lime cookies left?'

Tears pricked her eyes. She wished her sister could've heard the rare praise. 'I think so.'

'Cool.' He loped off, letting the door slam behind him.

'Boys don't do quiet.' Griff chuckled. 'It's a good thing a certain little lady isn't tryin' to sleep.' He crouched down in front of Nora. 'How're you doin' today? Having fun with Aunt Lyndsey?'

'We were just about to go on our walk.' A quiet surge of pleasure ran through her at his surprise when she explained the full story.

'William and Harold have always enjoyed fussing over her on the few occasions they've seen her, but Miss Grey? You've succeeded where the rest of us have failed. You're somethin' else, all right.'

Lyndsey found it hard to accept compliments and muttered something she hoped he'd take as thanks under her breath. 'I'm working up to offering to help her in some way. She's clearly struggling to even get around, and I'd love to convince her to give the rest of you a chance to prove you're decent people.'

'I'll do anything I can to help, remember?'

'I know. You've made a good start with Theo.' Griff's hair was tied back today, so it was easy to spot the tips of his ears turn bright pink.

'Maybe.' He lifted his broad shoulders in a shrug, tightening the sleeves of his faded green T-shirt to show off his muscles.

Lyndsey made a beeline for the fridge, grateful for the blast of cool air bathing her hot face. She lifted out the jug of lemonade and set it on the counter while she fetched three glasses.

'By the way, I found out why Theo fought with that kid at school,' he murmured.

'Oh my God, what was it?'

'I can't say too much without breaking his confidence, but a word in Deke's ear might be in order. He needs to make it clear to the boy that it wasn't Theo's fault his mother left. If Deke could bolster the kid up a bit and give him a bit more praise for being who he is, rather than who he isn't. You get the idea?'

'I do.' Lyndsey nodded thoughtfully. 'We can help with that, too.'

'We sure can.'

'Look, I'm really sorry I haven't—'

'Hey, we had an agreement, remember?'

'Becca and I are doing better.' She rattled off a quick rundown of the progress they'd made, around the house and in their relationship.

'It sure looks a hundred times better in here.' Griff glanced admiringly around the kitchen.

'Thanks.' Lyndsey gathered up her courage. 'I think the timing's as right for us as it's ever going to be . . . do you want to try again?'

'Are we talkin' friendly neighborliness, or . . . more?'

Lyndsey met his blazing eyes and melted like ice cream on a hot day.

'Cookies?' Theo bounded into the kitchen like an exuberant puppy. He'd changed into the black and gold Cornish T-shirt with the 'One and All' motto on that she'd given him when she arrived, which, at the time, he'd tossed to one side. 'Want me to go away again?' He smirked at them.

'No!' she and Griff chimed simultaneously, and next thing all three of them were laughing.

The sound of a car crunching over the gravel drew her over to the kitchen window on the side of the house where they usually parked. 'Becca's back.' Lyndsey turned to Theo.

'How about you help her in with the shopping bags?' From the corner of her eye, she caught a fleeting glance zip between Griff and Theo. The boy shrugged, nodded and ambled out the back door.

'What was all that about?'

'We talked.'

'Thank you.'

'He's a good kid.' Griff's voice turned husky. 'How about a date tonight?'

'Only if you fancy keeping me awake until two o'clock tomorrow morning?' Lyndsey quickly explained. 'Don't worry, I'm not serious.'

'Why not? It's not a problem, except for this.' Griff held up his bandaged hand. 'I'm not too adept on the cooking front at the moment, but there are still pizzas in the freezer.'

'I'll make us something. It'll be simple.' The warning made him smile.

'Perfect. See you later.' Griff brushed a soft kiss on her cheek. 'It's been a long week. I missed you.'

'Missed you, too.'

'That's enough snogging in my kitchen.' Becca breezed in. 'Theo tells me there's cold lemonade on offer and cookies.' He trailed in behind her, carrying the shopping bags.

'Absolutely. I'll get another glass.'

A short while later, she felt an unusual sense of ease. Theo was playing peek-a-boo with Nora and the strain was gone from her sister's face as she chatted animatedly to Griff about planting a butterfly garden next year.

'I hate to break up the party, but I've got work to do.' Griff gulped down the last of his lemonade. 'I'll see y'all later.' At the door he turned and winked at her.

Lyndsey blushed and tried her best to ignore Becca's satisfied look.

CHAPTER TWELVE

Griff knew he should exert some self-restraint and thought-fulness and allow Lyndsey to rest longer but leaned in to kiss her cheek, inhaling the intoxicating scent of her velvety skin. Hopefully she'd wake up and they could make love all over again. She'd been irresistible to him from the day they met, and last night cemented it.

'Oh my, what time is it?' Lyndsey yawned and stretched awake.

'Six o'clock.' He raised up on one elbow and pushed the dark, tousled curls away from her face so he could kiss her on the mouth. 'After you finished turning that prissy client into putty in your hands, we managed a few hours' sleep.'

'I hope I didn't snore?'

'Loud enough to make the rafters shake.' Griff struggled to keep a straight face. 'Don't worry, you were your usual quiet, thoughtful self.'

'Is that how you see me?' Her brow wrinkled.

'What's wrong with that?'

She pulled free of him and sat up, wrapping her arms around her bent knees. 'You aren't exactly gregarious your-self, are you?'

'Believe it or not, I used to be quite the party animal. In my yuppie days, I worked hard and played even harder. I wasn't a great guy, Lyndsey. These days, I appreciate "quiet and thoughtful" a whole lot. If more people were that way, the world would be a better place.' He grinned. 'If it's any consolation, you definitely weren't quiet and restrained when we did the horizontal tango.'

'The what?' She smacked him on the chest. 'You're appalling.'

'Let's just say it's a good thing there's a good bit of space between us and the neighbors.' A deep flush spread up her neck. 'I'm not complainin'. Far from it.' He slid a hand down to cup one of her breasts, and Lyndsey's sharp intake of breath made him groan. 'I love that under all your British modesty and coolness, you're . . .' His fingers stroked lower and lower. 'Insatiable,' he rasped.

Shifting off her briefly, Griff fumbled around for another condom and mentally urged himself to slow down. He'd always tried to be a thoughtful lover and not rush a woman for his own satisfaction, but this morning's battle was hard fought.

'Don't hold back. I won't break.' She gave a sly smile. 'Unless, of course, it's too much for your poor injured hand.' Last night she'd been cautious at first of hurting him, but he'd assured her the cut was almost healed up and made her blush when he insisted she was well worth a little discomfort. 'Before we came to bed last night I'd no idea how . . . *sensual* I could be with the right person.' Her breath came in short gasps and she wound her arms around his neck, kissed him hard and deep and pulled him down.

Griff gave in.

* * *

Lyndsey smiled when he sounded worried and asked if he was crushing her. If she said yes but she loved it, and possibly him too, Griff would probably freak. She usually jumped straight out of bed after sex to shower, not a habit that endeared her to previous lovers. Last night, she'd had no desire to wash off his musky, testosterone-laden scent lingering on her skin.

The desire simmering between them had bubbled away from the moment she entered the house last night. They gamely held it at bay for a while by eating together, a delicious lasagna she'd made following a go-to recipe that hadn't failed her yet, then by sitting on the porch to drink coffee until the sun went down. They'd talked about everything from the classic Westerns they both enjoyed to the various places around the world they wanted to see one day.

But when they shifted back inside and Griff casually asked if she wanted to take a nap until it was time for the video call back to England, all bets were off. She'd kissed him on the mouth and said three simple words.

'Oh, Griff, really?'

Now, in his magnificent king-size bed, where he'd made her feel so amazingly wonderful last night, Lyndsey snuggled back into his arms. Her emotions were all over the place today. Normally it was no hardship to push personal relationships to one side and concentrate on work, but over the last couple of months her priorities had subtly altered. The more involved she became — first in her sister's life and now with Griff — the more she felt constrained by the demands of her business. Last night it was as if he battered down the last bricks of the Berlin Wall, leaving her exposed, ecstatic and petrified in equal measures.

'Did I tell you the story behind this bed?' Griff murmured.

'No, but I'm sure it has one,' she teased.

'This is what they call a sleigh bed, and was carved from local white oak by one of the early pioneers in Williamson County. I discovered it at a local antique shop. It's very special.'

And so are you, she thought to herself.

He tangled his fingers in her curls. 'Your hair's so beautiful.' A lazy smile creased his face. 'Of course, the rest of you is too.'

'I used to hate it.'

'Why?'

'I longed for straight, blonde hair like Becca's.' She gave a wry smile. 'It was another thing to hate her for. Cornwall's not the most diverse place on the planet, so I stood out. I'd get teased unmercifully, especially at school.'

'I'm sorry.'

'That's when I started keeping it cut short.'

Griff started to open his mouth, but closed it again immediately.

'Go on. Say what's on your mind.'

'Don't take this the wrong way, because you're always incredibly smart and pulled together, but is this why you only ever wear white, black and gray?'

Her heart plummeted. She could blow him off by saying it made life easier, because then everything matched without having to think about it, but she refused to be dishonest with him.

'Theo called us both cuckoos in the nest, you know, and he's right. I was sure if I played down my Caribbean side I'd fit in better.' Lyndsey exhaled a tired sigh. 'It didn't work. Becca was still the lovable, blonde princess and I . . . wasn't.'

'But you've hashed that out with her now — right?' Griff asked.

She shook her head. 'I stuck with all the other stuff. The whole looks thing wasn't her fault, was it?'

'No, but you still might consider telling her. I'm guessing the more you understand each other, the closer you'll get. Isn't that what you want?'

'Yes, it is, but don't push me. We've taken big steps already. I don't hear you stepping up to mend bridges with *your* brother.'

Griff looked awkward. 'You're right. I'm sorry. I'll tell you about Jase another day. I promise.'

Now seemed the wrong time to push. They'd already put a dent in their wonderful night together, and she'd hate to ruin it completely.

'I suppose we ought to get you on home?' A trace of his sexy smile returned. 'I'd rather keep you here in my bed all day, but I guess it's not an option?'

'I'm afraid not. Maybe we should make a shortcut through the bushes for when we're desperate?' Lyndsey hoped he'd play along with her desire to push away the harder conversation they'd drifted into.

'Good plan. I'll get right on it when I can wield a chainsaw again.'

Reluctantly she threw on her clothes and sneaked longing glances at Griff as he did the same. They left the house and walked silently, hand in hand, until they reached Becca's front door.

'You can remind Theo that he promised to cut my grass later. It needs to dry up some first, so I reckon about eleven o'clock?'

'Was he really helpful yesterday or were you just saying that?'

'I wouldn't say it if I didn't mean it, Lyndsey.' He held her gaze. 'I'm not simply talking about things I've said about Theo, either, in case you had any doubts.'

'Good.'

Griff wrapped his strong, wiry arms around her and drew them into a lingering kiss. 'I suppose I'd better let you go. Tonight?'

'Oh, yes.'

'I thought I heard squirrels on the porch.' Becca flung open the door. 'Long work call, was it?' Her eyes danced with mischief.

'I . . . um . . . didn't want to disturb you creeping back in . . .'

'I'm glad you two have finally seen sense.' A wailing sound drifted from her phone. 'We don't need an alarm clock or a rooster with Nora around.'

'I'll get her up.' Lyndsey threw a regretful look at Griff. 'See you later.'

'You sure will.'

Her wicked sister made fake gagging noises when he kissed her again. 'Ignore her,' Lyndsey said, 'she's jealous.'

Griff laughed it off. 'How long until Deke's home?'

'Too long.' Becca rolled her eyes. 'We've still got about seven weeks to survive yet.'

Lyndsey's spirits sunk, and she couldn't look at the man who'd spent most of the night loving her. Once her brother-in-law returned, she'd have no excuse to stay this side of the Atlantic Ocean. Nora's shrill cries broke through her gloom, bringing her back to the here and now.

'I've got a baby to wrangle.' She tugged on Becca's arm. 'You've got breakfast to fix. It's your turn.'

'I'll see y'all later.' Griff ambled off, but Lyndsey stayed where she was and didn't move until he'd disappeared down the drive.

* * *

By twelve o'clock, Lyndsey was dying on her feet. She'd cleared up after breakfast, folded a mountain of laundry and made a healthy chicken, vegetable and pasta salad for lunch.

'For heaven's sake, sit down before you drop.' Becca gave her a shove towards the nearest chair.

'But—'

'But nothing. It's my turn to boss you around.'

'*I'm* supposed to be taking care of *you*,' Lyndsey protested.

'Remember what you told me the other day? If I didn't take care of myself, I'd be no use to my family? The same applies to you. You're wearing yourself out.' Her sister smirked. 'We both know you've had almost no sleep. How do you expect to keep going when you're running on empty?'

'Before you had Nora, did you have any idea how much work she'd be? Not that she isn't absolutely worth it, of course.' Lyndsey tried to deflect her sister's pointed questions.

'Did *you* know how much work running your own business would be before you started it?' Becca swiftly turned the tables back on her. 'None of us *know*. I didn't *know* when I married Deke that Theo would be so . . . challenging. I wouldn't ever say this to anyone else, but there were plenty of days I wished he wasn't around. I didn't expect to get pregnant immediately, either.' The color rose in her face. 'I don't regret any of it, but the timing could've been better.' Her expression softened. 'Thanks to you, I'm learning to embrace my new life.'

In the distance, Lyndsey thought she heard a door slam, but was distracted by Nora batting her tiny hand on her leg. Her niece was strapped into her bouncy chair on the floor, playing contentedly with a noisy elephant-shaped rattle. She crouched down to stroke her niece's soft pink cheek.

'Getting broody?'

'Broody?' Her face heated. 'Maybe.'

'Griff would make a great dad.'

'Griff? Are you mad?' Lyndsey's heart fluttered. 'He . . . I mean . . . we've slept together, and it was incredible and I love being with him, but . . .' She didn't point out the short amount of time they'd known each other, because months, weeks, days faded into insignificance when they were together.

'He adores Nora. And Theo? He's wonderful with him, too.' Becca looked sad. 'Much better than I've been. Theo was so sweet yesterday, though, and I'm sure that's down to Griff. It's my fault. I should've been more understanding from the beginning, but I let his natural resentment blossom and now it's a hard road to put things right. I'm determined things will be different from now on.'

'I'm sure they will.' Lyndsey stifled a yawn.

'You are going right now to take a nap.'

'I can't. You—'

'Will manage perfectly fine. You've taken care of the mountain of washing and prepared lunch. My house is tidy.' Her eyes shone. 'At least a large proportion of it is, and the rest is getting there. You certainly know how to do your job. When I video chat with Deke later, I'm going to give him a virtual tour so he can see what he's got to look forward to when he comes home.'

'That's a smashing idea.' Lyndsey debated how to casually throw in the conversation she'd had with Griff about Theo.

'Come on. What's going through that devious mind of yours now?'

Was this new understanding of how each other's minds worked an up or down side of them getting on better? The jury was still out. 'If I throw out some advice, could you trust me enough to think about it without needing to ask where I got the info from?'

'Probably.' Becca didn't sound certain, but half-hearted agreement was better than nothing.

'Theo's got the screwed-up idea his mum left because she thinks he's a loser and didn't want to be bothered with him any longer.'

'Oh, that's terrible.' Her bright blue eyes bored into Lyndsey. 'I'm guessing the trouble at school was to do with that?'

'I'm saying nothing more.' She mimed zipping her mouth shut.

'Deke needs to know so he can help put that right. I'll send him a private message now, so he can think it over before we chat later,' Becca said decisively. She glanced at the clock and frowned. 'Shouldn't Theo be at Griff's by now?'

'Yes.' Lyndsey pushed her chair back. 'I'll check on him when I go up, and if he's not there, I'll text Griff to make sure he turned up.'

'Thanks. Now clear off.'

Upstairs, she knocked a couple of times on Theo's door without getting any response. She popped her head in to find the room empty. After firing off a quick message to Griff, she dived into her own bedroom and debated whether or not to shower before trying to get some sleep. Before she was halfway through undressing, her phone buzzed.

Theo's not here. I'm still waiting for him.

An uneasy feeling settled in the pit of her stomach and her brain started to race. *If* the door she'd heard closing earlier was Theo heading over to Griff's, he might've overheard her conversation with Becca. *If* he'd taken some things her sister said out of context, who knew how he might react. Lyndsey dragged the rest of her clothes back on and raced down to the kitchen.

'Griff hasn't seen Theo and his room is empty.'

Becca stopped in the middle of pouring formula into a row of baby bottles lined up on the counter. 'He might've gone to Deke's studio. He's got his own key and likes to go there sometimes, to be close to his dad.' She frowned. 'I hate that he's let Griff down. I hoped we'd turned the corner.'

'Shall I go and check?'

'Yes, please, if you don't mind.' Becca exhaled a sigh. 'See if you can talk him around.'

She'd only ever been to Deke's workplace once, when he showed her around the old tobacco barn he'd converted into a state-of-the-art music studio. The sun beat down on her as she took the short cut across the grass instead of using the paved trail. It didn't surprise her to find the doors locked, but she went through the motions of banging and shouting Theo's name anyway. Her phone pinged with another message from Griff.

Any sign of Theo?
No.
I'm coming over.

Despite everything, a tiny smile played around her mouth. She needed him and he knew it.

CHAPTER THIRTEEN

Griff wrapped his arms around Lyndsey and hugged her, wishing he could brush away the strain etched into her weary face.

'I think Theo might've run away.' Her eyes filled with tears as she haltingly explained. 'This is going to crush Becca.'

'You might be jumping to conclusions.'

'Do you honestly believe that?'

Griff shook his head.

They made their way back to the house, where he winced at the sight of Becca's hopeful face when they opened the kitchen door. Her smile faded when Lyndsey shared the bad news that Theo wasn't at the studio and Griff hadn't seen him.

'The kid probably just wants to give us a scare,' Griff said. 'I did the same thing at Theo's age because I was angry with my dad for not letting me go to a party. We lived way out in the country, so I knew lots of great hiding places. My half-baked plan was to lay low for a while to frighten them.' He shrugged. 'But a bad thunderstorm started and that freaked me out, so I ran back home with my tail between my legs, blubbing like a baby.'

'I'm sure you mean well, Griff, but that's not exactly comforting.' Becca exhaled a sigh. 'Theo grew up in LA and isn't comfortable in the outdoors the way you were.' She threw her sister a despairing look. 'Where on earth do we start looking?'

'His friends?' Lyndsey suggested. 'We could phone around and see if he's been in touch with any of them.'

'Friends? He might have some at school, but I wouldn't know.' She sounded sad. 'He's never mentioned any names or invited anyone here.'

'Even that noninformation helps. Now we know he's probably not sneaked off to anyone else's house.'

Griff admired Lyndsey's ability to put a positive spin on the grim situation.

'It doesn't make sense for you to join the search, Becca, because you can't drag Nora around. Why don't you stay here, in case Theo comes home or tries to get in touch?' Lyndsey suggested. 'We'll start looking for him.'

'Shouldn't we call the police?' Becca's voice trembled.

'I'm not sure. What do you think?' Lyndsey looked up to meet Griff's eyes.

'I'm inclined to say wait a while. Maybe an hour or so? He's not a vulnerable small child.' If that piece of advice caused any harm to the boy, he'd never forgive himself, but he'd said it now.

'Oh God, we're doing a Zoom chat with Deke later. What am I going to say if Theo isn't back?' Becca's big blue eyes widened.

'Don't worry about that for now. One problem at a time,' Lyndsey said briskly. 'We've both got our phones, so we'll ring you with any updates and you can do the same.' She tilted Griff a nod. 'Come on.'

Before he had a chance to agree or disagree, she took off running and he caught up with her by the front porch.

'So how *are* we going to do this?' she said quietly. The certainty she'd impressed him with in the kitchen was nowhere in sight now.

'I know the wider area better, so why don't I hop in my truck and drive around? How about you thoroughly check out our two properties first? Mine goes quite a long way back behind my workshop, and it's pretty overgrown where I haven't cleared it yet.'

'Of course.' She squeezed his hand. 'In case you weren't sure, I couldn't handle this without you.'

'You don't have to,' Griff promised. He sprinted off down the drive and raced around to his own house. After picking up his keys and wallet, it made sense to take a few minutes for a quick sweep of all the rooms, in case Theo had sneaked in. He'd leave everything unlocked so if the boy came here seeking refuge, he'd find it. Griff jumped in the truck, but made no move to drive off.

He needed to put himself in the mind of an upset twelve-year-old with few friends, no means of transport and a simple desire to get away from a place where he felt unwanted. Griff doubted Theo would venture deeper into Paradise Valley, because he wasn't familiar with the area. It struck him as far more likely that he'd walk the few hundred yards to the main road to hitch a lift. Out here people still offered rides to strangers, a thought that cheered and worried him in equal measure. Most were decent enough and would take Theo somewhere safe, but there were bad people everywhere. Griff shuddered, then mentally gave himself a stern talking to. Panicking wouldn't help.

The truck protested when he put his foot down and jolted out of the drive. An hour later, when he'd driven a ten-mile radius around Paradise Valley without any sign of Theo, frustration set in.

* * *

Lyndsey tugged a bramble out of her hair and sighed at her grubby T-shirt. Pristine white a mere hour ago, it was sweat-stained and dirty now, with a hole in the back where it'd hitched on a tree branch. She'd started by checking every inch of her sister's property, and had just finished doing the same at Griff's. Back at the entrance to his drive, she hesitated a moment and debated which direction to try next.

'Are you okay?' A tall, statuesque woman wearing blue medical scrubs strode towards her, black and purple dreadlocks swinging in the air, her round purple-lensed glasses glinting in the hot sun.

'Yes, I'm fine, thank you.' Lyndsey hesitated. This wasn't the time to be politely, privately British. 'I'm not really, to be honest.' She introduced herself. 'My nephew Theo's gone missing. Do you know the Warners?' She pointed to Grey House. 'Becca's my sister.'

'Oh, right. Yeah, I know them. Well, I sort of do, I . . . sorry, let's try again. I'm Tiffany Hunt and I live over there.' She pointed to the gray brick house on the opposite side of the road. 'I've said hi to Deke a few times when we've bumped into each other, but I've never spoken to your sister.' A pop of heat flared on her ebony skin. 'I guess she's busy with the new baby and not outside much.'

'Settling in hasn't been easy for her.'

Tiffany rolled her dark eyes. 'Tell me about it! It's been a hard adjustment for me, too. Harold and William are awesome neighbors and always super helpful. Griff's great, too. But Miss Grey would happily kick my sorry ass back to Minnesota if she could.' She mused. 'Listen to me, rambling on. Tell me about Theo.'

Lyndsey trotted out a pared-down version of the story, skimming over the details of why he ran off in the first place. 'He's probably hiding somewhere to give us a scare, but we can't be certain.'

'Would you like a hand searching for him?'

'Thanks, that'd be awesome. Griff's out driving around in his truck.'

'How about I take my side of the road and have a good look around? I'll rope in the guys in the white house as well. They're always so generous when it comes to helping out.' Tiffany gave the dilapidated cabin at the end a wary look. 'Are you brave enough to venture on Miss Grey's land? I'm guessin' there's a whole lot of hiding places in there.'

'I've spoken to her a few times. I don't think she'll mind.'

'You have? Seriously? She came out on the porch the day my moving truck arrived, took a long, hard look at me and went back inside. If I walk by her house and she's in the garden, she pointedly turns away.'

'I'm sorry. She has a hard time accepting the Grey family isn't everything around here anymore. I'll tell you more about it later.' When they were the other side of this mess, and Lyndsey had to believe they would be soon, she'd work on getting this woman to help with the mission to charm Miss Grey with neighborly kindness. 'Should we swap numbers, so we can get in touch if we need to?' She pulled out her phone.

'Sure.'

After sorting that, Lyndsey marched towards Ruth Mae Grey's cabin with a renewed sense of determination. She stepped through the gap in the fence where there probably used to be a gate and picked her way gingerly through the long grass up to the sagging porch. It wouldn't do to start searching without asking permission, so she pushed away a flutter of nerves and knocked on the weather-beaten door. Griff told her when they had dinner at the Adamsville Grocery that the owner made a delivery here every couple of weeks, the only person known to see Miss Grey on a regular basis.

'Clear off or I'll get my shotgun. I won't stand no truck with trespassers.' Ruth's quavering voice drifted out.

'It's Lyndsey Carne, Miss Grey. I need to ask you a favor.' She held her breath and finally the door cracked open a few inches. Before the old woman could berate her, she rattled off the story of Theo's disappearance. 'I'd like to walk around the outside of your property, if that's all right?'

'The boy won't be here. He don't say boo to a goose when he runs by,' she scoffed. 'Frightened of me, I s'ppose.'

'He's a bit . . . troubled these days, and isn't the chattiest at the best of times.' Lyndsey added her nephew to the list of people who might help to alleviate this woman's appalling loneliness. 'So do you mind if I check?'

'You'll do it anyway, so I might as well say yes.'

It amused Lyndsey that the old lady had the measure of her and realized she wasn't a walkover. 'Thank you.'

'I'll come along. Make sure you don't do any damage.' The door creaked open further and Ruth Mae hobbled out, leaning heavily on her walking stick. As usual, she was dressed in another old-fashioned rust-black dress. To Lyndsey, the outfits always looked as if they'd arrived with the original pioneering Grey family.

She slowed her stride to match Miss Grey's halting steps and found herself talking about Theo and his problems.

'Being somewhere you're not wanted ain't much of it.'

The unexpected sympathy for her errant nephew touched her. 'Is that how you feel, surrounded by all these new people who've moved onto what was your family's land?'

Ruth Mae gazed off into the distance and said nothing.

'Perhaps you'd like to come over for a cup of coffee one day and meet them all properly? They may not be Greys, but they're good people.'

The old woman turned away. 'I'm tired. I'm goin' in. You can search the back by yourself. I hope you find the boy.'

'Thank you.' On impulse, Lyndsey touched her arm, shocked at the frailty of the bones under her fingers. 'I'll be sure to let you know when we find Theo, and I won't forget about that coffee, either.'

'Don't drink the stuff. Water straight out the tap does for me.'

She kept a straight face at the sly acceptance. 'We've got that, too.'

As soon as Miss Grey shuffled off towards the house, Lyndsey headed around to the back. This part was in even worse condition; the couple of sheds, a chicken coop and a small barn she spotted were all on the verge of falling down. Determined to do a thorough job, she checked them out and emerged covered in spider webs and decades of accumulated dust and dirt. She couldn't help smiling at the idea of Theo — another neat freak — coming in here.

At first she thought the buzzing noise she heard was bees, and glanced anxiously around. When it clicked that it came from her phone, Lyndsey yanked her phone from her pocket, hopeful for good news.

No luck. I'm heading back your way soon.

Griff's terse message made her spirits fade.

* * *

Griff parked outside the Adamsville Grocery and hurried inside. He'd kill two birds with one stone and ask if anyone had seen Theo while he picked up a cold Coke to slake his thirst.

'Hey, Buddy, how's it going?' he greeted the grizzled old man who'd run this place forever.

'Could be worse.' Buddy ambled out from behind the counter. 'Haven't seen you in a month of Sundays. Mind you, I did hear you were in with a cute little ole girl the other night though.' He winked. 'Missed that, didn't I? I were at my sister's in Leiper's Fork for supper.'

'I brought a friend to check out the music,' he mumbled.

'You could do with a good woman.' Buddy tugged off the faded orange baseball cap he was never without and scratched his bald head before settling the hat back in place. 'My Martha Lou kept me in line.' His smile dimmed. 'Fifty-one years we were wed, and there's not a mornin' now that I don't wake up and miss the ole girl.'

'It must be hard.'

' "Hard" don't begin to cover it, son.'

They stood silently for a moment.

'You didn't come in to hear me piss and moan.' Buddy straightened up. 'What're you after today?'

'Two things. First a cold Coke, then you might be able to help me with something. I know you keep your ears open and hear folk talking.' More than a few locals used him as a combination of therapist, police officer and minister.

'Just say I'm a nosy ole bugger and be done with it.' His loud guffaw made a couple of tourists checking out a display of local honey turn and stare.

'I'd never do that.'

'C'mon, I'll grab us a couple of cold bottles and we'll sit on the porch.'

A sliver of guilt wriggled in. He should take the Coke with him and hurry back to Paradise Valley, but an outside opinion might not be a bad thing, and he'd learned his friend wasn't a man to be rushed.

They settled in a couple of the rocking chairs whose seats were worn smooth by the imprint of thousands of backsides. Griff swigged half of his drink in one long swallow before telling Buddy about Theo. 'He's Deke Warner's boy.'

'Deke's a stand-up guy. He's been in here a bunch of times and always makes time to talk. It's all about the music with him, not all this celebrity garbage. I'm sure he tries his best with the boy, but it's a sorry mess when a kid don't feel like he belongs. Theo probably feels pushed out by Deke's new family.'

'Yeah, I know. You haven't heard anyone mention picking up a boy today, I suppose?'

'Nope, 'fraid not.'

'I'm worried about him, Buddy. We couldn't find anything missing from the house, so I'm pretty sure he left on impulse. He's probably got some money with him, but that's all.'

'I'll put the word out, if you like?'

'Yeah, that'd be great.' He gulped down the rest of his Coke and sprang up. 'Call me if you hear anything?'

'Sure.' Buddy levered himself out of the chair and clamped a reassuring hand on Griff's shoulder. 'I bet he'll come back with his tail between his legs when he's hungry.'

Griff prayed his friend was right. 'Thanks for listening.'

'Don't know I did much good, but they say a trouble shared is a trouble halved.'

Griff gave a curt nod, not trusting himself to say anything more.

Outside, he shoved his hand in his shorts' pocket and cursed when his phone wasn't there. Griff opened the truck and spotted it lying on the passenger seat, beeping like crazy. He picked it up and scanned through a string of missed texts from Lyndsey, unsure whether to laugh or cry.

CHAPTER FOURTEEN

'So when were you goin' to tell me you'd lost my son?' Deke's harsh tone of voice and his glare made Lyndsey cringe. She watched the last vestige of color drain from her sister's face. Theo was home safe now, but that didn't seem to take the edge off Deke's anger. 'I shouldn't have to hear it from a concerned employee at the British Airways counter at the Nashville airport.'

'We thought—'

'No, you didn't fuckin' think, that's the problem!' he yelled. 'I suppose you were too busy fussing over Nora to care what happened to Theo.'

'That's grossly unfair.' Lyndsey couldn't sit there in silence another minute. 'How dare you talk to Becca that way? She's been trying her absolute hardest while you've been away. You knew Theo was terribly unhappy when you left. Did you think a fairy godmother would wave a magic wand over him while you were gone?'

'No, but—'

'But nothing,' she snapped.

'Becca, I'm sorry.' Deke slumped, clutching his head in his hands. When he straightened up, his gaunt features were etched with pain. 'I didn't mean those things I said. I

121

know I'm a crappy father and a crappy husband. This is all my fault.'

'No, it's not,' Becca said firmly. 'We're both to blame. I'm sorry, too. More than I can say.'

'Things are gonna be different when I'm back home again. That's a promise.'

'You know I'm counting the days,' she whispered. 'I miss you so much.'

'I miss you too, sweetheart.' Deke sighed. 'I saw your message, and haven't been able to get it out of my head all day. I'd love to clear it up now, but I reckon it'll be best if I talk to Theo face to face about his mother when I get back.'

'You're probably right.'

'But maybe tomorrow y'all can give me a tour of our smartened-up house?' The ghost of a smile lifted some of the tension from his drawn features. 'Is that really our kitchen in the background behind you? I promise I'll try my darnedest to mend my ways and not be such a slob.'

'You and me both!' Becca laughed.

Lyndsey sensed they'd be better off without her there. 'I'll leave you two to talk. Griff's in the kitchen with Theo. I'll join them and listen for Nora, in case she wakes up.'

A couple of hours ago they'd been on the verge of reporting Theo missing to the police when Becca received a phone call from the airport. Her creative nephew had attempted to buy a ticket to London because he knew Deke's band would be performing there soon, but his naiveté let him down. The two hundred dollars he'd saved up didn't come close to covering the cost, and the airline would never have sold one to a boy his age anyway, even with the passport he'd stolen from his father's office safe. Griff drove Becca to the airport to collect Theo while Lyndsey took care of Nora. She'd immediately popped the little girl in the stroller and walked around to let all of the neighbors know that Theo was safe. She'd even persuaded Miss Grey to open the door for the second time that day to give her the news. For a fleeting moment, she could've sworn a mist of tears blurred the old lady's faded blue eyes.

'I suppose Dad's angry with me?' Theo sounded despondent.

She debated how to answer. Lyndsey didn't want to pile more agony on the boy, but he needed to realize the full effect of his actions so that he wasn't stupid enough to try something similar again.

'Hey, he loves you, kid.' Griff patted Theo's arm. 'He's glad you're safe. It's all that matters.'

Hardening her heart, she fixed her steady gaze on her nephew. 'No, it's not all that matters. You might've got a lift with someone who . . .' It wasn't easy to strike a balance between being too graphic while still putting her point across. 'You're twelve. That's old enough to understand not all people are good. You could've been hurt. Or worse.' Theo looked like a ghost. 'Can you imagine what that would've done to your parents?'

'Lyndsey, don't be too hard on him,' Griff urged.

'No, she's right,' Theo muttered. 'I just wanted to see my dad. He's been gone so long and I . . .' He dropped his head on his folded arms and the room filled with loud sobs.

Now she felt like the worst person in the world. Lyndsey tentatively put her hand on Theo's bony shoulder. 'I'm sorry I was harsh, but you frightened us all so much, and . . .' She startled when Griff's strong arms wrapped around them both. The scent of his air-dried clothes and the heat emanating from his big body acted like a warm blanket on her fraught nerves.

'Your dad wants to talk to you, Theo.' Becca appeared in the kitchen door, her eyes wide at the sight of the three of them holding on to each other. 'He needs to see you're all right with his own eyes. I . . .' Her hand flew up to her mouth.

'Don't cry, Mom, please.' Theo wriggled out of their arms and ran over to Becca. 'I'm sorry—'

'No, I'm the one who should be sorry.'

Lyndsey's heart overflowed with happiness. Seeing the two of them reaching out to each other was awesome enough, but Theo had never called her sister *Mom* before. Only the other day, Becca confessed that he painstakingly avoided calling her anything. The word might've slipped out unconsciously, but struck her as a major step forward.

'Come on, or he'll start to worry again.' Becca touched Theo's cheek. 'I promise I'll only stay a moment, then you can chat to your dad on your own.'

'I'd just as soon you hung around.' The ghost of a smile emerged. 'He might not yell at me so much if you're there. I totally get I deserve it, but it still won't be fun.'

'Let's brave him together, then.' Becca looped her arm through Theo's and steered him out of the kitchen.

Lyndsey met Griff's gaze, struggling to read his thoughts. 'Was I too hard on him?'

'No. I guess I'm a soft touch. I was too relieved to be mad at him.'

'Children need consistency. Limits. Consequences for their actions. Without that they . . . flounder.'

'Like Becca?' he murmured.

'Maybe.' For now, that seemed the wisest response, rather than going into the difference in the way their parents treated Becca — the family princess — and her. Lyndsey realized her mum and dad probably weren't even aware that's what they'd done, and would be horrified if they found out the effect it'd had on the sisters' relationship. 'She flitted through life pretty much unscathed until this last year. A whirlwind romance suited her, but dealing with the reality afterwards — not so much.'

'I reckon she's starting to see that now.'

'Let's hope so,' she said fervently. 'Anyway, I need to see about dinner, and I'm sure you've got work to do.'

'Tryin' to get rid of me?'

Lyndsey fiddled unnecessarily with her silver necklace.

'I hoped you might come over later?'

'I'd better not tonight. I should stay here.'

'Don't tell me you're goin' to stay chained up all weekend as some sort of penance? None of this is your fault, you know.'

'It's nothing like that. I have work to catch up on.' Nicola's hints that she couldn't manage The Right Place essentially on her own much longer were becoming more persistent. If she wasn't careful, she'd have no business to go home to. 'Tomorrow evening — if that suits you?'

'Seven o'clock. I'll pick you up.'

Their eyes met, and she knew she wasn't the only one remembering their night together. She'd given up trying to convince herself that pursuing this madness with Griff was well, mad. Lyndsey couldn't be her usual sensible, pragmatic self around him, so she might as well admit it.

* * *

An aggressive couple of hours spent hoeing his vegetable garden sweated out a good deal of Griff's frustration. Thankfully his hand was pretty much back to full strength now, but if he'd tried to work with glass instead of weeds, his moodiness would've made it an unmitigated disaster. Lyndsey was right to be shaken by Theo's escapade, and Griff was childish to hanker for a little more of her attention. He didn't consider himself a needy man; in fact, more than one girlfriend had complained about his lack of possessiveness and the correlation between the depth of his feelings.

He pulled up a couple of cucumbers and red peppers to add to the handful of green beans he'd picked earlier and strolled back into the house, dropping the vegetables on the kitchen counter. Griff's stomach rumbled, reminding him he hadn't eaten today. He wasn't in the mood to cook, but if he drove over to give Buddy an update on Theo, he could get a meal there. But he'd need a shower and clean clothes first, because even his old friend wouldn't let him in looking and smelling this bad.

On the way out, he threw Deke's house a longing glance.

* * *

Although it wasn't open mic night, the place was still busy. Friday's draw, which pulled in customers for miles around, was fried catfish, bought in direct from the Mississippi coast and cooked to Buddy's secret recipe. Griff's mouth watered thinking about the light, thin breading and tender fish. As a nod to Lyndsey's healthier-eating mantra, he'd order a side of green beans too, although as they were simmered the traditional Southern way with chunks of pork added for flavor, he doubted she'd approve.

Griff made his way to the restaurant at the back, heading straight for the bar, where Buddy was busy serving. His old friend spotted him and came out around.

'Good news, I hope?'

'Yeah. I would've called earlier but things were a bit tetchy.' He ran through what happened.

'Little devil.' Buddy tapped the side of his head. 'Pretty damn smart, though. You've got to hand it to him for thinkin' outside the box. Bet it worried his poor folks half to death, though.'

'You're not wrong there.' Griff had been too fast to condemn Lyndsey when she read Theo the riot act. They were her family. She and Becca had their ups and downs, but despite that, always maintained some sort of relationship — not like he and Jase. Even after all these years his parents still didn't know the full story behind their sons' estrangement, and at this point, he was resigned to letting it stay that way. 'Anyway, you're busy and I'm about to fall apart, so is there any chance of some food?'

Buddy's piercing stare bored through Griff. The old guy missed nothing, and knew something else was bugging him.

'Sure. Go see Fran and she'll fix you a plate. I need to bring more beer in.' He turned to leave, but stopped. 'Don't be a stranger, you hear me?'

Griff flushed and nodded. His appetite had disappeared, but if he didn't at least appear to enjoy his meal, Buddy would only hassle him more. He perched at the bar to eat, rather than at one of the empty tables. Being forced into unwanted conversation today wasn't on his agenda. Luckily, Fran was too busy with other customers to pay much attention when he left half his food, along with enough money to cover his bill and a generous tip.

Outside, the muggy air settled around him like a wet blanket. He thought wistfully about Lyndsey's tempting description of the year-round fresh salt tang in the air where she grew up in Cornwall, a stone's throw from the sea. He'd only ever been to the coast one time, when his family made a never-to-be repeated trip to Florida. They'd combined a couple of days enjoying the glorious white sand beaches with a visit to Disney World. Saving up for that trip meant his parents had to cut corners in other areas of their limited budget. Later, when Griff's career was soaring and finances were no longer an issue, he rarely took time off, always too afraid of someone even more driven and committed usurping his hard-won position while he was away.

The drive home was too short to clear his head, so he detoured to his workshop. He'd lose himself in work and try to finish the mosaic panel he'd been forced to abandon when he cut his hand. If he couldn't be with Lyndsey tonight, this would serve as the next best thing.

CHAPTER FIFTEEN

Lyndsey clicked the button to end the Zoom call and flopped back on the sofa. Nicola had been unusually vocal, making her unhappiness crystal clear when she admitted she hadn't booked her return flight. Helping Becca remained her number-one priority, which meant staying another six weeks until Deke came back. Thankfully, her parents didn't have a problem with her staying longer — far from it. They were thrilled she and Becca were getting along better, and her dad's health was the best it'd been in years, so she had no need to rush back for their sakes.

But the responsible gene that ran through her like a vein of rock wouldn't let her sit back and allow the business she'd worked so hard on to fail. The problem was that juggling so many balls made her dizzy, so something had to give.

The thought of putting a stop to her deepening relationship with Griff punched a hole in her heart so big Lyndsey was amazed it kept beating. There simply weren't enough hours in the day, so she'd have to make their date tonight the last one. There would be no dishonesty of the 'it's not you, it's me' variety. He would get the whole unvarnished truth, and that would be it.

Really? You think you can walk away that easily?

Not easily, never that. But her sister was relying on her and so were Deke, Theo, Nora and The Right Place.

What if this *is the right place for you, and Griff the right person?*

Lyndsey clapped her hands over her ears in a desperate effort to blot out the conflicting opinions battling for space in her head. She yanked off her clothes, threw them on the floor and headed for the shower. By the time she'd stood far too long under the pounding hot water, shampooed her hair, shaved her legs and dried off, slathering her skin with the fragrant gardenia-scented lotion Griff loved, a curious sense of resignation wrapped around her.

She'd make the most of this last night together, despite only one of them knowing that's what it was. His pertinent question about the way she dressed had driven her to go shopping. No black, gray or white tonight. First, she wriggled into her new coral underwear, a plunging bra and barely-there panties, and then added a figure-hugging silk shift dress in the same shade of coral, splashed with bright turquoise tropical flowers. The contrast with her dark skin brought out a sensuousness only Griff had ever seen in her. She kept her make-up to a minimum, putting the emphasis on her long, dark lashes and smoky eyelids. Hot tears stung her eyes as she stroked on a slick of coral lip gloss while imagining Griff kissing it away.

'Your date's arrived,' Becca yelled up the stairs. 'If you don't hurry up, I'll take your place. He's looking extremely yummy.'

Despite the ache in her heart, she could easily picture Griff's embarrassment. 'I'm coming.' Lyndsey rarely wore heels, so dared not hurry in her gold stilettos. She sucked in a deep breath at the sight of Griff hovering at the bottom of the stairs, staring up with his mouth curved into a blatantly sexy smile. Becca's 'yummy' description was spot on. He'd promised they'd be going somewhere fancier than the Adamsville Grocery, and his immaculate silver-gray suit, white shirt and sapphire blue tie reflected that. Lyndsey took his outstretched hand as she reached the bottom step and the tease of his expensive citrusy cologne cut another chink in her resolve.

She turned to Becca. 'Are you sure you—?'

'Yes.' The hint of steel in her sister's voice surprised her. 'We'll be fine, won't we, Theo?' Becca's hand rested on her stepson's shoulder, and it gratified Lyndsey to see him nod furiously. 'We're going to bathe Nora and tuck her into bed, so we can enjoy movie night and stuff ourselves with buttered popcorn.'

'Mom's letting me see the new James Bond.' He gave a conspiratorial grin. 'Don't tell Dad. He reckons it's too old for me.'

'She won't say anything.' A red-hot blush stained Becca's cheeks. 'My sister's good at keeping secrets, aren't you?'

For a second, she was home again, newly graduated from university and waiting to start her first job, coerced by her precocious thirteen-year-old sister into covering up the fact she was drinking and smoking with her equally delinquent friends. The sensible, responsible action would've been to tell their parents, but the never-ending need for her sister's approval had still been at the forefront of her mind.

'I never thanked you, did I? It's taken me all these years to realize how much you had my back and I treated you like—'

'It's okay. Not now, Becca,' she pleaded. Her emotions were on edge, and she didn't need them tipped over the cliff by apologies for things that were water under the bridge. Lyndsey plastered on her brightest smile and squeezed Griff's arm. 'Let's go paint the town red.'

'Happy to oblige.'

They strolled outside and she struggled to maintain her bright facade when the early evening sun picked out flashes of bright blue and rich golden brown in Griff's eyes as they roved appreciatively over her. He wrapped his arms around her and his long, lingering kiss sizzled all the way to her toes.

'If this was Christmas, you'd be the gift sticking temptingly out of the top of my stocking, begging to be yanked out and played with right away. They say patience is a virtue, so I'll be a good boy.' He stepped back, opening the passenger door of his beat-up truck with a flourish. 'Perhaps we'll do a reversal of the Cinderella story and it'll turn into a gold carriage at midnight.'

'I hope not. This is what won me over that first day. Your unpretentious vehicle . . . and you.' Lyndsey's voice broke.

'Hey, you're not goin' to cry, are you? Did I say something wrong?'

No, you're being your normal wonderful self, and I want you in my life so badly it hurts, but it's not going to work so we've got to stop now.

His face turned to granite.

'Of course not, I—'

'So, tell me if I'm right. Was it your plan to share my bed tonight, then walk out in the morning with nothing more than a thank you?'

The bitter words struck like repeated blows from a blunt object. Griff's scathing gaze bored through her skin, leaving Lyndsey nowhere to hide. If she stupidly asked how he'd guessed her intentions, that would demean them both. From day one, they'd been attuned to each other, so it made sense they'd end things the same way.

'I thought we were on the same page these days, but I guess I don't fit into your neat little plans for an organized life. I thought I'd finally got it right with a woman. Even started imagining how we might make this work long-term.' He grasped her wrist. 'Are you going to lie and tell me you didn't do the same?'

She supposed she could try to make him understand, but at the end of the day it wouldn't matter. Griff shook his head as she stayed silent.

'I didn't guess you to be a coward.' He let go of Lyndsey and slammed the door that he'd opened for her, then ran around to jump into his truck, leaving her standing there. Griff revved the engine and shot off down the driveway, kicking up a shower of gravel to sting her bare legs.

'What's going on?' Becca reappeared on the porch, holding Nora, wrapped in a white towel ready for her bath. 'Why are you still here?'

She stared helplessly at her sister and couldn't have spoken if someone paid her a million pounds.

* * *

The red mist cleared from his brain, and Griff jerked the steering wheel hard to the right and pulled off the road. He'd been so desperate to get away from Paradise Valley he was damn lucky he hadn't killed himself — or worse still, someone else — with his reckless driving. Paradise? That was a damned joke.

In the past, women hadn't always appreciated Griff's straightforwardness, but at least he'd never led one down the garden path before slamming it in her face. That's what he'd experienced tonight, and boy, did it ever sting. He'd tried his best to give her space, to be patient, but clearly it hadn't been enough.

He caught sight of his sad, disillusioned face in the rear-view mirror. Tonight, Lyndsey had wiped away every gain he'd made over the last few years with her fake smile and cruel plan to take him to bed again before dumping him. According to a slew of clichéd country music songs, he should head to the nearest bar and drown his sorrows in a whisky bottle. Not an option that held any appeal for him.

Flicking on his indicator, he turned the truck around and drove, well under the speed limit, back home. His gloomy mood lifted a few notches as he caught one of his favorite small birds homing in on a luckless worm in the freshly hoed vegetable garden. Its name made him smile to start with — tufted titmouse. A spiky blue crest resembling a mohawk gave it an eccentric appearance, along with a jaunty black patch above its beak contrasting with pretty silver-gray feathers.

He should probably eat, but the thought of food turned his stomach. Griff's feet took charge and led him, unsurprisingly, towards the workshop. Lyndsey's mosaic panel was waiting for him to work his magic. He had the last few pieces of glass to cut before the design was in place, then he'd be at the point of gluing everything down. Once that was complete, the panel had to be grouted, another exacting process, and left to dry before a final cleaning and polishing.

Something of his old doggedness, the persistence that made him so successful in his former job, resurfaced. He couldn't accept Lyndsey's stubborn conclusion that she didn't have room for their relationship in her busy life. He'd fight for her. Make her see they had something too special to toss aside. How to go about that was a million-dollar question, but perhaps when his homage to Lyndsey was finished, he'd know what to do about her, and them.

Griff shrugged off his suit jacket and hung it up out of the way. With his leather apron and safety glasses in place, he settled on his stool and set to work. He placed an uneven rectangle of azure blue glass in front of him and picked up his first tool, a brass oil glass cutter to mark the cutting lines for one of the waves, a process called scoring. The skills needed for this part of the job were the same as he'd learned in his stained-glass work, so by now they were second nature. After scoring the glass, he'd break it with running pliers, then grind down any lethal edges before repeating the sequence with the next small piece. If things went well, he'd end up with an abstract representation of the Caribbean Sea. If they didn't, he'd have more offcuts in the bin to work with another day.

The sound of an owl hooting outside made him stop and check the time. Two a.m. He took off his safety glasses and lifted his hand to rub his tired eyes. Inches from touching them, he stopped himself. Glass dust and eyes didn't mix. He'd made that mistake once when he was first starting out, and didn't plan on doing it twice. It would've been made worse by the fact that his fingers were also covered in grout from where he'd applied it to the gaps between every tiny piece. The mosaicist who'd taught him some of her tricks explained that many people chose to apply it with a palette knife or sponge, but she preferred the more intimate connection of using her fingers. It was a little riskier in terms of cutting himself, but tonight he'd emerged unscathed.

Griff heaved off the stool and began the laborious process of cleaning his workshop. Only when the last scrap of dust was eradicated did he walk back outside and lock up. Returning to an empty house wasn't an enticing prospect, although before Lyndsey, he used to relish the solitude as a welcome contrast to his old frenetic life. He put one foot mechanically in front of the other and trudged across the grass, stopping halfway to glance across the boundary separating him from Deke's house. The magnolia trees and hydrangea bushes between their two properties might as well be the Great Wall of China. He exhaled a weary sigh and kept going. Inside the house, he avoided turning on the lights because it emphasized the emptiness of the space.

His suit would need to go to the dry cleaners, but he threw the rest of his clothes in the machine to wash in the morning. After a long hot shower, Griff flopped on top of the bed, because he couldn't face getting under the covers. This morning he'd changed the sheets in hopeful anticipation of Lyndsey joining him; now, smelling their fresh air-dried scent would rub in her absence.

At six o'clock he was still staring sleeplessly at the ceiling when his phone buzzed with an incoming text. Griff glanced at the screen, shooting up in the bed when it showed the last name he'd expected to see. His finger hovered over the message. Reading it would doubtless open a can of worms he'd prefer the birds enjoyed. A swipe the other way would send it into oblivion.

CHAPTER SIXTEEN

Lyndsey glanced nervously over the table to make sure she hadn't forgotten anything, and tugged one corner of her grandmother's white lace tablecloth to straighten it. She'd discovered the delicate cloth when she helped Becca unpack one of many boxes she'd brought with her from London. Their mother gave it to her, along with Granny Amy's serviceable brown teapot, a delicate rose-sprigged tea set, and the silver cutlery Lyndsey remembered her grandmother lovingly polishing every week. The arrangement of pink rosebuds and sprigs of dark greenery in the center of the gleaming mahogany table came from Harold's garden. Her initial plan for a simple get-together to ease Ruth Mae Grey into being on speaking terms with all her neighbors had snowballed into this fancy Sunday afternoon tea.

'It's perfect, Li-Li.' Becca breezed in, slim and elegant in a sleeveless pale-pink dress. 'Stop fussing and get changed. I'll set out all the food. We've got enough for an army here already, and that's before William arrives with home-made scones. I'm sure Tiffany won't come empty-handed either.'

Lyndsey suppressed a smile at hearing her sister mention her neighbors so casually. Now that Becca often joined her and Nora on their walks, she'd got to know everyone

— except for Miss Grey. It'd seemed best not to push that yet, because Grey House was still a sore topic for the old lady. Lyndsey wasn't convinced Ruth Mae wouldn't change her mind about coming at the last minute.

'Do you really think sending Theo to walk Miss Grey over is going to be a good idea?' she asked Becca.

'Yes, it won't be a problem. She let him cut her grass this week, didn't she?'

'Well, yes but—'

'And gave him a cold drink and thanked him. That's progress.'

'It's a pity *all* the neighbors won't be here.'

'If this afternoon goes well, we'll do it again when Deke's back.' She pretended to misunderstand her sister.

'Don't be an ostrich.' Becca wagged her finger in Lyndsey's face. 'We both know who I'm talking about. I really thought you'd have come to your senses before now. I can't believe you've lasted a whole week. That's about five days more than I expected even your steely determination to manage.'

Dignifying that with a response would only encourage her. Lyndsey didn't need reminding of the precise length of time since she broke up with Griff.

You didn't break up with him. He caught on to your intention and stormed out on you.

'Have you seen Griff at all? Because I haven't.' Becca persisted. 'Theo asked where he was yesterday and seemed disappointed when I didn't have a proper answer. They were starting to get on well, and I don't want things to . . .'

She understood what her sister meant. Deke was making an effort to check in with the boy every day. Lyndsey had tapped into her nephew's interest in video gaming and coding and discovered a day camp where he could learn more about both. That would start on Monday in Nashville, and lasted for two weeks. Despite all of those things, the truce was built on shaky ground.

'I've no idea if Griff's around or not.' She refused to admit that every time she stepped outside she listened for the loud rattle of his old truck and peered through the trees into his garden. 'Leave it be, Becca,' she begged.

Her sister mimicked zipping her mouth shut.

'Could you chivvy Theo out of the house while I change? If he's late it'll annoy Miss Grey.'

'Yes, ma'am.' Becca mockingly saluted her.

Upstairs, Lyndsey left her sister tapping on Theo's door while she retreated to her bedroom.

The black-and-white check skirt and white blouse she'd ironed earlier hung on the wardrobe door.

She let out a sigh, remembering her reluctant admission to Griff that as a young girl she'd had the sad idea that playing down her Caribbean side would make people like her better.

Perhaps she'd go shopping again this week. Wearing the coral dress she'd ripped off after her would-be date with Griff wasn't an option, so she got dressed unenthusiastically. Although her hair was still comparatively short, its natural curls and kinks had started to emerge, and Lyndsey was determined to embrace them. A spritz of special oil she'd bought in a local beauty shop and quick tease with a wide-toothed comb and she was done.

A bell jangled in the distance, so she hurried back downstairs, barely beating her nervous-looking sister to the door. Theo hovered at the old lady's elbow, clearly unsure what he was supposed to do next.

Lyndsey said, 'Miss Grey. It's lovely to see you. Come in.'

For a second, Ruth Mae's face froze. Lyndsey couldn't imagine how hard this was for her, arriving as a guest at the house she'd grown up in and loved to the very foundations. Perhaps this wasn't one of her better ideas.

Miss Grey fixed her beady gaze on Becca. 'Well, girl, are you goin' to stand there gawping like a fish out of water, or invite me in?'

'Invite you in, of course. I'm delighted you came.'

She'd forgotten how charming her sister could be, and watched Becca take the woman's arm and lead her gently inside.

'Would you care to have a look around the house before everyone arrives?' Becca's offer deepened Ruth Mae's frown. 'I'd love to hear what Grey House was like when you were growing up. Lyndsey's told me you've shared a few wonderful stories with her already. I loved the one about your brother, Scotty, setting the nursery chimney on fire when he tried to get rid of his stiff Sunday clothes that he hated.'

'I didn't tell her so she could broadcast it to all and sundry.' Miss Grey threw an angry glare in Lyndsey's direction. 'I've no interest in traipsing around the place, either.'

Lyndsey heard the unsaid — that she couldn't face seeing what'd been done to her family's precious home.

Becca's smile faltered.

'Maybe another day you'd like to come over on your own,' Lyndsey suggested gently. 'You'll be welcome anytime.'

'We'll see.' There was an almost imperceptible softening in the old lady's stern expression.

Becca gave a nervous laugh. 'I'm afraid I'm habitually untidy and so is my husband, but my sister's been helping me sort things out. The dining room where we're having our tea was last week's project. Lyndsey has a business helping people to organize their homes and she's incredible at it.'

Lyndsey blushed at the unexpected public compliment.

'Theo, go to the kitchen and turn the kettle back on, please,' Becca said, and the boy ran off, clearly glad to get a reprieve.

The three of them made their way down the hall and Lyndsey hurried to open the dining room door.

'Oh my.' Miss Grey's hand flew up to her mouth. Her dark perceptive eyes swept around them.

Once the detritus of her brother-in-law's life had been hauled out of there, it surprised Lyndsey how much she loved the room's opulence. It boasted the most elaborate moldings and cornices of the whole house, a glittering antique chandelier hung over the highly polished mahogany table, and floor-length burgundy velvet curtains framed the elegant windows.

'The house was always packed with folk when I was growin' up, and you can't imagine the supper parties and so on we had in here. Scotty and I never used this room after Mother and Daddy passed away.' She sounded wistful.

'We want it to be full of life again,' Becca said. 'A real family home.'

'That's what it was always intended to be.' Ruth Mae nodded sadly, then straightened her thin shoulders. 'How much longer are you goin' to keep me standing here?'

The sisters smiled at each other behind the old lady's back.

'Come and sit down.' Becca pulled out a chair and Lyndsey noticed Ruth Mae's surprise and hint of pleasure at being shown to the head of the table.

Score one point to her clever sister.

* * *

'Is this *it?*' Jase stood by the truck and stared over at the cottage. 'I can't believe Mom and Dad talked me into living in this ratty old cabin with you in the middle of nowhere.' He scoffed. 'I suppose if I die of boredom it'll be easier for y'all.'

Griff gritted his teeth. He'd been guilted into inviting his brother here by their parents. Jase's original text was amazingly conciliatory, practically begging for his help. Of course, later on he discovered that his dad, who'd been at the end of his rope, had dictated it.

'I've done a lot of renovations to the inside, although there's still more to do. I needed to get my workshop up and running first.' Griff shrugged. 'I've got into gardening, too, and spend a lot of time outside when I'm not working.'

Jase scowled and pushed a lock of thick black hair away from his face. Griff always had the advantage of a couple of extra inches in height, but, although he'd left his scrawny teenage days long behind, could never rival his younger brother's athletic, muscular physique. 'Yeah, well, don't think you're gonna get me out there weeding. I've had enough of that kind of crap from Dad. He's been on my case nonstop because the rehab people told them to keep me busy.'

It had sobered him when he discovered the truth about the downward spiral in his brother's life over the last few years. He couldn't blame his parents for not sharing the news before, because he'd made it clear he wasn't interested. Things had come to a head now because Jase's therapist was concerned about him. His brother's recent success in kicking his drug habit might not stick if he stayed in the Knoxville area, around the people who'd supplied him with the painkillers he'd become reliant on after a back injury ended his minor league baseball career.

'Grab your bag.' Griff yanked his own battered brown leather case from the backseat and strode off to open the door. His gaze automatically drifted across to Deke's house. Did Lyndsey wonder where he'd disappeared to, or had she been too busy with her neatly organized life to notice he wasn't there? He'd asked Harold Morton to keep an eye on things, including watering his garden, while he visited his family. When he asked his friend not to mention it to any-one else unless it was absolutely necessary, Harold raised an eyebrow, but discreetly made no comment.

Jase trailed in the house after him, giving a scathing look around. 'Is this it? Mom and Dad used to boast about your swanky Nashville apartment and how you were in line for a head job at the boring company you worked for. You must've screwed up big time to end up in this dump.'

He wouldn't waste his breath defending his new home and lifestyle. He'd made mistakes in his old job, and regret-ted most the way he'd treated people, but had emerged from it all a happier, more contented man. Jase's athletic skills had made him wealthy and lauded for a while, but when his body let him down, he had nothing to fall back on. It hurt Griff deeply to see his brother broken and bitter. As small boys they'd played together, scrapping and fighting as kids do, but always having each other's backs at the end of the day. He knew the exact point where that had all gone wrong and remembering it still sickened him.

'It's a complicated story.'

'Takes all sorts,' Jase sneered. 'Where's my room?'

'At the back. I'll leave you to get settled. I've taken a couple of steaks out the freezer, so we'll throw those on the grill later.'

'Wow, you're literally killing the fatted calf for me? I'm honored.' Jase slung his bag over his shoulder and loped off down the narrow hallway.

Griff turned away before he said something he might regret later — and if he didn't regret it, he probably should.

* * *

Lyndsey let the chatter swirl around her while her heart ached with missing Griff. He should be there, sitting at the table with them.

'Are you going to pour the tea, Lyndsey, or are you leaving us to die of thirst?' Becca prodded her arm.

'Sorry.' Meeting her sister's sympathetic gaze was a mistake. Becca knew why she wasn't being her usual efficient self. 'Miss Grey, do you take milk in your tea? Or would you prefer a glass of water?'

'I was brought up right, young lady. At an afternoon tea party, it's proper to drink tea. No milk. A thin slice of lemon.'

Lyndsey caught William suppressing a laugh. It'd been a risk to put Harold and William either side of Ruth Mae, but she'd suggested it to Becca in the hope that the old lady's ingrained prejudice against the men's relationship might soften when she discovered they were all garden enthusiasts.

'Where did you get these flowers from?' Miss Grey asked Becca, pointing to the arrangement on the table.

'We brought them from our garden,' Harold piped up. 'Rose growing is a passion of mine. William is my right-hand man in the garden and does all the heavy digging.'

'I'm good at following orders.' William's cheeky smile broke through.

'He's also an excellent cook — the scones, clotted cream and strawberry jam are all home-made,' Harold boasted.

'I used to grow Double Delight hybrid tea roses here at Grey House.' Miss Grey touched a strawberry red flower with a creamy middle. 'And Mister Lincoln too.' She stroked a deep crimson bloom and sniffed the air. 'They're a red rose that can't be beat, in my opinion, and their scent is unmatched.' Ruth Mae asked what else they grew and the three of them chatted away happily. Even Lyndsey could tell the old lady's knowledge of Southern plants was encyclopedic.

'Perhaps you'd like to have a walk around our garden one day, Miss Grey?' Harold asked.

'I do believe I would enjoy that.'

Becca leaned over to join in. 'Miss Grey, I would love to bring the garden here back closer to what it used to be. There's nothing wrong with it now, but I can see it could be so much more. I'd love your help.' She smiled at Harold and William. 'And you too, of course. I'm particularly ignorant about roses.'

'As an Englishwoman, you should be ashamed to admit that,' Ruth Mae scoffed. 'You might not know, but my cottage traditionally belonged to the Grey House gardener. I found a box full of his plans tucked away in one of the closets with details of how the grounds were laid out, descriptions of every plant and his work calendar for the year, to take care of everything.'

'I'd love to see them sometime,' Becca said tentatively.

'Maybe.' Short and to the point, but it wasn't a no. They were making progress.

The doorbell chime broke in, and Lyndsey jumped up from the table. 'That will be Tiffany. She did warn us she'd be late because she was working until two.'

Out in the hall, she stopped to smooth down her shirt and take a moment to gather her thoughts before opening the door.

'Here I am, finally!' Tiffany breezed in, holding an ornate white china-covered cake stand carefully in both hands. 'Did the old lady turn up?'

'Yes, and you won't believe this, but she's rapidly becoming best friends with Harold and William. It seems she can turn a blind eye to them being gay because they're also excellent gardeners.' Lyndsey chuckled.

'Well, I'm no gardener, so she might not overlook my so-called faults quite as easily.' Under Tiffany's light words, Lyndsey sensed a layer of concern. 'Let's get this over with. Lead the way.'

She wondered how many times in her life this awesome woman had had to face situations where she wasn't welcomed with open arms. It put her own experiences in perspective.

'Miss Grey, this is Tiffany Hunt, your other neighbor.' Lyndsey watched the old woman's expression tighten.

'I sure am pleased to meet you, Miss Grey. Sorry I'm late, but I hope this makes up for it.' Tiffany set down the cake and lifted off the cover, revealing a vibrant red sponge covered in thick swirls of cream cheese icing.

'Oh my! A red velvet cake.' Ruth Mae's wrinkled face lit up. 'My mama used to make one every year for my birthday, although to tell the truth it was Miss Bessie who made it. She was the . . .' She stopped talking and looked wary.

'Is she the Black lady who helped your mama in the house?'

Tiffany's casual question flustered the old lady.

'Yes, but—'

'I'm sure she was dear to you.'

'Miss Bessie helped raise me and Scotty. We'd occasionally get a tap on the backside with her wooden spoon if we didn't mind our mouths and manners, but she loved on us something wonderful.' Ruth Mae's eyes had misted over. 'I sure miss her cooking. No one made biscuits like Miss Bessie — they were light as angels' feathers.' The old lady sighed. 'I see now a lot of things were wrong around these parts — especially when I was young. It's hard to teach an old dog new tricks, but I'm up for learning.'

Everyone around the table stopped talking and paid attention.

'Sit yourself down, do, and Ms Carne will fix you a cup of tea to go with this lovely cake.'

Lyndsey smiled at the way Ruth Mae had settled into a matriarchal role. Tiffany did as she was told with a smile, taking the chair opposite the old lady.

'I hear you're some sort of nurse?' Miss Grey said. 'Your folks must be mighty proud of you.'

'I'm a physical therapist at a clinic in Franklin. You let me know if you need any help, okay? I'm used to whipping stubborn old white women into shape.'

Ruth Mae surprised them all then by bursting into a peal of raucous laughter.

Lyndsey relaxed for the first time that afternoon. If only Griff was there, things would be just about perfect.

* * *

'Do you smell smoke, Theo?' Lyndsey turned around, stopping for a moment in the middle of making a salad nicoise for their dinner. No one wanted a heavy meal tonight as hot as it was, plus they were all still full from their extravagant afternoon tea. Well, maybe not *all* of them felt that way, she thought, watching her nephew stuffing a sausage roll in his mouth. After he returned from walking Miss Grey home, he'd helped Lyndsey clear the table — that included polishing off the last massive slice of coffee and walnut sponge and a handful of jam tarts.

'Yeah. Griff's back. He's barbecuing.'

'Oh.' She planted her trembling hands on the counter.

'Is it all right if I go over to say hi? He said it was okay to go anytime. Please,' Theo wheedled.

'I suppose so.'

'Thanks.' He raced out the door, letting it slam shut behind him.

Lyndsey supposed it really wasn't fair to use her nephew as a spy. Realistically, it wasn't possible to avoid Griff for the rest of her stay here anyway. Paradise Valley was hardly the big city, or even a small one like Truro, where it was perfectly possible to have minimal or no contact with your neighbors. Not that she planned to keep up that particular unfriendly habit when she returned to Cornwall. A lot of things needed to change, and that might be the least of them.

A pang of dismay struck her. She couldn't actually imagine slotting right back in to her old life as if her time here never happened — and the loving, funny, sexy man next door played a major part in that.

* * *

'Hey, Aunt Li-Li.' Theo bounded back into the kitchen. Somehow Becca's irritating pet name sounded sweet coming from her nephew. 'Griff's got his brother staying.' He swiped the dried-up scone she'd been about to throw out, pulled it apart and reached for the jar of peanut butter and a spoon. 'His name's Jase. Think that's short for Jason?'

His brother was here? The one he claimed to have no contact with and never spoke about?

'I asked Griff if he was comin' over to say hi, but he was kinda funny.' He wrinkled his nose. 'Did you two have a fallin' out or something?'

'We had a slight disagreement, that's all, but we're still friends.' She painted on a bright smile. 'I'd better get this salad finished or we won't have any dinner tonight.'

'I'm goin' up to play Fortnite.' His charismatic smile was Deke all over. 'You won't tell?'

She shouldn't conspire against his parents' strict limits on his game playing, but what were favorite aunts for? 'Half an hour. That's all. Becca and Nora will be home soon.' Her sister and niece had joined a group of friends from the parent and baby group for an early evening walk in one of the local parks.

'You're cool.'

You're the only one who thinks so.

'If you're looking for me after I'm finished making the salad, I'll be out watering the garden.' If Griff was determined to avoid her, she'd be reduced to lurking out of sight like a teenage girl pining for the boy she could never have.

But you could've had him; it's totally your own fault. This is what happens when you're mad enough to believe you can organize your life the same as organizing a house.

145

CHAPTER SEVENTEEN

Griff considered it nothing short of a miracle. Ten long days since he'd brought Jase back home with him and he hadn't killed his brother. Yet. He straightened up, wriggled his shoulders and frowned at the half-completed glass panel laid out on the bench in front of him. Although he'd never done any ecclesiastical glass work before, he'd been commissioned to make a replacement for a vandalized window in a local church. But between stewing about Jase and Lyndsey, his mind was all over the place, leaving little room in his brain for creativity.

By unspoken agreement, he and Jase stayed out of each other's way as much as possible. He divided his own days between his workshop and the garden while his brother seemingly did nothing. On Griff's lunch break, when he dutifully returned to the house, Jase was usually sprawled on the sofa watching sports and still wearing the ragged T-shirt and boxers he slept in. When he foolishly threw out a few tentative suggestions about things Jase might do to pass the days, Griff had his head bitten off. Judging by his brother's pallor, Griff guessed he hadn't stepped outside the door since they arrived. So much for everyone thinking that a change of scenery would get his younger brother back on some sort of constructive track.

And Lyndsey? He'd tortured himself wondering what exactly Theo reported back last week and how she might've reacted. On several occasions when working in the garden, Griff was convinced she was outside too, because he felt her presence so strongly. Perhaps if he was a better man, he'd hope she was contented with her decision to toss their relationship on the scrap heap, but he couldn't be that generous. He wanted her to hurt as badly as him. Sleepless. Unable to get pleasure from anything. Rehashing their time together until it stung like broken glass slicing through his skin. Perhaps then they might stand a chance.

'So what is it you do out here all day, apart from avoid me?' Jase strolled in.

Griff noticed it was before noon and his brother was dressed for once, although the ragged jean shorts and faded Metallica shirt weren't a huge improvement. 'Stop. Don't come any further.' He held up a hand. 'I'm not being a jerk for the sake of it, but you can't just walk in here.'

'Need an appointment, do I?'

'No, but for your own safety, you need to knock first.' Patiently, he explained the ritual surrounding his workspace. Hopefully, explaining that his neighbors were familiar with the routine made it clear the warning wasn't personal. 'I haven't started to lead this piece yet, so you're good on that score, but there's glass dust everywhere, so don't touch anything.'

'All right to look around?'

'Sure. Go ahead.' He selected a heavy piece of dark green glass and pretended to study the panel in front of him while surreptitiously watching his brother move around the room. Jase stopped in front of the piece he'd mentally titled *Essence of Love* — the work inspired by Lyndsey. After the grout dried, he'd cleaned off the stray scraps covering up the colored glass, then polished the whole piece with glass cloth. That brought it to life, the same as switching on a light bulb in a dark room.

'This one's different. I like it.' The inference behind Jase's words — that he wasn't as sure about the others — grated a little, but he chose to focus on the praise instead.

'Yeah, it's a change of direction. More personal.' He hoped his brother wouldn't dig too deeply into the inspiration behind the panel.

'Who is she? Must be pretty special.'

For a second, he couldn't speak, too shocked by the piercing insight. 'Yeah, she is,' Griff whispered. 'But we're not together anymore.'

'Not by your choice?'

'Nope.' He shook his head. 'How'd you see all that?'

'Contrary to popular belief, there's more to me these days than the guy who thought life began and ended with sports and girls.' Jase gestured to Griff's ponytail. 'I still had you marked out as a math nerd with a buzz haircut. What does our old man think of this?'

'Dad's eyebrows raised the first time he saw it, but he never said a word. I'm guessin' Mom threatened him.'

'I bet.' Jase looked puzzled. 'Tell me, how d'you get from being a numbers guy to this?'

Griff guessed what his brother was really asking was how you reinvented yourself when you were so far along on the path everyone expected you to follow. That question had a very long answer.

'Do you feel like telling me about it over lunch? I'm goin' a bit stir crazy.'

'Sure. I'll have to shower first. You go back to the house and I'll lock up and come join you.' This might be a first small step in the right direction. No doubt their parents' decades-long hope that he and Jase could become friends again was the biggest reason behind his brother being here now. That brought him back around to thinking about Lyndsey again, because she'd wryly admitted that her parents sent her to Tennessee with the same sort of mission in mind.

'Maybe over a beer you'll tell me about this woman, too?'

'Maybe. If I do, perhaps *you'll* tell *me* why you've continued to let me take the blame for crashing Dad's car and almost killing *my* girlfriend?'

Jase's face lost all color. It'd been festering between them since his brother arrived, but Griff never meant to spit it out this way. Perhaps it'd been inevitable, though? He waited for an answer.

* * *

Lyndsey dropped the last weed she intended pulling today in a bucket. Over the last week, she and Becca had worked together in the garden when they had any spare time. She was pleased when her sister showed an interest in livening it up, even if it did cut into what was left of Lyndsey's spare time. Although it was a little late in the season, they'd planted an interesting selection of summer flowers, but to keep it all alive and flourishing, they needed to water them daily. She'd added that to her own long list of chores but, interestingly enough, wasn't finding it a burden at all. Being outside, even when it was this hot and humid, and connecting with the earth was calming her, helping her cope better with life in general. Some of her neighbors back home had window boxes, but it wouldn't be as satisfying as this. When she admitted as much to Miss Grey this morning, Lyndsey got a knowing smile in response.

After the tea party, the old lady had accepted Harold and William's kind offer to help with her garden, and she'd invited Lyndsey over to see the improvements so far. In her typical determined way, Ruth Mae made it clear that she too had played her part, by supervising the two men's endeavors. Lyndsey had been amazed to see everything they'd done already: the newly tamed grass, the pruned-back bushes and the flower beds that were no longer buried under a tangle of weeds. She'd been pleased to find Harold and William there when she arrived, repairing one of the old sheds so it could be used for its original purpose. The only awkward moment came when Harold said they could do with Griff's help to make a start on repairs to the cabin itself.

'He usually wanders over for a chat if he's out getting the mail and sees me working in the yard, but seems to be avoiding us. Do you think we've done something to upset him?'

It'd been tricky to walk a tightrope between reassuring her new friends they weren't at fault without admitting her part in Griff becoming a hermit, or mentioning his brother. Lyndsey hadn't missed Miss Grey's perceptive look. Very little escaped the sharp-eyed octogenarian.

She'd better hurry up, or she wouldn't have time to get herself cleaned up before the rest of her family returned. Becca had dropped Theo off at his tech camp in Nashville before taking Nora to baby swimming classes at a local pool.

Raised voices drifted in through the shrubbery, and she lifted her finger off the hose fitting to stop the water spraying out. The deep gravelly voice was definitely Griff, but she guessed the other man speaking could be his brother. She edged closer and, although they were too far away for her to catch all that was being said, Lyndsey picked up enough to realize it wasn't a friendly conversation.

'Go to hell, Griff. I knew you'd never accept my apology in a million years, and that's why I didn't bother tryin' before. Give me a few days to make plans and I'll clear off out of your hair.'

There was no response from her one-time lover, and then somewhere in the distance, a door slammed. She let out a shriek as a blast of cold water gushed down her leg and tried fruitlessly to turn it off. When that failed, she struggled to redirect it, but a jet of water shot through the bushes.

'What the hell!'

Lyndsey switched the hose off properly this time before walking back over to push some greenery away to peer through. 'Oh gosh, I'm terribly sorry. I didn't mean to—'

'Half-drown me?' Griff swiped at the water dripping down his face. 'Tryin' to combine eavesdropping and watering, were you? That's a novel pastime.'

'Sorry. Dare I say hello and ask how you're doing?'

'Depends how brave you are.'

If she wasn't so attuned to his quirky sense of humor, she would've missed the thin strand of amusement running through Griff's attempt to sound angry.

'I made a jug of fresh lemonade earlier, and I'm happy to share it. Will that tempt you to forgive me?'

'Does it come with a sprig of mint and plenty of ice?'

Lyndsey blushed at his teasing reference to the day when she'd blatantly flirted with him.

'I'll be lousy company,' he continued.

'What's new? Come on over, if you want to risk it.' She spun around and strode off, heart racing. By the time she reached the porch steps, Griff was plodding up the drive, shoulders drooping as though the weight of the world was on them. 'Sit down and take the weight off your temper. I won't be long.'

'I'm surprised your sharp tongue doesn't cut you sometimes,' he muttered.

In the hall, she made the mistake of glancing in the mirror and cringed at her bedraggled reflection. Griff certainly wouldn't make any cracks about her immaculate appearance today. Six weeks without a haircut combined with Tennessee's humid weather meant she sported a shaggy mass of corkscrew curls. Instead of the make-up she started the day with, there were streaks of dirt and dried sweat. Her outfit didn't fall into her usual white/black/gray fashion palette, either. She didn't own any digging-in-the-dirt clothes, so she'd appropriated a colorful combination of old things belonging to her sister. Faded red shorts barely covering her thighs, a garish orange plastic belt and a skimpy, bright purple sleeveless tank.

Before she could be tempted to run upstairs for a quick shower and clean clothes, Lyndsey hurried off to the kitchen and scrubbed her face and hands at the sink. Spying the white plastic cake box on the counter, she gave thanks to the baking gods, or in this case, Becca. Yesterday her sister had baked four trays of millionaire's shortbread, keeping one for themselves and delivering the other three this morning to their grateful neighbors. She cut two pieces — one significantly larger than the other — and mixed their drinks to her guest's detailed specifications. Lyndsey carried the tray back out to the porch and stood for a second watching Griff hunched in the chair, frowning, deep in thought.

'Penny for them.'

He jerked his head up, then looked confused. 'Does that mean, "penny for your thoughts?"'

Lyndsey nodded.

Dark shadows lurked in his eyes before he covered them with a fleeting smile. 'Not sure they're worth that much.'

'Maybe not.' She set the tray down. 'You timed it well. These are courtesy of Becca, of course. I'm no baker.'

'They sure are a weakness of mine.'

Their fingers brushed when Lyndsey passed him a plate, releasing memories she'd struggled to repress of his strong hands stroking and exploring every inch of her in bed. Griff's color rose and it didn't take a psychic to realize the same X-rated video reel was replaying in his own head. To salvage a scrap of self-control, she tugged her hand back and sat down next to him.

'You went away,' she said accusingly.

'Yeah. I'm sure Theo told you my brother's here.'

'The one you didn't want to talk about?'

'Yeah, he's part of some things I haven't mentioned.' His brows knotted in a dark angry frown, which instantly disappeared when he bit into the shortbread. 'Wow. If your sister sold this in the stores, it'd make her a fortune.' Griff chuckled. 'How dumb am I? The wife of a multi-millionaire country music icon hardly needs to churn out a few cakes to keep food on the table.'

'It's not dumb at all. Becca is used to earning her own living. Supporting herself. That's another adjustment she's had to make, and it's tough.'

'Nothin's easy for any of us. Some lives might look that way on the surface, but dig a little and we've all got worms burrowing away,' he mused.

'Your brother is one of yours?'

'Yeah. It's a long story.'

'Maybe best kept for another day. Becca and the kids will be back soon. I'm sorry.'

'Me too.' Griff's humorless laugh spoke volumes. 'Why don't you tell me how the tea party went instead? That's a safer subject if we get interrupted. I hope it wasn't a complete bust?'

Lyndsey beamed. 'Far from it.' She rattled off the whole story, and got a kick out of seeing Griff's eyebrows shoot up and down with each new revelation.

'Wow! I'd never have guessed all that in a million years. You did great.'

'It wasn't all down to me,' she protested.

'You pushed the door open — somethin' the rest of us have tried to do for ages with no luck.' Griff smiled. 'It's one of the things I admire most about you. Your tenacity. You see problems and visualize a way to tackle them, then follow through.'

A hot blush warmed her face and neck. His compliment might not be the floweriest, but it was heartfelt, which meant so much more.

'I don't suppose . . .'

'Go on. Be brave.'

His eyes crinkled at the corners. 'Saturday night? Us?'

Perhaps she should say no, but that was never going to happen. 'All right, it's a—'

'Don't call it a date or you'll jinx us. A quiet friendly chat and dinner. I'll pick you up at seven.'

They stood at the same time, so Lyndsey caught the aroma of his plain soap, without the addition of expensive cologne today. Simple and unpretentious.

'I'd better go before I do somethin' I shouldn't,' he murmured, gazing at her like a castaway on a desert island tempted by a cold bottle of beer and juicy steak dangling barely out of reach.

Knowing it was foolish, she stretched up and brushed a fleeting kiss on his mouth. A flare of desire lit up his eyes and a struggle for control played out on his face.

'Saturday.' His deep drawl turned husky.

Lyndsey nodded, then watched his retreating figure and unconsciously raised her trembling hand to her face, stroking the prickle of heat where his stubble had grazed her chin. This thing between them seemed inevitable.

CHAPTER EIGHTEEN

'You don't need to leave.' Griff hovered in Jase's bedroom door.

'Don't I? We haven't spoken in five fucking days.' His brother stopped jamming his clothes in a black sports bag and scowled across the room. 'You seriously think I'm goin' to hang on any longer, waiting for you to grow up?'

'*Me* to grow up?' He couldn't believe what he was hearing.

'Yeah, you. I had the idea when I came here we might put an end to this . . .' Jase looked shamefaced. 'It was wrong to let you take the blame for the crash. I get I should've apologized years ago.'

One of his conversations with Lyndsey flooded back. Wasn't her admission that she'd held on far too long to childish and immature grudges against her sister, night and day different?

'How about we go for a walk and chat?'

'Is the walk necessary? It's a sauna out there.'

'Don't be a wuss. You grew up with this weather. What's wrong with you?'

His brother's face clouded. 'In case you've forgotten, I played ball up north for years. Tennessee summers aren't my thing these days.'

'Come out to the workshop with me, then. I've got a mosaic idea and you could help.'

'Me?'

Where the heck did that crazy suggestion come from? Griff had discovered contentment in working with his hands, but that didn't mean his brother would, too. However, if nothing else, it might give them something else to focus on outside of their long-held resentments.

'Fine, we'll do it your way.' Jase shrugged as if they both knew this was a complete waste of time, but he'd go along with it to keep the peace.

'Come on then.'

Out in the workshop, he wasn't sure how best to go about catching his brother's interest. 'You were pretty good at art when we were kids. What happened?'

'Sport and girls.'

Big mistake to ask *that* question.

'So what's your big idea?' Jase asked. Lingering by the off-cuts bin, he leaned down and picked up a cherry-red square of glass, lifting it to the light. 'This would make a great sunset.'

'It sure would. What else?'

His brother laid the red glass on the workbench and hesitated, giving Griff a puzzled look. Without another word, he went back to the bin and added other colors to the mix, in varying shades of greens and yellows.

'A baseball field as the sun goes down.' Jase's lip curled. 'Like it did on my fuckin' career.' He brushed the glass away with his hand, jumping back out of the way as the pieces crashed to the floor. 'Damn.' Blood seeped through his fingers.

'Let me see.' Later he'd reiterate his lecture on safety, but for the moment, he'd concentrate on comfort instead of condemnation. Griff unfurled Jase's hand and smiled at the small cut in the center of the palm. 'You're lucky. It's just a nick.'

'A nick? I'm bleeding like a stuck pig.'

'This is par for the course working with glass. The cut I got the other day puts this to shame.' Griff regaled him with the story of trying to catch a heavy piece of glass. 'Damned stupid. I knew better.'

'There's a lot of times we know better. Doesn't mean we pay attention.' The unmistakable undertone to Jase's words resonated around the room.

'Sit down and I'll patch you up.' After he fetched the first-aid box, he picked his brother's hand up again.

'If I'd gotten a criminal record, I would've lost everything, Griff. No college scholarship. No chance to turn pro.' Jase's voice shook.

He was too angry to look at his brother, so he concentrated on cleaning the wound with an antiseptic wipe before peeling the wrapper off a Band-Aid and smoothing it over the cut. Losing his temper now would be way too easy. 'And Hannah? You snatched my girlfriend out from under my nose, then almost got her killed.'

'I didn't *snatch* her from you. You won't want to hear this, but she told me she was tired of my serious brother with his talk of engagement rings and mortgages. Hannah was sixteen, for God's sake. She wanted some fun and knew she'd get that with me.'

Those careless words held the ring of truth, no matter how much he'd prefer to deny it. He'd known in his gut that Hannah was pulling away from their relationship and had made an immature mistake by struggling to tighten the bond between them in an attempt to hold onto her.

'I didn't know who else to call,' Jase pleaded. 'I didn't deliberately set out to get you in trouble. I panicked.'

A garbled phone call had sent Griff sneaking from the house to avoid waking their parents and out into the night, running as fast as he'd ever done before or since. A single car accident on a lonely country road a mile from their home at two in the morning. Their mother's car crashed headfirst into a tree. His brother reeking of beer. Hannah a hysterical wreck. Fortunately, neither were hurt apart from being badly shaken.

'You suggested the swap, remember?' Jase prompted.

'I wasn't thinkin' straight.'

'Yeah, well, I wasn't either.'

With a new clarity he saw neither of them was to blame — and both of them were. At the time, they couldn't have pictured the possible consequences ten or twenty years down the line. Amazingly, they got away with the deception. Griff calmly called the police, then their parents. He ordered Jase and Hannah to stick to the story that he'd been driving too fast after borrowing their mom's car to pick them up from a party and lost control on a sharp bend. His brother's golden life continued. Griff escaped with points on his license for reckless driving, a hefty fine and community service. Being forced to pick up trash from the side of the road in an orange safety vest wasn't one of the highlights of his life.

'I'm gonna tell Mom and Dad,' Jase said. 'It's way past time they knew.'

Should he urge his brother not to be stupid? The past couldn't be undone now. But it stung that he'd lived with his parents' disappointment all these years.

'Any chance we can give this brother thing another shot?' Jase asked.

'I suppose we might as well. You're the only one I've got.' He blinked away the tears pricking at his eyes.

'So, now we've put that to bed, you gonna tell me about this hottie you're after? I might be able to give you some advice. I haven't completely lost my touch where women are concerned.' A trace of his brother's swagger returned.

Griff always envied Jase's easy charm that let him get away with anything, although now he saw it hadn't done him any favors in the long run.

'I've got a date with her, tonight.' A slight exaggeration maybe, or wishful thinking? 'Her name's Lyndsey. She's British, and she's temporarily living next door with her sister's family.'

'Interesting.'

'I'll tell you the whole story and see what you think.'

* * *

Lyndsey ticked the last item off her to-do list. She'd been on the go since far too early that morning, after snatching a typical four hours of sleep. A long-standing customer back in the UK had needed an appointment by video link, so she hadn't crawled into bed until one o'clock. Since then her day had been rather like 'The Twelve Days of Christmas.'

One muggy five a.m. brisk walk around the neighborhood, essential to keep up her fitness levels, because the chatty ambles she took with Nora didn't really count.

Two flowerbeds weeded.

Three loads of washing done, folded and put away.

The day had continued on from there in a similar fashion. She flicked a satisfied smile around the sparkling kitchen that these days bore no resemblance to a germ-death-trap.

'So, are you going to tell me what made you stop being an idiot and give you and Griff another chance?' Becca strolled into the kitchen. Holding a sleepy baby in the crook of her arm, she selected a red apple off the dish with her free hand.

'No.' The curt response earned a surprised look from her sister. 'I might do later. We'll see how it goes.'

'If you don't roll in until tomorrow morning, that'll be all the answer I need.'

She didn't dignify that with a response. 'Where's Theo?'

'Upstairs working on a coding project.' Her sister's smile widened. 'He's got a friend over, who he met at camp. That was a smart idea of yours.'

'I'm glad it worked out. You never can tell.' Lyndsey didn't point out that she'd tried several tactics with her sister before hitting on the right one.

'Paul's staying to have pizza with us, then his dad's collecting him later.'

'That's really great.'

'So what're you wearing to lure Griff back into your bed — or his?' Becca's dismissive gaze swept over her. 'Not that, I hope.'

'What's wrong with this?' The loose linen trousers and soft white T-shirt were cool and comfortable.

'Uh, just maybe it's about as frumpy as I am. You looked awesome the other day in that gorgeous coral and turquoise dress.' Becca looked awkward. 'Maybe best not to wear that one again, in the circumstances, but we bought you lots of other pretty things when we went shopping.'

'You're not, and never have been, frumpy!'

Becca snorted. 'Liar. When you arrived, I could've featured in a "before" ad for a makeover company.'

Not any longer, Lyndsey thought. Her sister's hair gleamed again, the extra pounds had fallen off and there was a new brightness to her eyes. In her opinion, Becca was more beautiful than ever — softer around the edges than in her pre-marriage, pre-pregnancy days and radiating contentment.

'Deke won't be able to keep his hands off you when he comes home.'

A whoosh of heat flared in her sister's porcelain skin. 'That's the plan, although I can't compete with teenage groupies who are readily available.'

'Now you're the one talking nonsense.' An off-the-wall idea sneaked into her head, but she kept it to herself. Later she might consider sharing it with Griff and ask his opinion about whether it was completely mad. 'I don't want to over-dress tonight. It's not a date . . . not really. I don't want to give the wrong impression. He wanted to talk. That's all.'

Becca gave an unladylike snort with distinct overtones of Miss Piggy.

'Fine. I'll go and smarten up a bit.' Lyndsey left the room in as dignified a fashion as she could manage. Once she was out of sight, her shoulders slumped and her pace slowed. What were his expectations of this evening? She wished she knew. Going with the flow was so *not* her thing.

* * *

'Are you sure this is a good idea?' Griff joined Jase on the porch. 'It's still damn hot, and if she's sweaty and eaten up by bugs, it's not goin' to be the last word in romance.' He'd forgotten how disturbed Lyndsey became when her plans got changed. It tested his powers of persuasion when he rang her after lunch to ask if they could leave at five o'clock instead of seven. Her grudging agreement hadn't done anything to boost his confidence.

'It'll be brilliant. Take a can of bug spray and stop worrying like an old woman.' Jase took another long pull of his cold beer. 'I'll make sure to sleep with earplugs in tonight, and promise I won't wander out in my boxers to join y'all for breakfast.'

'I'm not bringin' her back here!' His face heated. 'Even if she was agreeable . . . and that's unlikely—'

'Oh, for Christ's sake, Griff, lighten up.'

His brother was right — not something Griff thought very often. He needed to dial his anxiety back a notch. 'See ya later and thanks again.'

'You might not be thanking me tomorrow.'

'Yeah, I will. No matter how it goes, I—' Griff stopped there. Jase's piercing stare ordered him to leave the emotional stuff alone.

Swinging his keys, he ambled down to the truck, scrutinizing it with a frown. It might've been smarter not to wash and polish it this morning because the vehicle's advanced age and battered condition showed up more now. He tried to reassure himself that Lyndsey had reiterated several times how comfortable she was with his regular unpretentious self, truck included.

Griff started the motor and lifted his hand to Jase in a wave as he drove off, making an immediate turn back up Deke's drive. He supposed it was too much to expect that he could pick Lyndsey up in peace. The welcome party was in position. Theo knelt in the flower bed under the porch, making a show of weeding, but stopped immediately to grin at Griff. Becca treated him to a satisfied smile from her prized vantage point in one of the rocking chairs, holding Nora on her lap. He could swear even the baby gave him a cheeky smile.

'Cinderella is on her way,' Becca trilled. 'Where's the ball tonight, or aren't you going to tell me, either?'

Ignoring the less-than-subtle dig, he took the steps in one leap and lifted his hand to rap on the door.

'No need for that. I'm ready,' Lyndsey said. Her accent became more clipped and precise the more nervous she was, and right now it could cut glass.

The incredible dress she'd worn for their best-forgotten last attempt at a date was etched in his memory. At the time, it gave him disturbing dreams about what might've been underneath and how the evening could've ended if they hadn't screwed up. And now? Griff's throat went dry. She'd taken his recommendation to dress casually to heart, but tonight's cotton off-the-shoulder, yellow-and-green-diamond-patterned, figure-hugging dress that barely skimmed her thighs had no less effect on his blood pressure. Dramatic gold hoop earrings dangled near her tempting bare shoulders and the pop of yellow polish on her toenails accented the flat gold sandals. He should try to pay her a compliment, but couldn't speak, so offered Lyndsey his hand instead. Their uninvited observers sniggered.

'Shall we go before the peanut gallery gets too raucous?' he suggested.

'The what?'

Griff chuckled. 'Must be an American expression. Back in the old vaudeville days, they called the cheapest seats in the balcony the peanut gallery. It's come to mean unhelpful advice from a rowdy group of hecklers.' He nodded at their company. 'Like this crew.'

'I'm not sure I appreciate the comparison.' Becca's haughty response only worked for a split second until she burst out laughing and Theo joined in, while Nora bounced happily on her mother's lap, waving her hands in the air.

'That's our cue to leave.' He wasted no time steering Lyndsey out to the truck and ushered her into the front passenger seat.

'I'm honored.'

'Why?'

Her eyes danced with mirth. 'I hardly recognized your vehicle today.'

'Very funny.' They were both still laughing when he pulled out of the drive.

'Are we going far?'

'It'll take about forty minutes or so. We could get on the interstate, but I reckoned you'd enjoy the scenic route more, and we're not in any great hurry, so we'll take Highway 96 instead. It's a two-lane road and the countryside's real pretty.'

'So it's still a secret?'

'Won't be when we get there.' His glib response made her smile.

They slipped into easy conversation, and Griff talked about the area they were driving through. If they ignored the electric poles and tarmacked roads, much of the undulating farmland would've appeared pretty much the same to the first settlers. When they passed one of his favorite old barns, he made her smile by reciting its full history. He spotted the first sign for their destination and turned off onto Cox Road, but she didn't say anything else until they passed another sign.

'Arrington Vineyards? I didn't know you could grow grapes in Tennessee.'

'We sure can. This particular place has been in business about fifteen years, and they make some award-winning wines.'

A few minutes later, he slowed down at the main entrance so she could better appreciate the acres of vineyards spread out in front of them.

'Oh wow, what a gorgeous spot.'

'They've sited the buildings perfectly to make the most of the views. It's been developed into quite a tourist attraction.' Griff followed the parking signs and swung into an empty space. 'I hope it's not goin' to be too hot. Jase seemed to think—'

'This was your brother's idea?' She tilted him a questioning look. 'Does that mean you've sorted out some of your . . . differences?'

A tug of emotion made his throat constrict. 'We're getting there.'

'I'm so glad.' Lyndsey's smile blossomed. 'Now, do I get to drink some of this world-famous wine, or did you just bring me here to . . . ?'

'Will it help if I'm honest enough to admit I'm not sure of my motives?' Griff shrugged. 'I do want to talk about Jase and other stuff, though.'

'Me too. But . . .' A rare hint of shyness crept into her voice. 'I made a mistake sending you away. Is there a chance—?'

'Oh yeah. Definitely.' His vehemence made her blush. 'More than anything in the world, I want a chance with you. I *need* a chance with you. We're both too damn old to play games, and I'm not denigrating your age or mine with that statement.'

'I know that, you silly man.' Lyndsey's breathing was audible. 'Let's go and do whatever you've got planned. See the sunset. And then . . . perhaps we'll see the sunrise together?'

'You won't here, because they close at nine o'clock. But that doesn't have to stop us.' Griff's hands slid up to surround her face, his fingers stroking her warm skin, and the sight of her smoldering eyes made his body tighten all over. 'If you listen closely, you'll hear that the Music in the Vines line-up has started already. There's a great bluegrass band on tonight, and an up-and-coming country duo. There's also a gourmet picnic basket with our name on it waiting at the vineyard — The Tuscan Picnic, no less, with all sorts of gourmet Italian goodies. I figure a few Frosés will be the perfect drink with it tonight.'

'What on earth's that?'

He flashed a grin. 'It's a frozen rosé drink. Perfect for a warm summer evening. Like you.' The vain attempt to keep the compliment light and casual failed, and she sighed his name and shook her head gently.

'Oh, Griff, what am I going to do with you?'

'I can give you a list if you'd like.' The swift response brought out her brightest smile. 'Maybe we should leave it there . . . for now.'

'For now. Mmm, that sounds promising.'

'Oh, it's definitely a promise.' Griff brought her hand to his lips and brushed a kiss over her sun-warmed caramel skin. He no longer cared what the original intention of this evening was, or wasn't. Wasting this second chance wasn't happening.

CHAPTER NINETEEN

Lyndsey tried to slip out of the narrow bed without disturbing Griff but a strong hand suddenly clamped around her waist. She smiled over her shoulder into his dancing eyes.

'Goin' somewhere?' His warm breath caressed her neck and delectable shivers ran right through her.

Before she went out last night, Becca slipped the key to Deke's music studio into her bag with a whispered aside that the sofa turned into a bed. Sometimes her husband slept there rather than disturb his family when working late into the night.

She wriggled around to face him. 'I need the loo, but don't worry, there's one here, so I won't abandon you for long.' Unable to resist, she stroked the soft stubble covering his square jaw. Remembering the rub of it all over her skin last night made her body tingle.

'You'd better not. I've got plans for you.' His playful fingers inched lower until she squealed and pushed them away so she could roll out of bed, even if it was in a somewhat ungainly fashion.

Lyndsey struggled to look serious, which wasn't easy with Griff splayed out over the bed in all his naked glory. His only tattoo — a stunning kingfisher inked in bright turquoise and gold, whose edges were defined in black like a piece of stained glass — perched on his right bicep and appeared to fly when he flexed his muscles.

'That's all very well, but we still need to finish the talk you distracted me from last night.'

'I don't remember you objecting.' A lazy smile creased his face. He frowned when she didn't respond and sat up, wrapping his arms around his bent knees. 'Sorry. That's me being an ass.'

Seeing she'd steered the conversation away from sex, it would be inappropriate to comment on his tight, muscular backside, which she'd admired earlier. That still didn't stop the thought floating through her head.

'Becca told me there's tea- and coffee-making stuff here, too.'

'Yeah, it's in the small room at the back.'

'You've been here before.' Her accusing tone brought back his wicked smile. 'You totally knew about the bed being here, didn't you?'

'Might've done. Deke showed me the place once and bragged on all the facilities.'

'Could you look any smugger?'

'Want me to try? I will if you like,' Griff teased. 'Or I could go fix us some coffee.'

'Tea for me, please. Whatever you can find will do.' So much for sticking to her clean, healthy diet. That flew out the same window as her promise not to get involved with Griff Oakes. With a sigh, Lyndsey picked her creased dress and yesterday's panties up off the floor and tugged them on. She fled to find the bathroom and made the mistake of looking in the mirror. Raccoon eyes from the make-up she didn't remove last night stared back at her. Her hair was a halo of wild curls that looked as though she'd been plugged into an electric socket. She rubbed her fingers over her face and neck, tracing the faint marks left behind by Griff's scruff. At least, thanks to her birth father, it didn't show up on her dark Caribbean skin as vivid red prickles. After making a half-hearted attempt to freshen up, she strolled back out and found Griff, still naked, leaning on the counter and waiting for the kettle to boil.

'I don't suppose it occurred to you to put some clothes on in case someone comes in?'

He laughed. 'You seriously think a pair of boxers would hide the fact we've spent the night here? I guess we might fool them into thinking we were working on a new musical masterpiece?'

'Very funny.'

Griff's smile faltered. 'In case you hadn't clicked, this is me avoiding the whole serious chat thing.' He tugged her closer and rested his large, warm hands on her shoulders. 'I'll go get dressed.'

While he was away, she made their drinks and carried them over to the silver-and-black guitar-shaped coffee table. Half a dozen soft crimson leather chairs were gathered around it; she could easily imagine Deke and his fellow band members hashing out their ideas here.

'That better?' Griff returned, wearing his own equally rumpled clothes, and struck a pose reminiscent of Michelangelo's David.

Despite her best intentions, Lyndsey giggled before mentally reprimanding herself and dropping down in one of the chairs. 'Off you go, then.'

'You don't mess around, do you?' He gave her a wary look. 'Let's get the toughest bit out of the way. There's a reason I hadn't spoken to my brother in years. I thought it was valid, and it kind of was, but . . . I shouldn't have held onto it so long.' Anguish spread over his face. 'I hope you'll get it and not write me off as a—'

'*I'm* not in any position to criticize *you*. You know about me and Becca.'

'Yeah, but it's not quite the same. Here goes,' he sighed, 'and be honest about what you think.'

A trickle of unease ran through her.

* * *

All Griff could think while he ran through the whole sorry mess was that she'd make an excellent poker player, because he tried and failed miserably to read her reaction.

'You had every right to be furious with your brother. Far more so than I ever did with Becca.'

'But?' he prompted, sensing there was more. 'Letting go is healthier — right?'

Lyndsey gave a slow nod. 'I didn't realize the crippling effect holding on to my resentments was having until I managed to pretty much put them behind me.' Tears shimmered in her emerald eyes. 'So much of who I'd become was tangled up with all the family stuff. It affected my career and everything.' She flung her hands open in a helpless gesture. 'Sorting out other people's possessions was a displacement activity when my mind was in a mess.'

'You're surely not giving up your business? It seems absolutely the right fit for you.' Griff couldn't hide his surprise.

'I don't know. Maybe. I'm not sure.' Frustration laced through her voice. 'We're supposed to be talking about you, not delving into my woes!'

'I hope . . . maybe the two are connected?' Griff's heart leapt in his throat when she didn't answer. 'Too quick? Way off base? Which is it?'

'None of those.' She cleared her throat. 'I suppose it's hearing you say it out loud. We haven't . . . I mean . . .'

'I'm sayin' it now because, well . . . I love you, Lyndsey.' Griff wasn't sure which of them was more shocked when the three simple words slipped out. 'Sorry. I—'

'Don't you dare take it back now!' Indignation burst out of her.

'I don't want to, but—'

'But nothing. You're braver than me. I've been wanting to . . .' Lyndsey toyed with one of her silky corkscrew curls. 'I've trained myself to always be in control. Never to give in to rash impulses. I found it's safer that way.'

'But is that any way to live life? If I hadn't taken the plunge, I'd still be juggling balance sheets and sitting through boring four-hour long meetings about budget projections and cost analysis.' He shrugged. 'I'm not gonna say I'm making a steady six-figure salary, but I get by pretty well. I can identify the birds at my bird feeder. One day I might have enough research gathered up on old Middle Tennessee barns to write a book. My vegetables are coming along pretty damn well. Last week, I helped Tiffany put up a new fence. Harold asked yesterday if I'd help him and William repair Miss Grey's roof.'

'Griff, I . . . really want to say the same as you did . . .' Her visible effort to swallow touched him.

'There's no hurry, although I hope one day you might—'

Out of nowhere, she flung her arms around his neck, locked lips in a searing kiss and wriggled over onto his lap at the same time. Through his wonderful confusion, it took a second to click that the words she was breathlessly reciting over and over were, 'I love you too.'

With a triumphant smile, she let go and beamed at him. 'In case you weren't sure, I've had enough of being a coward. This is me being out of control, rash and horribly, dreadfully unsafe.'

'Yeah, thought so. I'm a massive fan.' Griff hugged her back. 'How about we tidy up here, then I'll slink off to shower and throw on some clean clothes, and you go on back and make Becca's morning? I'll come back to rescue you, and we'll tell her our news together, if you like?'

'Tell her what exactly?' A wobble shook her voice.

'As much or as little as you want. In case you aren't sure, I want this — you — long-term. I'm not so sure how we'll make it work or what exactly it'll look like, but I'm okay with that if you are?'

Lyndsey looked thoughtful. 'Would you mind if we kept it to ourselves for now? Behaved as normal?' A mischievous smile lit her up. 'Well, normal with sex thrown in, because Becca's bound to guess that part.'

'Sure.' Griff squashed a trickle of disappointment. He had an overwhelming urge to shout their love from the roof-tops, but he'd pushed her far enough out of her comfort zone for one day. 'I'll wash our mugs if you make the bed.' The sparkles in her eyes glittered brighter than the summer sun. 'Don't do that, woman.'

'What?'

'The teasing eyes thing. You know I'd take you back to bed in a heartbeat, but—'

'Real life is waiting.' She exhaled a dramatic, resigned sigh. 'It's the penalty of falling in love when you're not a teenager. People give you a break, then, they put it down to uncontrollable hormones.'

'Were you that way?' Griff couldn't see it somehow. 'I sure was. I lost my mind at fifteen big time. Mandy Green was a blonde prom queen with curves in all the right places.' He shook his head. 'I never could figure out why she hooked up with me when she was two years older and could have any guy in the school by crooking her little finger. For a couple of magical weeks, nothing else existed for me but when I'd see her again. We made out like crazy in her parents' basement when they weren't home, and the afternoon she let me touch her breasts is etched in my brain. I thought I'd died and gone to heaven.'

Lyndsey's husky laughter filled the air. 'I do not need the details of you losing your virginity, thanks very much.'

'She didn't let me go *that* far! I was soon kicked to the curb and replaced by the muscle-bound, needing-to-shave-twice-a-day quarterback for the football team.'

'How sad. I suppose her toy boy days were over.'

'You're mean.'

'Yep. That's what all the men say.' Sadness ran through her words.

'You know I was joking, right?'

Her nod struck him as automatic rather than heartfelt. She said, 'I'm not a fan of dredging up my past love life, so can we leave it there for now?'

Griff itched to discover what brought on the change in her upbeat attitude, but he refused to ask. She'd been patient with him; it was his turn to repay the favor.

'Do you fancy having supper with me and Jase tonight?' The impromptu invitation brought back her smile.

'I'd love that. I'll clear up here. It's not much. You run along while I gather the strength to face my smug sister.'

He snorted. 'My brother's gonna be equally self-satisfied. The SOB even offered to put in ear plugs last night, so I could take you back to my place and . . .' Griff shut his mouth. Time to make a swift retreat.

CHAPTER TWENTY

Lyndsey chatted away to Nora while she struggled to wriggle the baby's tiny arms through the sleeves of an unbearably cute red-white-and-blue striped dress, which came with matching rompers. Her mother sent it in a parcel from England, along with more Minstrels for her and Becca, plus a couple of English computer magazines that Theo requested.

There was something incredibly soothing about discussing her thoughts and feelings with someone whose only response was to gurgle and kick her plump pink legs in the air. Before this, Lyndsey never had much to do with babies beyond the usual cooing over friends' offspring. Sadly, her friendship with the new mums inevitably faltered when the reality of their vastly differing lifestyles sunk in. Now she totally got why her friends' priorities changed so drastically.

Every day her love for her niece deepened; it was fascinating to watch Nora's personality reveal itself like a budding flower opening to the sun. At almost four months old now, there were clear signs of the person she'd one day become. Generally good-humored, unless she was tired or hungry, but very much knowing her own mind about what she did and didn't like.

'He loves me, Nora, and I love him. Should be simple — right?' She started on the rompers next, tugging them over the baby's adorable chubby legs. Most grown women never used the words *adorable* and *chubby* about themselves — how sad was that? Lyndsey hated to picture her beautiful niece in tears one day, because her legs didn't have the sought-after thigh gap flaunted by all the top models. 'But I've spent years building up my business in Cornwall. I know what I said to Griff, but what else am I any good at?' Frustration bubbled up inside her. 'It's all right for him. He's discovered a creative talent that pays the bills.'

Nora's velvety dark eyes latched onto her. 'You're right, sweet pea. I'm making excuses because I'm scared. It's nothing to do with the short time we've known each other, either, because I'd be just as skittish if we'd been dating for a couple of years.' She heaved a sigh.

Nora suddenly grabbed her finger and held on tight. 'Oh no, baby girl, don't you dare do that. I decided a long time ago I'm not cut out to be a mum. Griff's even older than me, so I'm sure he's got no interest in becoming a dad at this point.' Not that they'd ever actually discussed the subject. 'Oh, but he does worship you, Nora. He cradles you so tenderly in his lovely big, strong hands, treating you like the glass he handles every day. He's such a kind, thoughtful man who'd make a wonderful father.'

Nerves knotted her stomach. She was racing ahead of herself and needed to put the brakes on.

'Have you finished dressing madam yet?' Becca hurried in, fresh as a daisy in a bright yellow sundress. Her sister gave an understanding half-smile. 'I never expected it either.'

'What?'

'The fierce love I felt when the doctor placed Nora in my arms. It frightened me to death.' The admission came with a slight shrug. 'I would die for her. Kill for her. Anything to keep her safe.' She touched Nora's cheek and the little girl beamed. 'I'm convinced God makes babies start to smile at around two months old because by then you're totally exhausted and on the verge of losing it. The smiles bind you to them tighter than a sailor's knot.' A shadow blurred

Becca's smile. 'Poor Deke is torn all the time. He loves his music — it's an integral part of him — but these recent problems with Theo hit hard. He's seen the effect his absences have and doesn't know what to do about it.'

'But you and Theo are doing okay now, right?'

'Much better, but I know he misses his dad terribly.'

'You do, too.'

She'd seen how hard it was, even with help, to be a parent — especially to children of widely varying ages. Nothing about it was easy.

'At least we're on the downward side. It's not quite four weeks to go now.' Becca's brave words vied with her solemn expression.

The wild idea she'd had a few days ago popped back into her head. Lyndsey never did get around to asking Griff's opinion because they'd been too busy with other things. 'The band are performing in London the end of next week, aren't they?'

'Yes. Why?'

'There's nothing tying us here. We could pack up the kids and get on a plane. Go down to Cornwall first to introduce Mum and Dad to their new granddaughter, and let them get to know Theo properly. After that, we could travel to London and spend a couple of days with Deke before flying back in time for Theo's return to school. The first week of August sounds terribly soon for them to start back, but they finished so early for the summer holidays that I suppose it makes sense.'

'How long has this been percolating in your head?' Becca sounded suspicious. 'Is this a ploy to wriggle out of making a decision about you and Griff?'

Is that what she was doing? It hadn't been at the forefront of her mind . . . but was it burrowed somewhere she didn't even recognize, gnawing at her?

'Not at all. In fact, we could ask him to come too.'

Did she really say that out loud? By the way her sister's eyebrows shot up, she apparently did. Gamely, Lyndsey went on: 'He may have work commitments, plus he's got his brother staying, so I expect he'd think it's a mad idea . . .'

'I think it's terrific!' Becca scooped up her daughter with a huge grin. 'Right, Nora, let's get ready for our guests. With any luck, you'll soon be breathing some good fresh Cornish air.'

Oh God, she'd really gone and done it now.

'You need to leave soon to fetch Ruth Mae,' Becca reminded. 'You know what a stickler she is for punctuality. When I invited her to have tea with us at three o'clock today, I promised someone would arrive in good time to walk over with her. I hope Griff and his brother won't be late.' Becca frowned. 'Is it too much to hope she'll take a liking to them as well? I think I might've got a little smug after our first tea party was such a success.'

'I'm sure it'll be fine.' Lyndsey hurried to reassure her sister. 'Anyway, a little smugness on our part is deserved, I think.'

All they'd ever hoped for was a slight thaw on Miss Grey's part, enough to let her unbend and at least accept help from her neighbors, even if she would never consider them friends. But in the last two weeks, Paradise Valley had undergone a major climate change. Harold and William had worked like Trojans in Ruth Mae's garden, and even persuaded the old lady to have Sunday lunch with them last week. Apparently, they'd talked for so long it'd been nearly sundown when the two men walked her home. Miss Grey was warming towards Tiffany, too, after she showed the old lady a few gentle exercises to ease her sciatica. They all kept an unobtrusive eye on their elderly neighbor, and if no one saw any signs of life by mid-morning someone would find an excuse to go and check on her.

'I'm going to head off right now.' She squashed a trickle of nerves. How Ruth Mae might react to Griff and his brother was something no one could predict. Lyndsey had got on so well with Jase the other night at dinner that when she left, he apparently warned Griff if he was dumb enough to let her go, Griff would have him to answer to.

A wall of humidity hit her in the face when she stepped outside, and for the first time she longed for a break from the incessant heat. Miss Grey was ready and waiting for her, of course, not exactly tapping her watch but not far from it.

'Your garden is looking pretty.' Her praise softened Ruth Mae's expression. Lyndsey almost added that the house, with its watertight roof, new front door and tight-fitting windows was looking a thousand times better as well, but thought that might be a step too far.

'Mr Morton and Mr Puckett have worked hard.' Ruth Mae gave a tight nod. 'I like to give credit where it's due.'

They arrived outside the house as her sister greeted Griff and Jase.

'Lovely to see you, Miss Grey.' Becca turned to speak to them. 'Let's all go through to the conservatory. It's the most recent room Lyndsey and I have tackled, so I'm quite proud to show it off.'

It touched her to hear her sister bragging on the work they'd done together. With each area of the house they'd cleared, she'd seen Becca's confidence grow.

Becca nodded at Griff and Jase. 'We can have a nice cup of tea and a good natter, and you can meet these two lovely men.'

Jase stepped forward and offered the old lady his arm. 'Ma'am, I'd be honored to walk with you.'

Lyndsey suppressed a giggle. He sounded like one of the Southern gentlemen from *Gone With the Wind*. Two blobs of heat colored Miss Grey's thin cheeks, and she nodded at him. Griff caught Lyndsey's eye over the old lady's head and winked.

They walked through to the back of the house and stepped into the conservatory. Ceiling fans whirred silently over the newly scrubbed white wicker furniture, and they'd opened all the windows, so it was warm but not unbearably so. An abundance of pots and planters stood around the space, overflowing with colorful flowers, chosen according to Harold's advice for their intoxicating scents. Before the decluttering, it'd been knee-deep in moving boxes of Deke's that were never unpacked and assorted bits of broken-down old furniture that had been there since Ruth Mae's time.

'This room was my mother's pride and joy.' Miss Grey stared around, her eyes drinking it all in greedily. 'She was a green-thumbed lady and grew most of her plants from seeds or cuttings. This is where she brought her lady friends to entertain them. As a little girl, I'd be allowed to join them sometimes and . . . Oh my goodness, wherever did you find this?' She unhooked her arm from Jase and hobbled over to a child's small wooden rocking chair.

'It was over in the far corner under a pile of old blankets,' Lyndsey said.

'That was mine. I'd sit by my mother's legs and listen to them talk.' A secretive smile creased her face. 'They'd forget I was there sometimes, and I'd hear all sorts of things I probably shouldn't have.'

'Shall we all sit down?' Becca suggested. 'I'll go and make tea and retrieve my children. I left Theo playing with Nora in the kitchen.'

The four of them got settled, with Ruth Mae in the most comfortable chair with plenty of cushions tucked behind her back. Lyndsey wondered how best to get the conversation going, but her hero jumped in to the rescue.

'Miss Grey, we haven't ever met properly. I'm Griff Oakes.' He leaned across and offered his hand. The old lady took it briefly while raking him with her shrewd gaze. 'I'd love to hear more about the history of Paradise Valley and your family sometime. I've a particular interest in old barns and I love that Deke kept a lot of the original features in the one here when he converted it to his studio.'

'I suppose you know the Greys came about 1850 to farm tobacco?' Ruth Mae said. 'That would be my great-great grandfather, Thomas Scott Grey, and his wife Kathleen. Rounded up the whole family, they did, and moved here.'

'Yes, ma'am. It must've been a hard life to start with.'

Lyndsey waited for Miss Grey to brush him off, but the opposite happened and once Ruth Mae started to talk, they were treated to all sorts of fascinating stories. They heard about the barrels of sauerkraut the first settlers made to last them through the winter, to her pride in the fact no travelers were ever turned away if they stopped by the settlement needing food or a bed for the night. In this rural, thinly developed part of the state, there would've been nowhere else for them to go and people helped each other when they could.

'If I haven't bored you too much, you can stop by the house sometime to hear more.' Ruth Mae nodded at Griff.

'I'd be honored, ma'am. It's fascinating stuff.'

'Not many of the young are interested. They think us old folk have always been aged, but we had our hopes and dreams, too. My kinfolk wouldn't have settled Paradise Valley if they didn't.'

'It's what drives us all, ma'am. Without it, we're nothing.' Griff glanced at Lyndsey.

Her cheeks warmed and she was relieved to see Becca return carrying a loaded tea tray, followed by Theo, who held Nora in his arms. Lyndsey sprang up to help her sister and watched Theo tenderly place his sister down on a colorful alphabet quilt on the floor. He set up a wood arch, dotted with dangling toys over Nora's head and batted several of the animals to show her the noises they made.

'They tell me you're some sort of artist.' Ruth Mae addressed Griff again, a hint of disdain threading through her voice.

'That's right. I work in stained glass. In fact, I made somethin' for you.' He whipped out a flat oval object, encased in scarlet silk and tied with a length of wide red ribbon.

'For me?' Miss Grey took it cautiously from him and undid the wrappings to reveal a mosaic panel of a bouquet of roses. The sun streaming in through the conservatory windows brought the intense shades of red to life.

'It's stunning.' Lyndsey's breathless admiration made Griff's face turn ruddy.

'You've got a good eye.' Ruth Mae pointed out of the window. 'I used to grow those very roses out there years ago.'

Her wrinkled smile rested on him. 'You did your research well.'

'I had some help.' Griff winked at Lyndsey. 'I heard how much you admired Harold and William's roses at the tea party I missed.'

'Hopefully, we can grow them here again one day,' Becca said.

'I'd sure like to see that,' Ruth Mae murmured. 'I might even consider returning the bird bath for the front of the house. It's where it belongs.'

'That would be . . . amazing.'

Silence fell briefly on the group but it didn't last long. Nora swiped at her toys, kicked her legs in the air and giggled merrily.

'You're a very talented young man.' The old lady touched the mosaic and sounded approving.

'Li-Li, have you checked yet to see if Griff's got a passport?' Becca's eyes twinkled.

'What're you talking about?' He swiveled his head to frown at her sister.

Lyndsey frantically shook her head behind his back. She had been planning to pick her moment to raise the subject of him possibly joining them on their trip.

'Oh, um, nothing. Forget it,' Becca muttered and picked up the teapot. 'Who's for tea?'

She touched Griff's arm. 'We'll talk after this. Okay?'

'Yeah, sure.' His mind was clearly racing like a hamster on a wheel, but he cracked another broad smile and turned back to Ruth Mae. 'They'll turn your old house into a tea shop if we aren't careful.'

'There are worse things, young man — like seeing the place fallin' into rack and ruin. It's good to see it coming back to life.'

Emotion gripped Lyndsey's throat. They'd all come a long way.

CHAPTER TWENTY-ONE

'You sure you're okay with me goin' off to England?' Griff asked Jase.

He'd suspected at the time that Lyndsey hadn't expected him to agree so readily. The next day she came to see him, looking extremely worried and saying she needed to clear some things up. She'd sheepishly admitted that Becca and Tiffany had cornered her for a heart-to-heart chat about why she was getting cold feet. They pried out of her that the root of the problem was how scared she was by the depth of her feelings for Griff, because it felt out of her control — the complete opposite of the way she preferred to live her life.

Griff had brought a faint smile to her face when he promised she wasn't the only one experiencing some trepidation. He knew from what she'd told him that Lyndsey had rarely taken any boyfriends home, so he'd seen her offer as a clear sign she was ready to move their relationship to the next level. That both exhilarated and frightened him. Then he quietly told Lyndsey that the thought of losing her scared him far more than anything else, and she said the same in return. That's when Griff knew they'd be all right.

'Yeah. I told you so, didn't I?' Jase didn't look up from rubbing a glass cloth over his completed mosaic. 'There. What do you think?' His eyes shone with pride.

'It's a damn sight better than my first efforts, that's for sure.' Even someone who didn't know the heartfelt story behind the mosaic couldn't help but be impressed by its obvious power. 'Art of any sort helps get your feelings out in the open. I was going through a rough time at my previous job when I started working with stained glass. It sure helped me.'

'What happened?' Jase's cheeks turned red. 'You don't have to tell me. I get we're not close—'

'I sure hope we're gettin' there again.' Honesty was a two-way street. Time for him to step up. 'I was a selfish bastard. Oh, I gave the appearance of playing the game at work and being a team player, but really I was only lookin' out for Number One.' His shoulders slumped. 'My girlfriend and I were vying for the same promotion, and I screwed her over so they'd be sure to offer it to me. Luckily, I came to my senses and admitted what I'd done, so they allowed me to resign instead of tossing me out on my ear.'

He gestured around them. 'This saved me.' Griff pointed to a huge stained-glass panel hanging on the back wall — an abstract created entirely in black and red with vicious jagged edges. Even now, it made him uneasy to look at. 'That's how I felt at the time.'

'Hell, Griff, it's . . . scary. I thought you were the mild-mannered, nerdy one of us?' Jase chuckled. 'Still waters, I guess.'

'Yeah, you could say that.' He gave a wry smile. It felt good to have played a small part in helping his brother to start climbing out of the dark place he'd ended up. 'Maybe you'll get so hooked on this you'll turn pro too one day, like me?'

Jase shook his head. 'Nah, I don't see that. As a hobby it's great, but I don't see me having your dedication day in and day out.'

'So you got any thoughts about what you might transition into instead of playing baseball?' It was the one question he hadn't dared ask before.

'I've a few ideas. When I first started to have problems with my back, I did some coaching with talented high schoolers brought in by the team to see if they had potential. It was really satisfying. I've done a few sports reporting gigs on local radio, too.' He looked mildly embarrassed. 'One of the TV stations even approached me about being a commentator. At the time I blew them off, but . . .'

'Things change.' Griff closed his laptop. Time enough later to work on some new patterns. This was more important. 'Most people change careers multiple times these days. Some by choice, and others — like us — not so much. It's not the end of the world; it's often the beginning of a better one. You've got talent and personality in spades. You'll be fine.'

'You're not as dumb as you look, are you?' Jase's cocky grin returned. 'Probably just as well.'

Laughing together felt good.

'So don't worry about me while you're off romancing the lovely Lyndsey. I've plenty to keep me busy. I'll start putting out feelers for possible work, water your plants, visit Mom and Dad to make a full confession . . .' The break in his voice hinted at how hard that last point was going to be.

'You don't have to for my sake. Honestly.' Griff hoped his brother knew that he wasn't just saying that. He'd held on to his bitterness long enough.

'Yeah, I know that, but I need to tell them the truth for my own peace of mind.' Jase heaved a sigh. 'I can't move on with this hangin' over my head.'

He didn't argue. Doing the right thing wasn't an easy road to take.

* * *

'Aunt Lyndsey, can I ask you something?' Theo pushed the soil in around the last of their new plants.

Harold had recommended putting in a few quick-blooming flowers like alyssum, red poppies, zinnia and cosmos for a flash of late summer color, so that's what they'd bought.

This morning, she'd dragged Theo along to the nearest garden center, bribing him with the promise of road-testing, later, the video game he'd been working on with his friend. The boys wanted her advice, and although she was no expert, Lyndsey thought she might be able to give them a few pointers.

'Anything. That's what we agreed yesterday.'

It had definitely been a day for baring her soul. After her deeply honest conversation with Becca and Tiffany, she'd cleared the air with Griff. Discovering he was equally apprehensive had freed her. Weeks ago, she'd promised Theo that they'd talk about his 'cuckoo in the nest' feelings and her own similar experiences, but she'd allowed that to fall by the wayside, and yesterday seemed as good a time as any to put that right. When they ended their chat, Lyndsey told him he could ask her anything and she'd do her best to answer as frankly as she could.

'There is something . . . but Mom said it wasn't any of our business, when I asked her.' His face flushed.

'If it's on your mind and it's bothering you, then I want to know about it. If I can't answer, I'll tell you.'

'Are you and Griff goin' to get married and live in his place?' Theo blurted out. 'That'd be awesome.'

Lyndsey was stunned. Of all the questions she thought he might ask, that particular one hadn't made the list.

'We're enjoying getting to know each other better at the moment, Theo. We honestly haven't discussed what we might want to do in the long term.' That was the truth, although she'd laid awake many nights speculating along those lines. 'Okay?'

'Yeah, but I'm still gonna hope you do.'

'Hiya! You guys look busy,' Griff shouted, loping up the drive towards them.

She was grateful he hadn't arrived a minute earlier.

'Doesn't our trip planning meeting start soon?'

'Yes, Theo and I are finishing up here, then we'll be in.' Lyndsey stood and brushed a few specks of earth off her turquoise shorts.

'I don't suppose we could be reckless and just wing it?'

'It won't hurt to iron out a few details before we leave on Saturday. Are you sure Jase is okay with you going?'

'Yep. He's planning to go visit our folks for a few days.' Griff's smile lost a hint of its brilliance. 'He wants to straighten some things out with them.'

Lyndsey guessed he was referring to the aftermath of the car crash years ago. No doubt he didn't want to discuss that in front of Theo.

'Theo, would you mind putting the tools away before you come in?'

'Sure thing, Aunt Lyndsey.'

'I know you'll do it properly.' She shared a conspiratorial look with her nephew. The garden shed had been ramshackle and cluttered when she arrived, but they'd transformed it into a model of good order. 'Come on, Griff, let's go find your favorite girl in the whole world.'

He made a playful grab for her hand. 'She's right here. No searching needed.'

'Nora will be terribly jealous if she hears she's been usurped in your affections.'

Griff shook his head at Theo. 'Watch out, kid, for when girls try to catch you out. You've gotta be quick on your feet to keep up with them.'

'Most of the girls in my class are faster than me when it comes to running,' he said gloomily. 'I'm not much of an athlete.'

She stifled a giggle and was amazed Griff managed to keep a straight face.

'Smart women appreciate smart guys. You've got it up here where it really counts.' Griff tapped his forehead.

Theo turned beet-red, picked up their tools and scurried off.

'We've both embarrassed him now. We've forgotten what it's like to be twelve and in that awful in-between stage.'

'I shouldn't have forgotten.' Griff scoffed. 'It didn't help that my handsome sports star brother, who was two years younger, picked up girls effortlessly. They threw themselves at Jase, while I could only look on in envy.'

Lyndsey could sympathize. She'd resented her sister's ability to snap her finger and make the boys come running, too. Later, she'd come to see that the kind of boys who fell for Becca didn't interest her anyway. Reaching up, she kissed Griff on the mouth and he immediately cupped his hand around the back of her neck to draw her closer.

'Get a room, you two, and stop making this old married woman jealous,' Becca said light-heartedly, poking her head out around the front door. 'It's time for the travel summit — isn't that right, Li-Li? Nora's sound asleep, the tea is made and we've got millionaire's shortbread to go with it.' She smiled at Griff. 'You'll have an amazing time visiting British teashops, because they all serve their own versions of the recipe, so you can work your way through them and rate the best.'

'I knew there was a reason I wanted to come with y'all.' Griff hugged Lyndsey. 'Apart from seeing what I've been told is the prettiest place in the whole country, and meeting your folks, of course.'

A knot tightened in her stomach.

'They'll love me, honey, don't fret. What's not to love?' Griff winked, picking up on her unease.

'I've got a long list, but I promise I won't share it with them,' Lyndsey quipped. 'Come on in; let's make sure to get a piece of that awful shortbread before Theo scarfs down the whole thing.'

If she kept reassuring herself everything would be fine, she hoped it would come true.

CHAPTER TWENTY-TWO

Griff wandered into the kitchen to find Paul, Lyndsey's dad, there already and filling up the kettle. Now he wished he'd waited a while to come down, but although they'd arrived in London three days ago, jet lag was still kicking his ass, and he was in desperate need of coffee. He hadn't avoided Lyndsey's parents, but hadn't gone out of his way to be alone with them, either. He'd figured it best for them to get the measure of each other before any serious topics reared their heads.

'Should be another nice day for getting out and about,' Paul said, nodding at the bright blue, cloudless sky visible out of the window. 'What's on the agenda today? I'm sure there is one.' He chuckled.

To look at him now, it was hard to believe the man was seriously ill a few months ago. On Monday, he'd walked all around St Ives with them with no more need to rest than anyone else. Lyndsey's prediction had been correct. Griff *had* been enthralled by the pretty little town. The light *was* incredible. Long golden beaches stretching far out into the distance. Pastel-colored cottages clinging to roads so steep and narrow he was surprised people and cars didn't tumble down them. A picturesque harbor full of colorful boats bobbing around under a clear summer sky. The sketchbook he always kept tucked in his pocket was crammed with ideas for new glass projects.

'Even as a little kiddie, our Lyndsey always had a plan.' His scrutinizing gaze swept over Griff. 'I'm not sure you were one of the items on her list though when she went to help Becca.'

'I'm pretty sure I wasn't. She wasn't on mine, either. I reckon we were both pretty content with our lives, but . . .' He wasn't sure how, or if, to put his deepest feelings into words.

Paul eyed him thoughtfully. 'Some things can't be planned. I was a bit of a ladies' man when I met Maureen. Never more than one at a time, mind you.' His blue eyes twinkled. 'Although there might've been a bit of overlap occasionally.'

'You fell hard for her?'

'Oh yes, and I see you looking at my girl the same way.' He stepped across to close the kitchen door. 'You need to know it's never made any difference that Lyndsey's not my biological daughter. Not to me.' He gave an exasperated sigh and ran a hand over his thinning gray hair. 'Maureen and I wanted a little brother or sister for Lyndsey, so we tried for a baby as soon as we got married, but it never happened. We'd about given up when she finally fell pregnant. Because we were so thrilled, we thought Lyndsey would be, too.' Paul shoved his hands in his pockets and stared at the floor.

'But instead she felt left out. Second best. The one you got stuck with,' Griff murmured.

Paul nodded sadly. 'Becca was always a bit of a handful. Her mood changed like the Cornish weather from one second to the next.'

'So she played you both to her advantage, leaving Lyndsey out in the cold.' He wondered if he'd spoken too harshly. 'I'm sorry. That was rude.'

'Mebbe, but you're right. Will you tell me one thing?'

'Yeah, if I can.'

'The girls seem to be doing better together. Did we do right, pushing Lyndsey to go to Tennessee?'

'Apart from sending the woman I love spinning into my orbit? That's somethin' I'll be eternally grateful for, if you weren't sure.' He grinned. 'Yeah, I'd say you did good. Things were rocky at first, mind you. I'm not spilling any secrets by sayin' that, because they'd tell you so themselves. They seem to have found a middle ground that suits them both.'

Paul gave an appreciative nod. 'Little Nora's got us both wrapped around her tiny fingers already. I don't know how we're going to say goodbye when you take her away again.'

There was nothing Griff could say. All the video chats and pictures in the world weren't the same as real-life kisses and cuddles.

'I've tried talking to Theo, but he don't have much to say for himself. I s'ppose my funny accent confuses him.' He looked worried. 'I hope he isn't having the same kind of problems Lyndsey did.'

'He has had some trouble adjusting, but I'm pretty sure the worst of it's behind him now. He's a great kid who's had a lot of upheaval to deal with.' It wasn't his place to tell the whole story. 'Don't worry about him too much. Theo's a typical twelve-year-old, and they aren't usually the chattiest even at the best of times. You've got a point about the Cornish accent, because I don't mind admitting it's a challenge to me, too. Keep plugging away, Paul. He'll catch on eventually, like I'm startin' to.'

'You'm doing all right. Do you reckon the boy might enjoy going out fishing for mackerel tomorrow?'

'He might. How about we make it a guys' day out? I wouldn't mind having a try, too.' He'd only ever been on a pontoon boat on a lake before, never out to sea, but the idea appealed to him. It would also give him an opportunity to get to know Paul better.

'I'd be happy to have you come along. I didn't think to—'

'It's okay.' This was an opportunity for much-needed honesty. 'A short visit like this isn't enough for y'all to really size me up, is it?'

Paul gave a fleeting shrug, but said nothing.

'Lyndsey loves you both a whole lot, so how you feel about me — and us — matters to us both. I know this trip was originally put together for other reasons, but I jumped at the chance when it was offered to me too.'

'I'm some glad you did. Maureen was worrying herself half to death over who Lyndsey had got herself tangled up with — especially after that to-do with Tristan.' His color deepened. 'Have I put my foot in it?'

'Nope. You're good. I've heard all about it.' Griff's jaw tightened. He hoped he'd get away with the lie.

'He's a fine chap. We've known him all his life. Tris and Lyndsey were always good mates.' He looked rueful. 'Then she had the idiotic idea it wasn't a huge leap from there to being a romantic couple. He was more than willing to give it a go, so they tried for a bit, but it didn't work. Daft girl. You can't make yourself fall in love with someone. It's sad, but he didn't take it well when she came to her senses.'

'I don't suppose he did.'

They fell silent.

'Why's the door closed?' Lyndsey breezed in. Griff loved seeing her first thing in the morning, devoid of make-up but glowing with vitality. Her slender figure was wrapped in her new favorite emerald green robe and her shiny black corkscrew curls cascaded around her face. 'Are you two up to no good?'

'Your dad's offered to take me and Theo out mackerel fishing tomorrow.'

'Right.' She didn't sound convinced that there wasn't more to it.

Griff held her gaze and watched a faint blush brighten her cheeks. She'd picked up the hint to leave it alone, at least for now.

Lyndsey gestured to the teapot. 'Is it still drinkable?'

'Oh, I haven't got around to making it yet.' Her father's admission sent her eyebrows shooting into her hairline.

'Honestly, you're both hopeless.' She brushed past and switched the kettle back on, gathered up mugs and fetched milk from the fridge. 'We're leaving here at half nine, so that way we make it to the Eden Project before they open at ten.

That gives us time to see the highlights, at least, before lunch, then get back here for Nora to have a quiet afternoon nap.'

'I think I'll give it a miss, love,' Paul said.

'Have we overtired you, Dad?'

Griff had heard that the extensive tourist attraction, with its massive biomes and surrounding gardens, was well worth seeing, but a lot of walking.

Paul shook his head. 'It's not that, but I've been there enough times already.' He brightened. 'Why don't you leave Nora with me? The rest of you won't have to rush around that way.'

'I think it's a great idea, but I'm not her mum, so it's not up to me. You'll have to ask Becca.'

The touch of wistfulness threading through her voice brought Griff up short. Was he running ahead of himself by mentally making plans for a future with Lyndsey? There were a whole lot of things they hadn't discussed, and children was one of them. When he was solely focused on his career, he'd freaked out when girlfriends assumed the next step in their relationship was a proposal, followed by the white wedding of their dreams, a house in the suburbs and a family. But now that his mindset was in a far different place, he needed to do some re-evaluating. Griff noticed Lyndsey frowning at him and could've kicked himself. She'd read his mind as usual, but misinterpreted his thoughts. This wasn't the right time or place for an explanation, so he had no choice but to hold his tongue when her expression closed down.

'I'll go and ask her.' Lyndsey fled the kitchen.

Paul gave Griff a puzzled stare, as though he knew something crucial happened, but couldn't for the life of him work out what it was.

* * *

Compartmentalizing was Lyndsey's thing. After all, she did it every day — literally — at work. If she couldn't pull it off now, her mother and sister would guess something was up between her and Griff. And there was no way she'd clearly know how he felt until they had a chance to speak in private.

If anyone asked a couple of months ago if she was pining for a baby, Lyndsey would've laughed her head off and told them not to be ridiculous. Her lack of interest in having children was one of the arguments she used when making it clear to Tristan they'd never be anything more than good friends. Tristan's large boisterous family were his pride and joy. No one doted on their nieces and nephews more, and he'd never made a secret of the fact he couldn't wait to have his own children. When she told him bluntly that she had no interest in that direction, it shook him. Suddenly the love he professed for her came with conditions, and that was one of them.

But all that was before she met Nora and fell head over heels in love. At first, she tried to rationalize it as nothing more than a simple family connection. But that changed. As she spent more time with her niece, watching her change and grow with every day, it shone a light on another gaping hole in her life. Did Griff feel the same way, though? She'd seen him with Nora enough to know he adored her too, but earlier, he'd looked distinctly worried. If they weren't on the same page, what did that mean for them?

'You look as though you've lost a pound and found sixpence.' Becca's careless remark made tears spring to her eyes. 'Spill the beans.' She draped an arm around Lyndsey's shoulder. 'Remember we're supposed to be best mates, now.'

Guilt grabbed her by the throat. They'd wasted so many years because of stubbornness on both their parts. Everything poured out uncensored.

'You silly girl.' Becca rested her forehead against Lyndsey's with a sigh. 'You can listen to *my* advice for a change. When we're at Eden, I'll steer Theo and Mum off at some point, so you and Griff can talk. You won't get a chance here, because we're on top of each other all the time.'

'I don't remember the house feeling this small when we were growing up.' The three-bedroomed cottage was bursting at the seams with five adults, one almost-teenage boy and a baby. 'You sure you're okay with Dad looking after Nora?'

'Absolutely. He'll enjoy having her to himself to spoil, and if he wants, he can take a nap when she does. There are bottles made up in the fridge, so he should be good.'

They fell silent for a moment, thinking how fortunate they were to have their father well again.

'Now, let's go.'

For once, Lyndsey followed her bossy sister's instructions and didn't mind one bit.

* * *

'Warm enough for you, is it?' Griff playfully whipped out a handkerchief and dabbed at Lyndsey's brow. 'Makes you want to rush back to the hot, humid Tennessee summer, doesn't it?' He slipped his arm around her waist. 'Don't take this wrong, because I'm over the moon to get you to myself for a few minutes, but are you gonna tell me what's behind your family's sudden disappearance?'

A minute ago, he'd miraculously found himself alone with Lyndsey in the tropical biome, after Becca announced she was off with her mother and Theo to the Mediterranean biome. Theo was supposedly mad keen on attending a workshop about the people whose behind-the-scenes jobs made the Eden Project such a success.

'Can't fool you, can we? Let's find somewhere cooler to chat. How about we get a coffee downstairs?'

'Sure.'

'Don't look so worried. It's not a date with the guillotine.'

Griff kept to himself that was how it felt. 'I was only wondering if they'll have any millionaire's shortbread, so I can see how it rates.'

'I should've guessed. Come on, Mr Greedy.' Lyndsey linked her arm through his and they wended their way back to the stairs.

Luckily, it was too early for most people to be thinking about lunch, so there were plenty of empty tables scattered around the expansive space.

'You pick a quiet spot while I get our drinks,' Lyndsey suggested. 'I don't need to ask what you want to eat.' She wandered off towards the cafeteria counter.

Griff selected a table by one of the huge picture windows overlooking the outside gardens. He retreated into his own thoughts and various depressing scenarios ran through his mind. Yesterday, Lyndsey went off on her own to Truro and spent the morning at her business, coming back looking very thoughtful. Maybe she'd come to the realization The Right Place *was* where her future lay, and there wasn't room in her life for him after all. People sometimes got swept up in things, and it took a dose of cold, hard reality to open their eyes.

'It's all right; you don't have to look so worried — they had plenty left.' Lyndsey unloaded a tray in front of him and slid a plate of shortbread in his direction.

'My day is complete.' Griff bit into the chocolatey, caramel-laced, buttery deliciousness and chewed thoughtfully.

'Well?'

'I'll give it a nine. It's close to perfect.' Sometimes the shortbread layer was either too hard or too crumbly. The caramel could be runny or stodgy. The chocolate too cheap. None of those negatives applied here. 'You've always got to leave some room for improvement, a bit like with women.'

The corners of Lyndsey's mouth twitched with amusement. Griff gulped a swig of coffee, then picked up on her nervous smile. He set down the mug and ignored the remaining shortbread. 'So, apart from enjoying the pleasure of my company, what's on your mind? Being back here has stirred it all up, hasn't it?'

'In a way.' Lyndsey fiddled with a paper napkin, twisted it in a tight roll, unraveled it and started tearing it into shreds. 'We've talked around what the future might look like for us, and don't think I'm pressing you—'

'But?'

'At work yesterday — at the shop, it . . . didn't feel like the right place for me any longer. Does that make any sense?'

'Is there some other career you think would suit you better?'

'I'm not sure it's that exactly.' She returned to fiddling with the remnants of her napkin, straightening bits out and frowning, as if she'd dumped a pile of jigsaw pieces out of the box and wasn't sure how to start putting them together. 'You know I've never lived out of Cornwall, Griff, except for my time at university, and then I only ventured as far as Plymouth.'

'You're scared of change. I get that.' He reached for her hands, feeling them tremble in his.

'But you threw in a great career and took the plunge to change everything about your life.'

It was time to tell her the complete truth.

CHAPTER TWENTY-THREE

Lyndsey's troubled mood lifted as she gazed at the sea stretched out in front of her, glittering in the early morning sun like a handful of diamonds tossed on a blue silk sheet. After lying in bed rigid and sleepless all night, she finally gave up shortly after five o'clock. As quietly as she could, she'd gathered up the clothes she wore yesterday and crept out of her old childhood bedroom, now shared with Becca and Nora. She sneaked past what Griff and Theo laughingly called the Man Room and inched down the steep, narrow stairs. As soon as she stepped outside and took a few breaths of the cool, salt-tinged air, she began to feel better. By the time she reached the cliffs overlooking the beach at Carlyon Bay, her brain fog had thankfully started to clear.

'I told you I left my old job because I wanted to pursue my stained-glass work full-time, but that wasn't the complete truth. If I hadn't resigned, they would've fired me, Lyndsey.'

Griff's shocking confession yesterday had struck her hard. She clearly remembered everything else going on around them in the Eden Project café receding, from a noisy argument between two fussy children and their parents about eating ice creams before lunch, to the clatter of a waitress busy clearing the nearby tables. She'd focused all her attention on listening to the gray-faced man hunched over in front of her, his husky voice roughened by nerves.

'I'll spare you the details, except to say that I'd got so caught up in the fight for a promotion I felt I was owed that I trampled over other people without a second thought. One woman in particular was far better qualified and I knew it, but I didn't let that stand in my way. I was shitty enough to ignore the fact we'd been dating for a couple of months and made up lies about her. I almost got away with it.'

It'd been almost impossible to wrap her head around the fact Griff hadn't always been an honorable man. She'd pretended to take the news well when he promised he'd confessed everything to his bosses before it was too late, but deep down, she'd been massively conflicted. Lyndsey knew she'd disappointed him when she suggested they went to find the rest of their party and then avoided being left alone with him for the rest of the day. When Becca asked a lot of pointed questions later, she'd brushed them off by explaining she had a lot to think about. She let Becca assume their discussion about children hadn't gone the way she hoped.

Now she saw how judgmental she'd been, especially as he'd never flinched when she confessed some of her own darker secrets.

Lyndsey heard footsteps nearby and jerked around. 'Where did you come from?'

Griff had materialized on the path, like a genie popping out of a magic lamp. He looked as ragged and sleepless as she felt.

'Same place as you. Number twenty-four White River Road.' His laconic response pulled the whisper of a smile out of her.

'How did you—?'

'Know you were here? I followed you.' His tired face creased into a satisfied smile. 'My wayward brother used to steal out of the house all the time, and I brought him back more than once without our folks finding out. One creaky floorboard and I'm wide awake — not that I was really asleep anyway. You know full well why that was.'

Heat prickled her neck.

'I should've told you everything about leaving my old job before. I'm sorry.'

'You've got nothing to be sorry for. I do, though. I was an uptight cow.'

Griff's eyes twinkled. 'I wouldn't phrase it that bluntly.'

'I'm right, so don't you dare argue.'

'No ma'am. Wouldn't dream of it.' He hesitated. 'Your dad mentioned something — or rather, someone — yesterday, and took it for granted I knew what he was talkin' about. I didn't correct his assumption, but—'

'Tristan, I suppose?' Lyndsey sighed when he gave a sheepish nod. 'I should've done that myself. I'm sorry. It was crazy and cost me a good friend. I'm not sure what got into me.' She plucked at a ragged hole in one sleeve. 'No, I do know. It was my last fling at being jealous of Becca for stupid reasons. She seemed to have it all — again. We both know that's not true, and everyone's "all" is different anyway.'

'It sure is,' he said fervently.

'I was never trying to hide it from you . . . but I felt such an idiot afterwards. All I wanted was to forget all about it, so I pushed it to the back of my mind.'

'Yeah. I know how that feels. Does this Tristan guy live around here still?'

'Yes, at the other end of the village, but don't worry he won't tackle you in the pub or anything like that.' Lyndsey's promise made Griff smile. 'Mum even told me this morning that he's got a new girlfriend.'

'I reckon we need to forgive each other and move on?'

'Sounds good to me.' Lyndsey smiled back at him. 'I'm afraid we should probably go back home. My dad's an early riser and so is Nora. If we're missed, it'll set off alarm bells.'

'Nope, it won't.' He sounded smug. 'I left a note saying I was taking you out for breakfast and promised we'd be back by lunchtime for this afternoon's mackerel fishing expedition. I reckoned a couple of hours on our own wasn't too much to ask for.'

'Well, aren't you the smart one?'

'Occasionally.' Griff's hand snaked around her waist. 'Found you, didn't I? I reckon that makes me the smartest guy around.'

'There's only one snag.'

'What's that?'

'I didn't bring any money, and the nearest café is a couple of miles away over a challenging, very hilly section of the path.'

'Oh, ye of little faith.' He was really grinning now. 'I slipped my wallet and phone in my pocket. Called a taxi on the way here, too, so we'll find one waiting for us about five minutes back along the road. He'll take us wherever we want.' Griff waggled his eyebrows. 'We could even check into a hotel for a few hours?'

'He says hopefully.' Lyndsey grimaced at her own crumpled clothes, then shook her head at his faded gray sweats and old red T-shirt. 'Looking like this?'

'A takeaway coffee will do me. Just give me — us — this well-deserved slice of time. Please?'

'I can't resist a man who begs. We'll go to The Sailor's Rest in Port Glyn. It's a no-frills sort of place, and they cook an awesome breakfast. It's too early in the day for many visitors to be around, so it'll be full of locals.'

'Sounds good. You might need to act as my interpreter, though, if anyone decides to chat with the strange Yank.'

His warning made her laugh. She'd been forced to intervene and explain a few Cornish expressions already. Over the years, hers and Becca's accents had smoothed out, but her parents remained staunchly Cornish. Their broad accents and uniquely local turns of phrase had defeated Griff on more than one occasion.

'I expect I can manage that. Let's get our cholesterol fix for the day.' She took a deep breath. 'There's more we need to discuss, but our chaperones might allow us out on a date tonight if we're extremely lucky.'

Lyndsey didn't intend to talk about their future and what it might involve over their bacon and eggs.

* * *

Griff clambered off the boat and his knees buckled. He bent low and clasped them with his hands while sucking in several deep breaths to stave off another wave of nausea. He'd never been more relieved to place his feet on dry land.

'We'll make a fisherman of you yet, boy.' Paul beamed at Theo, who'd leapt off first and was proudly holding up a string of nine mackerel. 'Not so sure about your poor mate, here.' He threw a rueful nod in Griff's direction. 'He hasn't the stomach for it.'

As soon as the small boat chugged out of the sheltered harbor and started bouncing over the choppy waves, he'd been toast. The big greasy breakfast he'd enjoyed with Lyndsey, and Maureen's delicious pasty from lunchtime, were soon history. He'd spent the rest of the seemingly endless trip either hanging over the side of the rocking boat or clinging onto his seat desperately trying not to be sick again. The amazing thing was that Theo, not the most outdoorsy sort usually, took to it like the proverbial duck to water. Or in this case, one of the ever-present squawking seagulls. Theo's shaggy dark brown hair was salt-stained and tousled, and he'd caught the sun, but Griff had never seen him look happier.

'Can we go out again tomorrow?' Theo begged.

'Course we can, boy, but we'll leave this chap home.' Paul clapped a hand on Griff's shoulder. 'Don't worry. Lyndsey will dole out the sympathy in a minute. That girl can do most anything except go to sea.' His warm rumbling laughter broke out. 'I took both girls out once and Lyndsey were like you — heavin' all the time and pleading to go home. Becca weren't much more than about five, I s'ppose, but she were like Theo and loved every minute. That was one more thing to set them against each other, 'cause Becca was a little minx and teased her sister to death over it.'

'Siblings can be a blessing and a curse,' Griff mused.

'You've got one brother, Lyndsey said?'

'Yeah. We've had our ups and downs, but we're pretty close now.' One day he'd share the full story with Paul. 'Should we head on home? I'm supposed to be taking Lyndsey out tonight.' Right now, the thought of eating, or doing anything beyond collapsing on his bed, struck him as ludicrous.

'You'll be all right. A hot shower and a bit of a sleep and you'll be right as rain.' The reassurance came with a wink. 'Lyndsey will nurse you up.'

Back at the car, Griff fell gratefully into the front passenger seat and immediately opened his window. With any luck, the fresh air would mitigate the nauseating smell of fish filling the car, thanks to Theo's prized haul. The twenty-minute drive back to St Lanow felt like two hours.

'Hail the conquering heroes.' Lyndsey breezed out to meet them, fresh and sparkling in a poppy-red sundress. Becca followed close behind, with her mother who was proudly carrying Nora. 'Oh dear.' She grimaced at him. 'You won't be throwing in your stained-glass art work to become a Cornish fisherman, then?'

He made a huge mistake and shook his head. Everything kept on moving even after he tried his best to stand still. Griff pushed Lyndsey aside and barely made it to the closest unfortunate hydrangea in time to unload the last few dregs from his stomach.

'I know they say it's good to have interests in common when you fall in love with someone, but this is a bit extreme.' Becca collapsed in fits of laughter.

'Let's get you inside so you can have a lie-down.' Lyndsey gently steered him towards the house.

'I need to shower.'

'Mmm, I won't argue with that.' She playfully wrinkled her nose. 'You go up first, so I can steady you if you get wobbly.'

The short flight of stairs might've been Mount Everest where Griff was concerned, but he finally heaved himself up over the last step.

'Why don't you get your clean clothes from the bedroom, then I'll hang around outside the bathroom while you're showering, in case you feel woozy?'

'You just want to sneak a peek at my bare ass.' Griff's half-hearted complaint made her grin. He even managed a fleeting smile himself. Maybe he'd live after all.

'You have a problem with that?' Lyndsey gave his rear end a sharp tap.

The rest of the family were moving about downstairs and he was swamped with fleeting regret that he wasn't well enough to sneak a kiss.

'Don't worry, I'll be okay. It's starting to pass now that I'm getting used to a nonmoving floor under my feet again.'

'All right, but be sure to yell if you need anything. I want you well for tonight.'

Griff wished she meant for something more fun than whatever she was so keen on discussing, but wasn't dumb enough to say so out loud.

* * *

Lyndsey watched Griff wend his way back from the bar with their drinks and wished this was nothing more than an enjoyable uncomplicated date. All she wanted was to enjoy the perfect summer evening with the man she loved, but too many worries were on her mind and needed to be sorted. She'd purposely chosen to come to the Pengooth Inn because the low-ceilinged, whitewashed pub was well off the beaten track. It was highly unlikely they'd bump into anyone she knew on this remote part of the north coast halfway between Bude and Tintagel.

'There you are.' Griff set down two glasses. 'A soda and lime for my designated driver, and I'm following the landlord's recommendation by trying a pint of Tribute. They said it shouldn't take long when I put in our food order.' He pulled out a chair and dropped down next to her. Shafts of sunlight danced in through the window and caught the golden streaks in his hair, loose around his shoulders tonight.

How she restrained herself from reaching over to touch him she'd never know. He'd laugh himself senseless if she called him beautiful, but in her eyes, he absolutely was.

'So, you gonna get the bad news over with?'

'I never mentioned any bad news,' she protested.

'You've had a grim expression on your face every time you bring up the subject of "talking," so I put two and two together. Did I make five, or is my math spot on?'

'It's . . . tricky, and maybe it's too soon to discuss this, and I should shut up and enjoy what we've got without worrying—'

'You're killin' me, honey.' Griff's eyes blazed. 'I sure hope you didn't bring me four thousand miles to turn around and dump me?'

'Oh God, no!'

'That's okay then. Anythin' else we can work through. Relocation. Work. Whatever. We love each other, so as long as we're honest, it's all good.' The corners of his mouth lifted and he slipped one hand behind her head, drawing her close for a kiss. 'I'll kick it off if you like. I used to run a mile in the opposite direction when girlfriends started talking about weddings and having kids—'

'Me too.' Lyndsey felt her cheeks flame. 'Well, in my case I'm talking about boyfriends obviously. I was totally focused on growing my business.'

'But you've changed.'

Lyndsey frowned. 'Yes, sorry.'

'Don't be.' Griff's drawl turned raspy. 'I noticed you goin' all soft and gooey with Nora the other day, and it couldn't have made me happier.'

Now she was puzzled.

'I know I acted a bit weird at the time, but I needed to think things through, to be sure I wasn't projecting my own feelings onto you.' His long fingers stroked her cheek, heating it under his touch. 'See, I want those things now, too.' Griff's smile broadened. 'I need more than stained glass to keep me company. Make a life with me, Lyndsey.'

'Do you mind spelling it out, so I'm absolutely sure we're not misunderstanding each other again,' she whispered.

He sheepishly glanced around the busy pub. 'This wasn't how I'd planned on doin' this.'

'You had a plan?'

'Yeah, of course I did.' He sounded offended. 'I intended asking for your folks' blessing first. Buying a ring. Finding the perfect scenic spot to go down on one knee and . . . oh, to heck with that. I love you, Lyndsey. Be my wife. We can have one kid, a whole bunch or none, and it'll be fine with me. All I need is you there when I wake up and when I go to bed at night.'

She was totally different from Becca, who'd dreamed about her perfect proposal and wedding since she was five years old. Every time there was a wedding at the village church her sister would drag Lyndsey along so they could be waiting outside for when the ceremony was over. Her sister would critique everything from the bride's dress to the mode of transport waiting to take the couple to the reception. Lyndsey's fantasies, on the other hand, had revolved solely around becoming an independent, financially successful woman. Now she saw all of those things were wonderful ambitions, but a well-rounded life needed more. The man gazing across the table at her with love blazing from his eyes was her 'more.'

'Yes, please, to absolutely everything.' Lyndsey beamed.

'Come here.' He patted his knee and she hopped over, flinging her arms around his neck.

A bored teenage girl plonked the plates and cutlery down in front of them. 'One sausage, chips and baked beans, and one salmon salad.' She rolled her eyes in barely veiled disgust and slouched away.

'No doubt she thinks anyone over thirty has one foot in the grave and shouldn't be snogging in pubs.' Lyndsey laughed.

'Yeah, well that's her problem. I'm gonna kiss my new fiancée whether she likes it or not . . . the waitress, I mean.

You'd better like it, or we're in trouble before we even get goin'.'

'After I have a sample, I'll give my verdict.' Lyndsey pursed her lips.

'One sample coming up.' Griff didn't hold back. She'd noticed a number of stares, sly smiles and winks coming their way from the other customers, but happily ignored them. It was several blissful minutes before they came back up for air. 'So, you still gonna marry me?'

'It's a definite yes.'

He glanced over at their food. 'You still interested in eating, or would you rather go spread the good news to your family?'

'What do you think?' Lyndsey hopped off his lap, grabbed her handbag and beamed at him. 'Come on. There's probably some fried mackerel left if you get hungry.'

'I can promise you I won't be *that* hungry!'

CHAPTER TWENTY-FOUR

Griff hugged his future mother-in-law. 'I promise I'll take good care of her.'

'We know that, my 'andsome, or we wouldn't let her go off with you now!' Maureen smacked a kiss on his cheek.

The guard blew the whistle, so he grabbed their two suitcases and leapt onto the train. He'd already helped Becca and the children on first to get them settled in their reserved seats.

'Lyndsey, they're getting ready to lock the doors,' he yelled.

Griff's heart was heavy watching her cling onto her parents one last time. The tears etched on her face gave Griff a glimpse of the magnitude of what they were embarking on. Starry-eyed twenty-somethings swept away by the romance and adventure of it all might be able to push away worries about problems that could arise in the future; he and Lyndsey weren't those people.

'I'm here,' Lyndsey said breathlessly, leaping on the train and clutching hold of his arm. 'Let's find somewhere to put these bags and . . .' Her sharp eyes pierced through him. 'What's wrong?' Before he had a chance to reply, she gave a sad head shake. 'Yes, I'll miss my mum and dad, and worry about them, and they'll do the same for me, but I love you and so do they. They're happy for us.' She touched her empty ring finger. 'You are *so* not getting out of buying something extremely sparkly to go here.'

'That's not what . . .' Griff glowered. 'You're teasing me and it's nothing to joke about.'

'I'm not stupid and so blinded by love I can't see the dark clouds lurking on the horizon.' Her expression softened. 'There'll be hard times. Choices I'd rather not have to make. But that's life. When I told you I was done being a coward, I meant it.' Lyndsey's gentle laughter reverberated through him. 'Maybe this is a bit drastic, but small changes were never going to be enough for me.'

The train jerked, picking up speed, bumping her into him. A broad grin spread over her face when he wrapped his arms around her to stop them both toppling over.

'It's the train's way of telling us we need to sit down and eat our pasties while they're warm.'

'Knowing our luck, Theo's devoured them already,' Griff said. In Cornwall, the boy seemed to have lost his normal teenage-boy appetite and found a horse's instead. Maureen had loved nothing better than feeding him, and Paul had joked that he'd be sorry when they left and life went back to ready meals and salads.

'He better not have.' Lyndsey let go of him. 'Are we good now?'

'Always.' Griff picked up their cases and followed her.

Jase hadn't even pretended to be surprised when he rang yesterday to share their good news. His brother was in Knoxville visiting their parents, and had put him on speakerphone so Griff could talk to them, too. Their mother's happy scream almost burst his eardrum, but it was his dad's gruff expression of pleasure that tugged at his heart the most. Larry Oakes wasn't the sort of man to tell his sons he loved them, but showed it day in and day out with his unswerving support and caring — especially when they didn't deserve it. There'd been a brief veiled mention of the main reason behind Jase's visit when his dad said he'd always suspected there was more to the car crash story.

'We'll talk about it more when you bring your young lady to see us. Make it soon, yeah?'

'Sure thing, Dad, or maybe you and Mom would like to make the trip to Paradise Valley instead? We'll make a plan after we get back. Let us get over jet lag first and give me time to buy an engagement ring.' Those had been Lyndsey's only stipulations when he raised the subject of meeting his parents.

'There you are!' Becca waved at them from halfway down the carriage, so they made their way to join her. 'We decided you'd either missed the train or decided to stay behind. I was afraid you'd left me to deal with this pair on my own.' She ruffled Theo's hair and laughed when he half-heartedly pushed her away. 'Thankfully, our little drama queen fell asleep a few minutes ago.'

Griff sniffed the air and spotted crumbs around Theo's mouth. 'If you've been eating my pasty you're in big trouble, young man.'

'Not guilty!' Theo nodded at Becca, then grinned broadly. 'Only 'cause she said you'd chop me up into tiny pieces and use me in one of your weird mosaic things.'

'Not a bad idea. I'll remember that if you cause me any hassle down the line.' Griff dropped down in his seat. 'I wanna hear what we're doin' for the next two days in London.' The sisters exchanged despairing smiles. 'Hey, I'm sorry. I'm not going to apologize for being a typical American, wanting to cram in as much as possible.'

'You'll have plenty of other chances,' Lyndsey explained. 'Promise.'

'I'll hold you to that.' He pointed to the bag of food. 'Give me a pasty and I might shut up.'

'Oh, for heaven's sake, you're as much a baby as Nora.' Becca whipped out a large white paper bag and passed it over, the savory aroma making him salivate.

Griff pulled the golden brown, warm pasty halfway out of the bag and took a gigantic bite. Life was really great sometimes.

* * *

'Please tell me you're finally worn out?' Lyndsey begged.

She'd been elated this morning to discover they'd have the whole day to themselves while Becca and the kids spent much-needed time with Deke, but that was before Griff rattled off the list of places he wanted to see. He'd completely ignored her promise that they could return as often as he wanted. They'd set off first thing after breakfast and relentlessly ticked off the Changing of the Guard at Buckingham Palace, the Tower of London, Westminster Abbey, St Paul's and Tower Bridge. Their last stop was the London Eye. When they clambered off that a few minutes ago, she'd grabbed his hand, dragged him to an empty bench and forced him to sit down with her.

'I guess I am pretty tired.'

'Thank heaven for that. Anyway, we need to start heading back to the hotel. Don't forget we're on babysitting duty.' They'd agreed to take care of Nora so that Becca and Theo could see Deke's concert at the O2 arena. 'Hopefully, she falls asleep easily so I can be right behind her. I'm knackered.'

'I reckon I can un-knacker you . . . at least enough to wear you out again.' He teased a finger along her chin, lifting her mouth to his for a lingering kiss.

'Do you seriously think I'm going to have sex in front of my baby niece?'

'She'll be asleep,' he wheedled. 'We can go in mine and Theo's adjoining room and leave the door open, so we'll hear her if she wakes up.' Griff's hand strayed behind her neck and his fingers massaged her tired muscles until she moaned. 'You can have a long, hot bath first.'

'I'd fall asleep and drown.'

'I should've phrased it more accurately — *we* can have a long, hot bath first. Deke didn't stint when he booked the rooms. Their suite has the most enormous tub I've ever seen.'

'You've had this planned all day,' she said accusingly.

'It has spurred me on.'

'I'll consider agreeing to your rather seedy suggestion on one condition.'

'What's that?'

'You spring for a taxi to the hotel. I refuse to walk any further or be crammed on the Underground or any more crowded buses.'

'Yes, ma'am. Anything you say, ma'am.'

'That's quite enough groveling for one day.' She leaned against his shoulder.

Who would've thought when she flew out of London a couple of months ago that her world would be turned upside down in the best possible way?

* * *

'You lookin' forward to coming home soon?' Griff asked Deke. He glanced back down at his plate of breakfast and poked a fork in the fried egg. Out of the corner of his eye, he noticed Lyndsey shudder as the yolk spread satisfyingly over the plate. One of the many things he'd discovered during this trip was her violent dislike of runny eggs — hers needed to be cooked to the point of turning into rubber before she'd touch them.

They were all eating a late breakfast together before Deke flew off to Paris for the band's next show. It'd amused Griff to see Lyndsey arrive at the table with the collar of her bright pink blouse turned up. He suspected he'd got a little . . . enthusiastic last night and left traces of his unshaven face where everyone might notice.

'Can't wait.' Deke squeezed Becca's hand. 'She knows that.' The meaningful look he gave his wife stirred Griff's curiosity.

'Well, go ahead and tell them. You know you're dying to.' Becca managed to sound exasperated and indulgent in the same breath.

'I've been rethinking my priorities. Touring isn't conducive to a settled family life. My first marriage is proof of that.'

From what he'd heard, Theo's mother had her own problems that would've almost certainly wrecked the marriage without any help from the Deke Warner Band. It was decent of his old friend to take the lion's share of the blame for his son's sake.

'Before y'all arrived, I had a few heart-to-heart sessions with the other band members. We've been together for years so they know me pretty well. They were disappointed but not surprised to hear I'm lookin' at taking a different direction. It's up in the air right now whether they'll replace me as front man or break up. I want to start my own record label in Nashville. It's bound to still involve some travel, but I'll be home most nights.' Deke stretched an arm around Theo's shoulder. 'This guy needs a real father, not an occasional visitor.' He smiled indulgently at Nora, bouncing around happily in Lyndsey's arms and chewing on her new Peppa Pig stuffed toy. 'This little munchkin's given me a second chance. I hope I'll get things right sooner with her.'

'It must've been a tough decision to make, but for what it's worth, I reckon it's the right one,' Griff said.

'I'm sure you didn't expect this fallout from your suggestion that we all make this trip?' Becca directed her question at Lyndsey.

'No, but I could see we were all at a crossroads and needed to check our road maps.' She burst into giggles. 'Goodness, I'm sounding terribly American already.'

'Nothing wrong with that,' Griff asserted.

'It sounds okay in a Southern drawl, but I'm not so sure about in my British accent.'

'Give it time.'

'I've offered you the rest of my life. What more do you want?' Lyndsey teased.

'Hey, that's an awesome line for a song.' Deke's eyes lit up.

'I thought you were retiring from performing,' Becca chided.

'I am . . . at least on big stages. That doesn't mean I won't be tempted by the occasional open mic night somewhere, and I'm damn sure I'll keep writing songs until I'm old and feeble.'

'You mean as opposed to just feeble?' Theo joked with his father.

'Anyway, I think it's *all* awesome,' Griff said with conviction. 'Let's toast to the future!' He raised his coffee cup and even Nora joined in, picking up on the infectious happiness around her and waving her arms around madly.

CHAPTER TWENTY-FIVE

Despite knowing how ridiculous she was being, Lyndsey's stomach was in turmoil. She touched the ring Griff bought for her yesterday — a sparkling round cut diamond surrounded by glittering emeralds — feeling like a child at Christmas who couldn't stop playing with their favorite new toy. This was another thing she'd never pictured for herself, unlike her sister, who knew every detail of the engagement ring she wanted about two decades before accepting Deke's proposal.

'I hear my folks' car. You comin' out with me?' Griff tilted her a questioning smile. 'It's gonna be fine.'

'Of course it is. I can't wait to meet them.' That was true, but still it did nothing to lessen her nerves.

In the end, his parents had decided they felt like a trip to Nashville, so any second now she'd be face to face with Sylvia and Larry Oakes. She almost wished Jase was here too, but he'd made a tactical retreat and decided to leave the four of them alone while he took Tiffany out for lunch. It had amused them both no end when Jase pounced on Griff the minute they got home and asked his brother's opinion on whether he should ask Tiffany out on a date.

Apparently, the two met at an impromptu barbeque Harold and William threw the previous week for their

213

Paradise Valley community, and flirted over the hamburgers and hot dogs, no doubt to everyone else's amusement. Griff hadn't been able to resist teasing Jase — after all, it was the first time his charismatic younger brother ever asked him for dating advice. But he'd hurried to assure Jase that as far as he knew, Tiffany didn't have anyone special in her life, and told him to go for it. The first date went well, and now they were out again together today.

'I love that dress,' Griff said, smiling down at Lyndsey warmly.

She'd initially dressed in a simple white shirt and black capris, thinking the comfort of one of her old familiar stand-bys would be reassuring, but then succumbed to Griff's last-minute plea for her to change. The vibrant hot pink sheath splashed with exotic green leaves accentuated her coloring, something he was helping her to learn to celebrate. Lyndsey clasped his outstretched hand and they stepped outside together.

Tomorrow was the first of August, so the constant wall of heat and humidity was supposedly at its peak. She could only hope her deodorant was up for working overtime.

A dark red truck, only marginally newer and less battered than Griff's, stopped in front of them. The doors were flung open and before she had a chance to say hello, Lyndsey was engulfed in a warm hug.

'I'd about given up hope of my boy ever findin' someone crazy enough to take him on!' The woman loosened her grasp, and her inquisitive brown eyes swept over Lyndsey. 'He was right on. You're a looker, all right.'

There was really no reply she could make without sounding weird, so she contented herself with smiling. To return the favor, she checked out Griff's mother. He certainly didn't get his tall, rangy build from the woman who barely reached Lyndsey's chest, and whose tight blue T-shirt and jeans were stretched over generous curves. But Sylvia's amused smile was the mirror image of Griff's — so much so that it knocked her off-kilter for a moment. She shifted her glance to the man standing quietly to one side. The only clue to Larry Oakes being in his early eighties was his slight stoop and thinning gray hair; apart from that, he and Griff could be clones.

'I'll get your bags. You go on inside with Lyndsey.' He'd persuaded his parents to stay for a couple of nights to give them more time together, so Jase was consigned to sleeping on the sofa.

Sylvia bustled on ahead and settled herself on the sofa. She patted the cushion next to her and encouraged Lyndsey to sit down.

'Go help Griff,' she ordered her husband. 'I want a few minutes with this girl.'

Lyndsey's heart thumped. She'd faced one or two boyfriends' mothers in the past, but those encounters never meant as much as this one. Despite knowing Griff loved her and that they were solid no matter what, Sylvia Oakes' opinion still mattered. Now she had an inkling how he must've felt in Cornwall, faced with her own curious parents.

'What would you like to know?' A flash of respect lit up Sylvia's eyes when she took the initiative. 'I'm sure there's a lot Griff hasn't told you.'

'He's a man. They don't tell their mothers much, especially when it comes to women.'

Lyndsey rattled off a brief biography, then felt herself blush. 'Sorry. This isn't a job interview, and I didn't mean to treat it like one.'

'Don't you fret.' Sylvia patted her hand. 'I remember meeting Larry's folks the first time. His father was a sweet old soul, but his mother was another story. She put the fear of God in me. I tried not to take it personal, because I knew deep down no one would've been good enough for her only child.'

'Did you win her over?'

Griff's mother chuckled. 'I forced down two hunks of her dry-as-sawdust coconut cake, praised it to the skies and asked for her recipe. She fell for it hook, line and sinker.' She wrinkled her nose. 'Only problem was, then she made the damn thing every time I visited.' Sylvia shuddered. 'I can't bear to eat the stuff now.'

'Well, I haven't baked, so you don't have to do anything like that today. I promise I'll try my best to always be honest with you if you'll do the same in return.'

Sylvia nodded. 'I like you. Nothing wrong with bein' straight and sayin' what you mean.' Her smile broadened. 'You're not just a pretty face. I see why you've won over my boy.'

'He's won me over, too. I love him so much.'

'That's all I needed to hear. He's a good, decent man and I can tell he worships you. Nothin' more a woman needs, is there?'

'Is it safe for us to join you now?' Griff edged back in the room with his father peering over his shoulder.

'Sure it is. I told her a few home truths and she's changed her mind about marryin' you!' Sylvia threw back her head and roared with laughter.

'Thanks a bunch, Mom.' He bounded over and perched on the sofa arm next to Lyndsey. 'I was afraid she'd bring you to your senses.' The kiss he seized was borderline unsuitable for public consumption.

'My senses flew out the window the day I met you. There's no hope, I'm afraid.' Her patently fake sad head shake made everyone laugh.

'Let's hope they stay gone.' Griff kissed her again before turning to his parents. 'How about some lunch? We've got tuna salad and home-grown tomatoes and cucumbers from my garden.'

'Sounds good, son.' Larry's expression turned serious. 'Then we need to clear the air some.'

Lyndsey watched Griff's smile fade. This was the first time he'd seen his parents since Jase told them the truth about the car crash and its aftermath, so it was set to be a difficult conversation on both sides.

* * *

Despite the soaring heat, Griff always found he could breathe and think more clearly outside. When he'd suggested taking their drinks on the porch after lunch, Lyndsey threw him a puzzled look and his mother muttered that he'd always been a strange child. His father was the only one to give an approving nod.

'We should never have believed that cock-and-bull story you spun in the first place.' His father leaned forward and his thick eyebrows furrowed in concern. 'I might've guessed you were coverin' up for Jase. You were always a more loyal brother than the little devil deserved.'

'I'm glad you know the truth now, so it's all good. All I ever wanted was an apology from Jase and the chance to regain your belief in me.'

'You never lost that, son.'

The veil of tears shimmering in his dad's eyes threatened to unman him.

Larry tapped his chest over his heart. 'You're here. You and Jase. Nothin' you or anyone else can do or say's gonna change that. I'll be lookin' out for you both when I'm six feet under, too, so don't you forget it.' Next thing, his dad's arms were around him in a tight hug.

'What's up with you guys? Hasn't Lyndsey passed the Oakes' test?' Jase's teasing voice startled him.

He hadn't heard his brother's car arrive, but a quick glance told him that was because it wasn't in the drive. For a moment he was confused, until he saw Jase was holding Tiffany's hand and worked out they'd walked over from her house. Today, an intricate weave of braids added at least another six inches to her height, and paired with her multi-colored African floor-length cotton dress, her appearance was stately. When no one answered Jase's question, his brother's face fell.

'Would you prefer us to go away again?'

'No, son.' Larry managed a faint smile. 'We've been sayin' a few things needed airing, that's all. Bring your young lady on up here so we can meet her proper-like, and then fetch a couple more chairs. You'll want some cold drinks, too. Comin' out here was your big brother's idea.'

'Yeah, he's dumb like that,' Jase said indulgently. 'Come on, Tiff, it's your turn to face my folks.'

'They're not monsters!' Lyndsey sounded quite fierce.

'I'm sure he was only joking.' Tiffany's defense of his brother amused Griff. Jase needed someone in his corner. She hitched up her dress and marched up the steps. 'Mr and Mrs Oakes, I sure am glad to meet y'all.' A chuckle slipped out of her. 'I've been livin' here long enough now I'm starting to talk more like a Southerner. In case he didn't tell you, I'm from Minnesota originally, but I got tired of the cold winters.'

'For heaven's sake, don't you go callin' us Mr and Mrs Oakes. That makes us sound like Larry's folks, God rest their souls. We're Sylvia and Larry.' His mother sprang up and flung her arms around Tiffany.

A few minutes later, Griff smiled happily around his crowded, noisy porch. This was all he'd ever wanted. His family close again. The woman he loved by his side. In his opinion, there wasn't much more a guy could ask for.

* * *

Lyndsey snuggled back against Griff's solid chest. Now they were finally alone and the sun had gone down, she was more than happy to linger out on his porch. They'd wrapped up the day with a barbecue at Becca's house to take full advantage of her sister's larger grill and spacious kitchen where they could all squeeze around the table together. Now Nora was in bed and Theo was making the most of his last few days before school started again to stay up late working on his latest computer project.

Becca was lounging in a bubble bath while enjoying a private video chat with Deke. He'd insisted the time difference didn't matter because he was too hyped up after the night's concert for sleep. They were counting down the last week until he'd be back home again.

Jase and Tiffany had invited Griff's parents to her home for coffee and dessert. It had momentarily thrown her poor friend when she mentioned the coconut cake she'd made, and Lyndsey and Sylvia burst out laughing. After they explained the full story, Tiffany had happily challenged Mrs Oakes to reserve judgment until she'd tried her version, made from her grandmother's recipe with fresh coconut, and supposedly moist and light as a feather.

An owl hooted in the trees as the last slivers of daylight faded away.

'Do you reckon Deke's studio needs another visit?' Griff's hands slid around her waist and he trailed kisses down her neck. 'We might want to check everything's okay out there before he comes back next week.'

'That would absolutely be the responsible thing to do.'

'It sure would. We could discuss our wedding plans, too, before my mom and your sister take over. If we're not careful, they'll be on the phone to your mother behind our backs and we won't get a say in anything.' He swung her around to face him.

'That discussion won't happen if we . . . you know . . . it didn't last time.'

'I swear I'll behave and not do this.' A firm hand caressed her back, inching lower and lower. 'Or this.' The other hand shifted to her breasts, stroking and teasing until she arched into his touch. 'At least until we've agreed on a quiet wedding in St Lanow, followed by an amazing honeymoon somewhere tropical, where all you need to pack is a few sexy bikinis. And afterwards, a big party back here, to celebrate with our friends and family who couldn't make it across the pond.'

'You've clearly thought about this.'

'Haven't you?'

She flushed. 'Well, yes, but not in as much detail as you, by the sound of it.'

'Am I on the right lines?' Now he looked worried. 'If you want anything different, that's fine by me. I'm not tryin' to—'

'Shush. Kiss me.'

'Yes, ma'am.' Griff never needed telling twice, one of the many things she loved about him. 'It was a damn good thing your folks sent you here,' he whispered. 'See what you've done for me.'

'Ah, but see what you've done for me in return.'

'I'd call it a draw. We're both in the right place now.'

Lyndsey wasn't arguing with that.

EPILOGUE

The following spring in Tennessee

'I've got something for you,' Griff whispered in Lyndsey's ear. 'Let's sneak away.'

'Mr Oakes, you're incorrigible.' She jabbed his ribs. 'In case you've forgotten, we're married now, so we don't need to run off to have illicit sex in Deke's studio.' A flare of heat lit up her face. 'I can't even step foot in there now without remembering . . .'

'Give me some credit.' He chuckled. 'I've got a gift for you that I'd prefer to give you on our own. I couldn't really take it to Cornwall for the big day.' Sometimes it amused him how spot on he'd been when he guessed how they might want to celebrate their wedding.

He could picture Lyndsey now walking arm in arm with her father down the aisle of the small, ancient St Lanow church; its granite stones must've seen thousands of such ceremonies over the seven-hundred-plus years of its existence. She'd worn a sleek, scoop-necked dress made of heavy cream satin, the rich color flattering her Caribbean skin. No veil. Cream rosebuds woven through the shiny mass of natural curls brushing her bare shoulders.

'Or haul it all the way to Hawaii and back here afterwards.' They hadn't exactly clashed, but they definitely had a back-and-forth discussion before settling on their honeymoon destination. They'd batted a few ideas around.

'Absolutely no way.' That was her immediate reaction to his suggestion that they should go to Dominica and track down her birth father's family. She hadn't wavered, insisting she had no intention of contacting people who'd never shown the slightest interest in her. Rather than argue and make her unhappy, he'd shut up at that point. Griff still thought it would settle the last hints of her lingering insecurity if she could at least meet Luis Reyes' family, but he could bide his time. As he'd told her at the start of their relationship, he was a patient man.

'Isn't it nearly time to cut the cake?' A broad smile lit her up. 'Our second wedding cake, that is. The high-octane American version. Ten layers of chocolate overload, made to *your* specifications this time. I did appreciate you manfully eating the fruit cake I know you hated in Cornwall.'

'Hey, babe, I'd do anythin' for you; don't you know that by now?' Although he'd conceded afterwards that their traditional English wedding cake was marginally better than the American fruit cakes he detested, it didn't mean he wanted to eat another slice anytime soon.

She touched his mouth, tracing the outline of his lips with her finger. 'Oh yes. You've proved that. I still can't believe you managed to turn a derelict hardware shop into the new branch of The Right Place in a matter of months.' They'd been lucky to snatch up the building, which was within walking distance of the center of Franklin, at a bargain price. The previous business had closed several years earlier, and it'd started to fall into disrepair because no one wanted to take it on.

'You worked damn hard, too.'

'It was a team effort.'

'Have you heard from Nicola recently?' he asked.

'Yes, she's doing great. The Truro shop has doubled its profits since she took over. I lost my focus on it after I came here.'

'That wasn't your fault.'

'I'm not complaining, just being realistic. Anyway, her success is good for our bank account, too.' She'd negotiated a franchise agreement with her former employee, giving her a continuing percentage of the revenue.

Griff checked the time. 'We've got twenty minutes yet before we need to cut the cake. Plenty for what I've got in mind.' Her eyes glittered. 'I know I told you I wasn't thinkin' of that . . . although . . .' He stroked his hands down to the jade silk belt cinching in her waist. For today's party, she'd chosen a jade-and-white-striped fifties-style tea dress rather than wear her wedding dress again. But at Ruth Mae Grey's insistence, Lyndsey modeled her wedding dress for the old lady to admire yesterday, so she could see her as 'a proper bride.'

'There's no "although" about it.' Her air quotes made him laugh. 'Come on, then. Show me your secret before you burst.' She grabbed his hand and pulled him towards the front door. 'I assume it's at our house?'

'Yeah, in my workshop.'

Their guests were out on Becca and Deke's patio enjoying a selection of their original wedding reception foods mixed in with local Tennessee specialties. That'd led to a curious combination of Cornish pasties, sausage rolls, scones with jam and cream at one end of the buffet table, and then country ham biscuits, pimiento cheese sandwiches and Moon Pies (a chocolate marshmallow confection reminding Lyndsey of Wagon Wheels) at the other. Deke and Theo were also on grill duty and cooking hamburgers, hot dogs and British bangers they'd sourced at a local butcher.

'Where d'you think you're goin', big bro?' Jase caught them halfway across the hall. 'You've been married for weeks now. Hasn't the novelty worn off yet?'

'Nope, I'm pretty damn sure it never will.' Griff grinned. 'Haven't you got anythin' better to do, like chase after your own lady?'

'She's taking care of Ruth Mae. Theirs is the most unlikely friendship I've ever come across, but it proves what an awesome woman Tiffany is.'

'You goin' to make an honest woman of her anytime soon?' Griff teased. 'Your job's going well, isn't it?'

'It's all good. They're a great bunch of folk at the Sounds.'

As luck would have it, Nashville's minor league baseball team had been searching for a new coach and youth coordinator, and Jase's experience proved a perfect match. Griff's only concern had been that the temptations of the city might undo the good work his brother had done turning his life around. He'd been relieved when Jase took up Buddy Earl's offer of renting a small flat over the Adamsville Grocery. The commute didn't seem to bother Jase, and judging by the number of mornings he'd spotted his brother's car parked outside Tiffany's house, the flat wasn't getting a whole lot of use anyway.

'And as for Tiffany . . .' Jase's face turned bright red. 'Where were you off to anyway?'

'My workshop,' Griff said, 'but if anyone asks, you haven't seen us. I promise we won't be long.'

'Fine. I'll use my charm and charisma to smooth over anyone's ruffled feathers.'

'Thanks, bro.' Griff steered Lyndsey out before anyone else could delay them.

* * *

Even though it'd been touch-and-go a few times, she'd made it through their wedding in Cornwall and today's party without crying, but now tears pricked at her eyes. Hopefully, her waterproof mascara would live up to its promise.

'I've called it *Essence of Love*.' Griff's voice turned hoarse. 'I made it when we were at odds, and I was afraid this might be all I'd ever have to remind me of you.' He picked up her hand and touched it to the stunning mosaic on the workbench in front of them. 'The vivid blues are the Caribbean Sea, the shards of emerald your eyes.' He slid her fingers closer to the top. 'Those heat-drenched yellows and oranges are the sun.'

'It's incredible.' Lyndsey stroked along the border, formed by a variety of miniature tiles in complementary colors. 'The detail is stunning. It's definitely going in our bedroom.' She slid him a teasing smile. 'Unless you were planning to sell it and make a fortune?'

'Never!'

They both laughed, before she suddenly slammed her mouth shut and looked embarrassed.

'No secrets, remember?' Griff teased. 'Mine was acceptable, because it's a gift. We're allowed some leeway with those.'

'Mine is sort of a gift, too.'

'So, where're you hiding it?'

Lyndsey took hold of his hand and pressed it against her stomach. 'It seems us Carne girls don't drag our feet when we find the right man.' She watched Griff's expression settle into a frown . . . before a smile skittered across his face.

'Do you mean what I think you mean?'

'Get ready for sleepless nights. No sex for months, because I'll be too tired and fat. Do you want me to go on?'

'I'll take all that happily. A baby? Really?'

'Yes, really, and don't be silly enough to ask how it happened. You're old enough to know the answer to that one. Those tiny bikinis have a lot to answer for.' She twisted a smile. 'We didn't exactly try very hard to prevent it, now did we?'

'I'm over the moon, but are you happy about the timing?' Worry crept into his voice. 'With your new business and—'

She kissed the rest of his question away. 'I'm still a bit shell-shocked, but thrilled. I'll hire more help with the business when I need to. It's very early though, so to be on the safe side, let's keep the news to ourselves a bit longer.'

'Whatever you want, sweetheart.'

'We'll leave the mosaic here for now, and hang it indoors later. You couldn't have given me anything more special.'

'Neither could you.' He slipped one hand down to caress her stomach.

'Hey, you two.' Jase banged on the door. 'The natives are getting restless out here.'

'We're coming!' they shouted together.

* * *

'Congratulations! Ruth Mae just told me your awesome news,' Tiffany said with a broad smile.

Lyndsey wasn't sure how to react and slid Griff a nervous glance. All of their Paradise Valley neighbors were sitting together, and now everyone's eyes were on her.

'Are we missing something?' Becca swept Nora up in her arms, rescuing the little girl before she toddled into the table.

'According to Miss Grey, you're goin' to be an aunt later in the year,' Tiffany explained.

'What?'

Lyndsey withered under her sister's shocked gaze.

'Is this true?'

'We've only just found out ourselves,' Griff said, slipping his arm around her. 'We were goin' to wait a bit before telling y'all.'

'How on earth did you guess?' Lyndsey asked Ruth Mae.

'I've seen enough expectant mothers in my time to spot it a mile off. You've got that look about you. I would've said if it's a girl, you can name her after me, but it won't be.'

'It won't?' Griff's amusement was clear.

'Nope. You'll have a little boy first.'

'First?' Lyndsey squeaked.

Miss Grey held out her champagne glass to be refilled. 'If Paradise Valley's goin' to keep on, it needs new blood.' She bestowed another wrinkled smile on Tiffany. 'You and that young man of yours are gonna have some pretty babies, too.'

Tiffany's jaw gaped open and Jase turned the color of a boiled tomato.

'Well said, Miss Grey,' Harold chimed in, and his partner quickly agreed. 'They'll have all of us as honorary grandparents,

226

to spoil them rotten.' His eyes held a hint of sadness. 'We would've loved kids ourselves. These days we'd be allowed to adopt, but when we met thirty years ago, it wasn't possible.'

Griff gave his shoulder a sympathetic pat, because what was there to say? He twined his hand with Lyndsey's. 'It looks like we've started something.'

'We certainly have.'

Life was a lot more interesting when you weren't quite sure what might come next.

THE END

THE CHOC LIT STORY

Established in 2009, Choc Lit is an independent, award-winning publisher dedicated to creating a delicious selection of quality women's fiction.

We have won 18 awards, including Publisher of the Year and the Romantic Novel of the Year, and have been shortlisted for countless others.

All our novels are selected by genuine readers. We are proud to publish talented first-time authors, as well as established writers whose books we love introducing to a new generation of readers.

In 2023, we became a Joffe Books company. Best known for publishing a wide range of commercial fiction, Joffe Books has its roots in women's fiction. Today it is one of the largest independent publishers in the UK.

We love to hear from you, so please email us about absolutely anything bookish at: choc-lit@joffebooks.com

If you want to hear about all our bargain new releases, join our mailing list: www.choc-lit.com

ALSO BY ANGELA BRITNELL

NASHVILLE CONNECTIONS
Book 1: SUGAR AND SPICE
Book 2: WHAT HAPPENS IN NASHVILLE
Book 3: CELTIC LOVE KNOT
Book 4: THE WEDDING REJECT TABLE
Book 5: LOVE ME FOR A REASON
Book 6: YOU'RE THE ONE THAT I WANT
Book 7: HERE COMES THE BEST MAN

LITTLE PENHAVEN
Book 1: ONE SUMMER IN LITTLE PENHAVEN
Book 2: CHRISTMAS AT LITTLE PENHAVEN

PEAR TREE FARM
Book 1: A CORNISH SUMMER AT PEAR TREE FARM
Book 2: A CORNISH CHRISTMAS AT PEAR TREE FARM

STANDALONES
SUMMER IN PARADISE VALLEY
SPRING ON RENDEZVOUS LANE
A LITTLE CHRISTMAS PANTO
SUMMER AT SEASPRAY COTTAGE
CHRISTMAS AT MOONSHINE HOLLOW
A SUMMER TO REMEMBER IN HERRING BAY
CHRISTMAS AT BLACK CHERRY RETREAT
NEW YEAR, NEW GUY